J.E. REED

RUNNING
WITH THE
WOLVES

THE CHRONOPOINT CHRONICLES

INDIGO
Livonia, Michigan

Edited by Catherine Jones Payne
of Quill Pen Editorial

RUNNING WITH THE WOLVES
Copyright © 2018 J.E. REED

Published by Indigo
an imprint of BHC Press

Library of Congress Control Number:
2018930086

ISBN: 978-1-947727-31-1

Visit the publisher:
www.bhcpress.com

Also available in ebook

To my loving husband,
whose patience knows no bounds,
and whose encouragement could make anyone
believe in changing the world.

①

RUNNING
WITH THE
WOLVES

UNKNOWN

REALM: 1
DAY: 1

Lying in bed, the chatter caused her mind to stir from that blissful place that lingers on the edge of dreams. It was too loud, too early. She rolled over, the fog slowly clearing as voices turned to song, birds greeting the morning sun. Strange how they'd never woken her before.

She groaned, reaching for a pillow, but something stung her fingertip, and she jolted. A small droplet of blood formed on the tip of her index finger. Her heart thundered as she looked at the culprit and then her surroundings.

This wasn't her room.

Instead of cool sheets and a soft bed, she lay on dead leaves and grass, the musty forest scent filling her nostrils. White walls were replaced by an endless array of trees that blotted out the sun, save for a few rays that fought their way through.

She blinked, pushing herself up.

Am I still dreaming?

Her finger pulsed as she scanned the vicinity, and fear crawled into her mind.

Nothing.

No fire, no tent or tracks. Nothing that indicated civilization existed.

Surely someone had to be here, someone could explain—wait, had she been abducted?

Who would want to kidnap her? Why wasn't she bound if that were the case? The list of reasons for waking in the middle of a forest were slim. Abduction, a lapse in memory, a vacation gone horribly wrong.

She stood, using a tree for support, but dizziness rocked her back. She leaned her head against the trunk, waiting for the spell to pass.

Small specks flew across her vision. Abduction seemed the most likely of scenarios, but where were her captors? Could a drug explain her lapse in memory?

The last thing she could recall was dressing for bed. The girl examined herself, pleased to find shorts and a tee-shirt rather than pajamas. Brown hair hung loose around tan shoulders, and nothing around her wrists indicated she'd been bound. The only odd possession she carried was a little bracelet with leather threaded around a small blue stone. White veins traced a sky-colored surface like cracks of lightning.

Unease settled in her gut at the name etched on its surface.

KIUNO

It was a surrogate name. Something she used for gaming and online activities. Few knew her—

She paused. Her name. She couldn't remember her name...

What's going on?

Her throat tightened as she slumped against the tree again, fighting back tears. She was alone and didn't know her own name. What were the odds?

She took a deep breath, trying to steady her racing heart.

Stay calm.

A forest in mid-summer wasn't so bad.

Summer? Wasn't it only January?

Her heart pounded faster as she realized one of two possibilities. Either time had passed without her knowledge, or she was further from home than she imagined.

Calm down. Think.

Summer, okay. Food would be easy. She'd spent a lot of time camping and experimented with a few survival techniques. That would help as long as she could remember them.

She glanced back at the name on her wrist. She tried to picture her husband calling when dinner was ready or when he needed her to fetch something from the house, but every time the recollection came close it eased away again. Like a cloud hanging over her mind. Maybe she'd recall it later. For now, Kiuno would have to do.

Knee-high foliage surrounded large trees, and fur covered vines snaked their way up the trunks. Thick air caused sweat to roll down her neck. She needed to find water.

Kiuno made her way through the foreign forest and allowed herself to become lost in its beauty. Heavy, snarled roots spread across the ground, connecting each tree in an endless network. Small animals eyed her with curiosity before scurrying beneath the brush.

It would have been the perfect painting.

Hours passed, and the temperature continued to rise as mosquitoes and other insects nipped at her skin. Beauty was turning to nightmare.

Kiuno stopped to catch her breath and plopped on a fallen log. Sweat rolled down her face as she tried to lift her hair for some relief. She was no stranger to the outdoors, but didn't remember camping ever being so miserable.

She looked at the sun. Had someone noticed her missing yet? Surely her boss would call home regarding her absence. Her husband would know something was up.

Standing, she took another breath, wiped the sweat from her brow and started walking again, the dry patch in her throat a nagging reminder. Using the tree roots, Kiuno slid down a small hill and finally heard the sound she'd been searching for. Running water.

She made her way around a few more trees to find clear water cascading down a rocky cliff that stood twice the size of any person. The river stretched twenty feet across and flowed with a steady pace. Thick brush and cattail lined the bank, and a large piece of rock lay just below the falls, its previous fixture visible above.

Rushing to the water's edge, Kiuno cupped her hands, the cool liquid easing her scratchy throat. She splashed more on her legs to ease the itchy bites.

Deep colored pebbles lined the river bank with small water plants growing between them. Little fish played among the foliage and larger stones. If she could catch one that would resolve her growling stomach.

Before worrying too much about food, Kiuno hoisted herself onto the fallen rock, slipping a few times on the green moss. She looked down river, hoping for some sign of civilization, but it only renewed her sense of dread. Forest extended for miles.

Her stomach flipped, and she sank down, drawing her knees into her chest.

Trapped. Alone.

Kiuno stayed there for some time wrestling with ideas. She had water, first priority taken care of. The river would provide food, and it wasn't as though she'd be there forever.

Despite some optimism, her nervousness grew with the looming shadows. Beings seemed to form and vanish as evening played on her fears. It was too late to build a fire, but at least a tree would be safer than the ground.

Glancing between branches, Kiuno found one that split, creating a nook just big enough for her to squeeze in. She rested her back against the biggest branch and watched the orange glow dip below the horizon. Her stomach growled, her skin itched, and every sound made her jump and recheck her surroundings. She curled into herself, trying to reason the shadows were nothing more than the reflections of trees.

SANCTUARY

REALM: 1
DAY: 2

Sleep eluded her, every sound playing on the nightmares that could materialize any moment. Branches cracked nearby, wolves howled in the distance, and even the cricket's song added to her terror.

Loneliness and fear lingered at the forefront of her mind.

Kiuno jolted.

Sweet relief flooded through her at the faint sign of dawn. She jumped to the ground, careful of her footing and stretched the stiff muscles in her back and legs.

With morning, her fears were soon forgotten as she made her way to the river, splashing water over her face. She took in a breath, the crisp air refreshing.

Her stomach growled painfully as a fish broke the water's surface. Priority two.

The thought of catching one brought to light the memories of her husband's laughter with her previous attempts. They camped throughout the summer, and she was always trying something new. Her ideas usually resulted in his amusement, and they'd head back to their campsite empty-handed, but this time there was no backup plan.

Making a pole or net didn't seem to be an option, but perhaps a spear would do. Even if she caught one, Kiuno still needed a way to cook it. Raw fish wouldn't kill her, but it didn't sound appealing.

She made her way deeper into the trees gathering a variety of small twigs and sticks. In theory, she knew how to create a spark, doing it was another matter. It usually resulted with her hands blistering, which would be problematic given the circumstances.

Once satisfied, Kiuno tossed her load beside the river and cleared a space. Igniting the forest wouldn't help her chances of survival.

She pulled a few cattail pods to use as kindling and peeled them apart to reveal the fluffy white interior.

Using one foot to hold a log she chipped a notch in it then placed a second stick in the small hole. Moving slow at first Kiuno rotated the stick between her palms, adding enough force for friction.

Smoke was visible in moments.

She couldn't be sure if the wood was different or another miraculous reason empowered her success, but she didn't question the matter.

The tiny ember gave her a glimmer of hope. Carefully, Kiuno placed the small, red glow into the white fluff and blew the flame to life.

Success.

With a fire going, she picked up a larger branch and started chipping away at it with a rock. It was tedious and took the better part of the afternoon, but she finally had a spear. Whether it would work remained questionable.

She waded into waist high water, the need for sustenance overriding the fear of what might be lurking in the depths. After what felt like an hour, she turned back to the bank.

Still another hour passed as she stalked the tall grass until she found what she'd been searching for.

Holding the spear high, Kiuno held her breath as she crept forward and threw. As soon as the spear hit the water she dove, sure she'd missed until something moved beneath the sharpened edge.

At least her luck hadn't run out.

Thankfully she knew how to fish and clean her catch. She removed her shirt and shoes to allow them to dry by the fire and set to cooking her meal.

Bland fish was far better than an empty stomach, and feeling satisfied, Kiuno nestled against a tree as the afternoon wound down. A sense of loneliness stirred as her heart ached for home.

Kiuno slept on the ground, hoping the flames would keep any wandering predators at bay. The fear that she might be stuck in the wilderness for an extended period clawed at her mind.

People often mentioned staying put when lost, but she wasn't sure anyone knew where to start. Once they did there was no telling how long it would take for them to locate her. Perhaps her best option would be to keep moving.

Kiuno curled into herself as the fire crackled and popped and prayed for something to come of tomorrow.

STRANGE NOISES woke her in the middle of the night, and she decided a tree might be safer after all.

The fire dwindled to red coals by morning, and she waited for the sun to fully rise before climbing down.

Her foot slipped on a moss-covered branch, and she reached to brace herself, cursing when her fingers couldn't grasp anything solid. Kiuno's body collided with the hard earth, and a knotted root made itself known in the middle of her back. Tears sprang to her eyes as she gritted her teeth.

Kiuno limped to the river and turned her face to the sky. The sun bounced off the clouds in a vibrant array of orange with pink streaks shooting through the center.

Another perfect painting.

Kiuno closed her eyes.

She was alive. Despite the uncomfortable circumstances, she still had a chance.

Kiuno traced the etched letters on the stone. Someone was responsible, someone knew she was here. Why go through the trouble if they were just going to abandon her?

Several people knew the name Kiuno, but only a select few knew the woman that hid behind it. Was she being punished for something?

A far more ominous thought flashed through her mind. What if she hadn't been kidnapped at all? What if this was hell, and she was trapped in an endless convoluted purgatory? It was a place that reminded her of the things she feared most: abandonment and loneliness.

Kiuno shook her head trying to force the thoughts away.

She made quick work of another fish and spread the embers to cool before moving on. She wrapped the leftovers in a leaf and stuffed it in her back pocket.

After snacking on berries, Kiuno kept a steady pace throughout the afternoon and only stopped to splash water over her face.

Then she saw it.

It was faint at first, so much so that she thought her eyes were playing tricks on her, but rising against the blue sky, a thin wisp of smoke reached for the heavens.

Her heart jolted, and she ran from the river, grabbing her spear along the way.

Finally.

The trees opened to a thick meadow, and she relished in the cool breeze that raced across the tall grass.

Thorns grabbed at her bare legs, further irritating the skin, but it was a small price to pay for the glimmer of hope that moved closer with each step.

The land sloped downward, and she trudged through a muddy rut before climbing a steep hill and locating the source of the smoke.

Kiuno froze.

Standing thirty feet tall and made entirely of stone, a wall surrounded a small village, the thin cloud of smoke curling from its center. It looked like something from European history.

Kiuno's heart hammered as she stared at the rooftops inside. An open gate stood to her left, the only apparent entrance.

What the hell?

Overwhelmed, she collapsed letting her legs stretch out before her.

A stone wall? Was this some kind of joke?

How far had she been taken from home? How long had she been unconscious?

Rising, she slid down the hillside and made her way toward the looming structure. Loose stones lay scattered along the outskirts like rich pieces of a long-forgotten history. Gray hues gave some life to the grim structure, but grass grew between the stones, almost as if the meadow were reclaiming lost territory.

Her hands shook as she traced over the rough edges, feeling the uneven blocks and wondering who'd first placed them.

Would they welcome her or even speak her language?

At the gate she paused, her gaze fixated on the ominous structure. Rusted thick iron bars crossed one another all the way to the top where they angled to form eerie jagged spikes.

Despite the fear, a soft murmur coaxed her inside. A sweet sound that promised to chase away the loneliness that tried to consume her.

A dirt path led to the middle of a tiny village, if it could be called such. Small wooden structures that appeared ready to collapse stood in the center.

She merely stood there gaping.

People were everywhere.

Some sat huddled in the tall grass while others used the buildings as protection from the sun.

Kiuno caught a few peering up, but they quickly looked away. None seemed concerned with the newcomer.

She examined each face. The same expression written on both young and old. Wide eyes revealed a look of someone cornered or captured. A few cried while others appeared as statues that hadn't moved in days.

The most unnerving detail was their state of attire. Each wore something that resembled the normalcy of her life. She'd been expecting something a little more foreign.

Getting her bearings, Kiuno turned to examine the small buildings and noticed a stone basin that rested behind the dwindling fire. She approached the people gathered around it and felt her stomach turn at the sight of the stale liquid.

"E-excuse me." The man before her glanced up, seeming to determine she wasn't of much interest before returning to the water. "I was wondering if you might be able to help me."

"No."

"But I'm lost."

He huffed. "Does it look like we're any different?"

She took a step back. "I just thought—"

"You thought wrong." She caught sight of a bracelet around his wrist before he stomped away.

Her heart sank.

We? As in everyone?

Kiuno turned back toward the gate shifting her gaze across the sea of faces as her heart hammered. Had they all been abandoned out here?

She wandered to a patch of grass and plopped down, pulling the berries and fish from her pocket.

"Where did you get that?" She looked up to find several people watching her, or rather, the food she held.

"Out there—" Kiuno was thrown forward, the fish ripped from her hands, and her face smashed into the ground. Someone held their knee to her back while several scrambled through the dirt, kicking it in her face.

Kiuno fought against her captor, using her hips to knock him off balance and struggled to her feet. She ran her tongue over her lower lip, revealing a bitter metallic taste.

"Check her for more." A man twice her size pointed, and she raised her hands in a vain attempt to ward him off.

In seconds, more hands were rummaging through her pockets and ripping at her clothes. She desperately tried to force them off and kicked one in his stomach, but her head crashed against the ground again before she was dragged from the chaos.

"Leave her be." Her rescuer placed himself to her front.

"She has food."

"Maybe that's because she worked for it." The deranged man's gaze fell on her again, and a desperate expression told her she needed to run. He lunged, but another male, this one younger, broke from the crowd to plant a fist in his jaw.

"If you weren't a coward you wouldn't be starving," he yelled. Another fight ensued that the older male quickly put to rest.

Moments later the group turned away mumbling their displeasure, and warm brown eyes turned to her. "Are you all right?"

She looked at his hand, her own shaking, before she took it. Once on her feet Kiuno nodded and wiped the blood from her mouth. He looked her over, and once satisfied, turned to his companion. She stood there for a moment allowing her heart to slow.

Kiuno glanced at the gate, bewildered. Perhaps she should go back in the forest. She took a few steps before stopping again when the looming shadows reminded her of the fear. Kiuno didn't want to face another night alone. She might be better off in a tree but...

Kiuno moved toward the far wall and stomped the grass beside it. She'd be content there for the night. The grass would give some coverage, but hiding was out of the question.

The man's reaction surprised her. Were they incapable of gathering their own food? She licked her lip, the area already swollen.

More fights ensued as the sun set, and she was glad to be away from their chaos. The cool wall eased her throbbing head.

As the last bit of light faded, Kiuno shifted her position and the night sky made her still.

Thousands of stars shimmered in their own wondrous glory, each twinkling against a vast expanse of blackened night. The Milky Way stretched across the dark void, giving it a soft glow. Though only half full, the moon shone brighter than any she'd ever seen. It was as if this land had never been touched by the modern age.

"Something else, isn't it?" Kiuno startled, looking down to find the man that helped her earlier. She guessed him to be in his mid-forties, a bit younger than her father.

He threw her a soft bundle. "In case you need something to lie on."
A blanket?

"Aren't there others who have more need for this?" Her mind wandered to the young faces in the crowd.

"There's plenty, about the only thing plentiful in this place."

Kiuno hugged the blanket feeling as if it were the only real thing she could cling to. "What's wrong with them?"

"Hunger mostly."

"Are they incapable of gathering?"

He chuckled. "They're afraid to leave the wall."

"So, they'd rather starve?"

He shook his head. "They'd rather someone get it for them."

He had to be joking. Kiuno sighed. "I guess there isn't anyone that actually lives here is there?"

"Afraid not. You're the first new face we've seen in days."

Silence filled the space between them as she tried to wrap her mind around the situation. She thought he might leave, but he stomped the grass to her right.

"What are you doing?" she asked.

"Would you rather someone search your pockets while you sleep?"

Kiuno chewed her lip. "What's to stop them?"

"I'm bringing in the little food they have."

"Thanks," she said, shuffling her feet, "for before."

"Don't mention it."

Silence lingered around them again.

"What's going on?" she whispered.

His smile shifted. "I'm not sure. Everyone has a bracelet, but there are people from all over the world."

"How long have you been here?"

"A week."

"Do you know your name?"

He shook his head. "Only what's on the bracelets."

Her shoulders slumped. "How is that possible?"

He shrugged. "Don't worry too much. We'll figure things out. What name are you going by?"

She looked at her bracelet. "Kiuno."

"You can call me Elliott."

His eyes rose to the void above as he lay back and folded his arms behind his head. After a moment, she mimicked the action.

A shooting star caught her attention, and it drew her into the captivating beauty of lights flying across the endless dark.

Where am I?

SURVIVAL

REALM: 1
DAY: 4

She wanted to go home. She wanted her own bed with new clothes and a warm shower. But most of all she wanted her husband. What did he think about her disappearance? How long had they been searching for her?

Kiuno turned away from Elliott when the tears fell and fought to keep her sobs quiet. A deep shiver ran down her spine as she tried to take another breath. Her heart ached, and if she could admit it, she was scared. Not knowing what her future might hold was the most terrifying thing about this whole situation.

She woke with sunrise and leaned against the cool stone, hugging her knees to her chest as she listened to the cries of others waking to this nightmare. They were all lost, hungry and afraid of what might come, or what might not.

Elliott stirred. "Couldn't sleep?" She cast a glance his way, but turned back to the gate, hoping someone with answers might walk through.

"I did." Silence stretched between them.

He cleared his throat and stood. "Would you like to join me this morning?"

"What for?"

"Food, we can't put it off anymore."

She wondered if yesterday had been the last straw or if he'd given up on the possibility of being rescued.

"Sure." Kiuno stood, wiping the dirt from her pants.

"Excellent, I've already arranged for a meeting outside the gate. I have something to take care of first, so I'll meet you there."

"Have you already gone out?" she asked looking at the iron bars and wondering what kind of history lay beneath the rust.

"Not far. I had other concerns." Judging from yesterday she could only imagine.

"There's a river just over the hill. It's not far."

His eyes brightened. "Good, I was hoping there would be a water source nearby." Kiuno nodded and watched him join the crowd at the water basin. She rubbed her sweaty palms against her pants, took a breath, and headed toward the gate.

It felt as if a hundred eyes followed her every move. She risked a glance and found the one who attacked her yesterday glaring as if she were the cause of his discomfort. Kiuno ran her tongue over the tender part of her lip and picked up the pace.

Outside the iron gate, a familiar green meadow welcomed her. The grass expanded on all sides, with the forest encircling it in a protective embrace. The wind shifted through the grass in waves, reminding her of the sea.

Several people sat at the edge of the hill and waved when she drew near. She returned the greeting with an awkward smile.

Instead of joining them, Kiuno opted to lean against the wall and watch their interactions. She wasn't sure if any of them had been involved with yesterday's events. Risking a glance to her left, her skin prickled when she caught sight of a young man glaring.

Midnight hair hung over savage eyes that tried to bore into her. His right cheek appeared bruised, the area slightly swollen. He'd been the one who defended Elliott yesterday. She averted her gaze and sighed. First impressions were not her strong suit.

Elliott arrived a short while later with four others in tow. Those seated stood to greet him, eager to get things underway. At least there were people willing to help.

His gaze shifted over them, his eyes taking in each individual. "Thank you for coming. I'll keep this short. Our survival will depend on us. We're the only ones capable."

"You mean the only ones willing." All eyes turned toward the one leaning on the opposite wall. His position remained unchanged, but that cold glare on Elliott caused her skin to crawl.

Elliott smirked. "Yes, the only ones willing. At least for now. I know there aren't many of us, but once we demonstrate our capabilities more will lend a hand." The boy scoffed, but Elliott ignored him. "We're going to split into teams. Some of you will set up snares while others scavenge. We'll meet back here by noon."

When no one commented he continued. "Kikyo," he indicated the one with the bruise on his cheek, "has experience with hunting and trapping. The two of us will be teaching you as we go."

Elliott's gaze shifted to her. "Kiuno, you'll accompany Kikyo today." He looked back to everyone. "I found some knives in the corner of a storehouse. You should all keep them on you, just in case. Get as many snares up as materials allow."

The way Elliott carried himself spoke of prior leadership. No one questioned him even when he paused to ensure all agreed. What experience did he carry?

Kikyo stepped forward to take one of the knives. "I'm not fond of this arrangement." Elliott didn't appear surprised. "Send me out with a group of boys. She should be—"

"Not fond of working with a girl you mean," she stated. Her face flushed when he cocked his head in mock amusement.

"Look," Kikyo said, "it's not my intention to offend you, but I don't have time to play babysitter to some girl who feels she has something to prove."

Kiuno clenched her fists and let her eyes trail down his frame. A head taller than her, lean yet muscular, but the same age as herself. He was in no position to judge anything.

When he turned back to Elliott her temper flared. "I'm more than capable of learning."

His smirk vanished. "I beg to differ."

"Try me." He shifted, pinning her in place with his icy glare, but she stood firm.

Elliott laughed. "It seems things are settled." He handed her rope and walked toward the others. It was only then Kiuno realized she was the only female among them.

Kikyo clicked his tongue and grabbed two bows from the ground. He threw one to her, which she missed, and he shook his head again. She'd have to impress him if she wanted his help.

As she followed Kikyo toward the trees Kiuno wondered why Elliott paired them together at all. If this Kikyo was so against teaching a girl why force him? It wasn't as if someone else couldn't do it.

The air turned muggy as they entered the forest, and she noted the small animals that scurried through the underbrush. If they were setting up snares then they'd be catching several of them soon.

"I hope you learn fast." His tone made her blood boil, but Kiuno held her tongue. *Don't say anything if you have nothing nice to say, don't say anything, don't say anything.*

She let out a breath when he bent down to pick up a few twigs. Curious, she stepped closer to watch as he broke them into smaller pieces.

It wasn't until he led her to a sapling that the explanations began. The sapling acted as a spring to pull the loop tight and toss the animal in the air. With careful precision, he placed the sticks in the ground.

Kiuno studied the contraption before he gestured her deeper into the forest. Kikyo picked up another set of twigs, this time showing her the exact length and how they were placed in the ground. The middle piece served as the leverage. Once an animal disturbed that particular piece, the tree would snap up, trapping the prey.

The next snare was hers to set.

Kikyo was awkward, shifting to avoid contact, but he wasn't unpleasant. When she wasn't certain, he instructed her where to move a piece and helped bend the tree so she could place her first trap. He smiled at her success, and they moved on.

After monitoring two more, he let her set them alone, the two moving down different paths. Kiuno was sure she lost him a few times, but he always popped up just as she started to panic. It was as if Kikyo were reassuring her he was still around.

When the twine ran out, she assumed they'd head back, but Kikyo kept walking. She opened her mouth once, only to stop herself. Kikyo seemed the type to get upset with questions. His determined footsteps told her there was a route in mind, so she'd wait.

"This should be good." Kiuno glanced around confused until he slung the bow from his shoulder and let an arrow fly. It struck dead center in a tree. She wasn't even sure he'd aimed.

"That's only about ten yards. Don't expect to make the first shot."

Her confidence crumbled as she pulled the bow from her shoulder praying she could mimic his action. How hard could it be?

She tried to stand with her feet apart, but her positioning must have been off as he kicked her shoes until satisfied they were in the correct position. Her eyes were drawn to the arrow still firmly in the trunk. She notched her own. It was power evoking. Primal. She could do this.

Kiuno took a breath, pulled back hard and released only to watch the arrow fly off at an awkward angle. It landed several yards from the intended target.

Her face flushed, and the sting to her pride felt far worse than the sting to her arm. She tucked the injury close and clenched her teeth.

Kiuno braced for the criticism. To be told this wasn't worth his time, but slender fingers wrapped around her wrist and examined the area. He tied a piece of leather over the welt.

Without a word, he repositioned her feet and gave her another arrow. Kikyo stood behind her and assisted in the draw back. He raised her elbow, pushed her right hand closer to her face and bent the front arm before indicating for her to release. It still missed, but at least it was straighter.

"Better. Again."

She took another, feeling her confidence grow. Again, he moved her body and helped pull the arrow back.

They continued until her arms were too shaky for the draw.

Kiuno's spirit soared as they made their way back. He didn't talk much, but Kikyo had been more help than she'd expected, and she found his company pleasant. Maybe she'd judged him too soon.

Elliott waved them over when they broke from the tree line. They were the last to arrive.

"Finally, thought you two might have gotten lost." Elliott looked between them.

"We walked further than I planned," Kikyo said.

"I trust your student did well?" Elliott's gaze appeared hopeful.

"She'll do."

Kikyo joined the others, and Elliott ushered for her to do the same. "We've done a lot already, but there's still something that needs to be tended to. I'm sure you've noticed the water basin is running dangerously low. Thanks to Kiuno, I found a river. The land flattens on the far side of this hill and circles to the water."

"How are we carrying it?" she asked.

"With those." Elliott pointed to several large potteries hidden in the grass.

"They just happened to be in the storehouse?" Kikyo asked.

Elliott nodded. "Behind the last of the blankets."

"Convenient." Kikyo's tone didn't go unnoticed. After several long moments, Elliott picked up the first and balanced it on his shoulder. She followed suit.

Despite how dry her throat felt after trudging through a dense forest, Kiuno couldn't convince herself to drink the stagnant poison within the walls. There were too many variables that might end her life. Contaminated water would not be her undoing.

They followed Elliott along the hillside and into a thin line of trees. Upon seeing the water, everyone laid their pots against a trunk and ran to the edge, splashing the cool liquid over their skin. She wondered if some of them had refused to drink the basin water as well.

Kiuno washed the sweat from her face and filled her pot.

Without handles, it made the journey more difficult as she hoisted the heavy load over one shoulder. Walking back reminded her of a time in her childhood when she'd been asked to carry a bucket half her size to the horses. Her father had laughed endlessly at how soaked she'd been.

Though not as bad as her childhood, Kiuno still spilled some along the way, leaving her shirt drenched before they made it back. Each walked inside single file, and one would have thought they were bringing gold to the indigenous.

Several of them stood to help, licking their parched lips. A child clung to an older woman's skirt and backed away when Kiuno placed the pot before them.

Deciding it might be better to give them space, Kiuno moved away from the crowd and took a moment to rest in the grass. Several people gathered around Elliott, and she prayed they were asking him how to help. Maybe he was right, they just needed to be shown all wasn't lost.

With the commotion dying down, Kikyo found Kiuno and extended a hand to hoist her up. His palms were rough and calloused, making her wonder what kind of life he'd lived back home. He didn't speak, and they started back for a second load.

After their fourth trip, the entire group collapsed by the riverside. It'd been a good hour of hauling water, and they'd filled the basin past the brim. This final trip was just to top off the pottery.

Kiuno sat against a thin tree and felt the cool breeze brush past her skin. It grazed the tree tops, making the branches sway over the river. The steady flow of water carried her beyond this strange land and into a sea of colors. Only the occasional fish broke the slick surface.

With the silence, birds came to join them in the trees, several she didn't recognize. Vibrant colors of blue and green shown when they spread their wings. It was a perfect setting. If only she had a canvas to capture their beauty.

With eyes closed, cold water shocked her senses, and she jumped in surprise spluttering to find her assailant in hysterics, Elliott's warm eyes filled with mirth. Several others joined in his playful mockery.

"Anyone up for some fishing?" Kiuno tried to make a stern face, but her stomach growled in response to his proposal. It'd only been yesterday that she'd eaten, but she had to remember that most hadn't had a satisfying meal in days.

Elliott instructed them on how to make a spear and where the best fishing grounds would likely be. He split everyone along the bank, and within minutes she heard shouts of victory.

A little while later they sat around a fire with full stomachs. She voiced her guilt about eating when the others had nothing, but Elliott assured the group there would be plenty by tomorrow.

"Tell us about yourself Kiuno," Elliott said.

Startled, she found all eyes staring. "I-I'm not really sure what to say."

He turned to Kikyo. "What about you?" Blue eyes rose for a moment, but drifted as if uninterested. Elliott sighed. "Kids. They make things so difficult."

"Why don't you tell us about yourself?" she offered.

Elliott leaned back. "Not much to tell. Spent a few years in the military and have a daughter about your age, but retirement is boring. I spend most of my time in the basement modeling airplanes."

Kiuno laughed. "Modeling doesn't seem your style."

He shrugged. "I needed something with a slower pace to occupy my time." Kiuno tried to envision this authority figure sitting on a stool while wrestling with a glue gun. "Your turn," he encouraged.

She twiddled her thumbs. "I don't know. I like to paint."

"Professional?"

Kiuno shook her head. "Not yet. I've had a few people interested, but it's hard to let my pieces go after spending so much time on them."

"What's your style?"

"Landscape."

Elliott looked around. "You'll have plenty of inspiration once we get home."

"No kidding."

Elliott rose and made his way to the water, splashing it along his arms. She took the opportunity for revenge. Sneaking up behind him, Kiuno planted her foot in his backside and shoved him headfirst into the water.

She was thrown in next, and several more joined in their merriment. Elliott broke the surface laughing, and she tried to swim beyond his reach, but he caught up, dunking her under the surface.

They wrestled and splashed one another for the rest of the afternoon forgetting about the worries they would face tomorrow.

When she finally climbed onto the bank Kiuno removed her shoes and wrung out her hair.

"Vengeful much?" Elliott asked, still laughing.

"I had to repay the favor." She grinned.

Tired, yet refreshed the group made their way back to the village. Kiuno's clothes were damp, but they would dry by morning. The only thing that would be soaked for a while were her shoes. She carried them, opting to walk the woods barefoot.

They were welcomed back once again, and Elliott divided the remaining fish between the children and those in desperate need of substance. She hoped Elliott was right about more food tomorrow. Perhaps with full stomachs their minds would clear.

Kiuno made her way back to the wall and collapsed on the blanket. Kikyo claimed they wouldn't work with the bow for a few days. Her body had to acclimate to the usage. Truthfully, she wasn't sure she'd be able to lift her arms tomorrow anyway.

"Hey." Elliott slumped against the wall beside her, looking just as exhausted.

"Hey."

After spending the day with him she didn't feel as awkward in his presence.

"Kikyo's warmed up to you."

"He was surprisingly patient."

"I figured."

She tilted her head, curious. "What made you so sure?"

"Kikyo, like the rest of us, is stressed for obvious reasons. His manifests into aggression. If I'd paired him with one of the other boys, a fight would have broken out, therefore I put him with you. I figured nothing more than verbal aggression would come of it, and even then, he'd feel guilty for it later."

"He was better after we entered the forest."

Elliott nodded. "What we're going through is nothing short of a disaster. People handle such extremes in their own way."

"How would you say I'm handling it?"

Elliott cocked his head to study her. "Denial."

"What?"

"You're still hoping this isn't real and that hope is preventing you from acceptance and panic."

Kiuno opened her mouth to argue, but closed it again when she realized he was right. She was still hoping for it to be a dream.

Feeling the need to keep conversation going Kiuno switched the subject. "A lot of people approached you when we came back."

"They want to help. Come morning I'll have everyone check their snares and send a few of you fishing. If everything works out, we'll be having a feast by noon."

"You think so?"

He nodded. "It'll help take down a lot of the aggressive behavior." Elliott sighed. "They're scared and have every right to be. Feeding this many will be a challenge. Kikyo is heading out to hunt bigger game tomorrow."

Her demeanor fell as night settled. "How long do you think we'll be here?"

He leaned forward to unlace a boot. "Honestly, it's hard to say. We know what we need to do. That's enough for now."

Silence settled around them as the last bit of light faded. Nothing seemed real. As if she'd been thrown into a fantasy. Once they were home, the excitement would fade, and it'd just be another story. Hopefully one she'd soon forget.

FEAR

REALM: 1
DAY: 5

Good morning." Elliott's voice woke her, and she cracked one eye to find dawn had barely risen. She groaned and rolled over.

Everything hurt.

He laughed. "Rise and shine we have work to do."

Maybe he should poke at the people who hadn't pulled their weight yesterday. Her body felt like a lead weight though the others probably felt the same.

Huffing, Kiuno rolled to her feet and trudged behind him as they made their way to the gate. He waited, still laughing at her and handed her a blanket that would serve as their bag.

"Where's Kikyo?" she asked.

"Hunting."

"Oh." Kiuno chewed her lower lip. Did he go alone?

Once they reached the trees Elliott stepped aside. "After you."

Kiuno was afraid she might not remember the path, but those fears were put to rest when they came upon the first trap.

A rabbit dangled from its back leg and struggled harder when they approached. She'd always had an affinity toward small furry things and had to turn away when Elliott ended its suffering. This was necessary. This was survival. That knowledge didn't stop the guilt from welling in her gut.

The next few traps were empty, and she hoped they weren't the ones she'd set. Elliott simply bent the trees, replaced the sticks and moved forward.

After a few successes, the two stopped before a scattered mess of fur and blood.

Elliott knelt. "Seems predators got them."

"You don't think they're still around do you?" She looked between the trees.

"I'm sure there's nothing to worry about." He stood, wiping the sweat from his brow.

"I'm more worried about Kikyo."

She ignored the smirk playing on Elliott's face. "No need. He didn't go out on his own."

An hour later their bags were full, the traps reset, and Elliott led the way back to the open meadow; the heat of the day rising fast.

A small crowd welcomed Elliott through the gate and he picked people to help skin the rabbits under his guidance. Kiuno's stomach twisted during the demonstration and she vomited, much to Elliott's amusement. He sent her away with the assurance that she'd get used to it. She scoffed at him, it wasn't as if she'd be here long enough. They'd be back home with a microwave and frozen food soon.

With the meat over a fire two more surprises arrived. The group of boys sent fishing returned with several pots full, while Kikyo walked through the gate dragging a deer.

Unable to assist in preparing the large animal, Kiuno helped with the fish. She had plenty of experience in that at least.

While working, Kiuno glanced around and smiled. Strangers were finally talking and sharing stories. Bouts of laughter echoed across the yard as everyone helped prepare dinner. Elliott had been right.

Later that afternoon, she sat beneath a porch, thankful to be a thoughtless shadow. Those that'd previously attacked her paid no attention with full stomachs. It was the first time they had the chance to relax.

Kiuno watched Elliott introduce himself and speak with everyone. He seemed genuinely interested in their thoughts. Maybe getting to know them was his way of keeping control and meeting their needs.

That evening he joined her in their usual spot and fell against the wall in exhaustion. Kiuno expected him to comment about the day and express how much they'd accomplished, but he stayed silent.

"Something bothering you?" she asked.

Elliott waved one hand across the area. "Everything. No matter how hard I try to piece this together I can't come up with anything reasonable." He let out a long sigh before continuing. "Something was brought to my attention today, but…I don't know what to think about it."

Kiuno leaned forward. "What is it?"

"Does the name Chronopoint mean anything to you?"

Chronopoint—A real-time strategy game that focused on building a fortress and defending one's territory with the help of an alliance. She was the leader of one alliance, and one of the best in her chosen realm.

With the help of her allies, they'd spent two years building to be the strongest. People once thought of as friends had grown to become like family. She couldn't imagine the chaos they were facing now. Maybe they'd called for a stalemate with rival alliances due to her absence. She was sure her phone was blowing up back home.

"It's a game."

"Something you played often?" he asked.

"Yes."

"And you used the name Kiuno?"

She nodded. "But I use that for everything. What does a game have to do with any of this?"

"Some feel they've only used their given names for that game in particular."

Kiuno laughed. "Are you trying to tell me we were kidnapped because of a game?"

Elliott couldn't hide his smirk. "That's what these kids are trying to tell me."

"That's the most ridiculous thing I've ever heard. Did you even play?"

"I dabbled with it."

Her smile faded. "You used the name Elliott?"

He nodded, and she looked out over the area. "I knew a lot of people in that world, but I don't recognize anyone here."

"Would you be able to recognize them by their face alone?"

She thought about it and shrugged. "I guess not, but I haven't heard any names that ring a bell either."

"No sense in getting worked up over a theory then."

Silence fell between them, and she wondered how much merit he was giving to the assumed theory. Was it possible to track people through a mobile game and if so, how had they been transported?

"There's a few people interested in starting a search party."

"Kikyo?"

"No, he's our best hunter."

She sighed with relief. "When are they going?"

"Probably tomorrow afternoon. If they don't find anything in a few days they'll come back, fill us in and head in another direction."

Silence fell between them as she watched the sun sink on another day. Homesickness had set in hard. She wanted her bed, to cuddle with her cats and eat cold pizza while watching T.V. She wanted to see her husband and forget this whole mess ever happened.

TWO TEAMS of three set out the following afternoon. One group headed north while the other moved south. If she'd managed a few days on her own, surely, they wouldn't have any trouble.

Everyone bid them farewell and waited.

A week crawled by.

Then another.

By the third, people were restless and another group, this time with five, headed north.

They never returned.

Kiuno stood by the gate staring into the trees as the sun faded once again. It'd been three weeks, and she wondered how eleven people could disappear without a trace.

Despite the worry that clawed at their minds, the rest of them were forced to move on. They had a shaky routine that comprised of hunting, fishing, and collecting water. No one wandered far though she felt Kikyo pushed the limits. He was always watching at the top of the gate. A guardian statue waiting for news to break through the trees.

Two days in a row she woke with Elliott already gone. Curiosity got the better of her, and she followed him. If nothing else killed her, boredom certainly would.

When she rounded the gate, he was stretching.

"What are you doing?" she asked.

"Figured in light of the situation it would be best to get back in shape."

"Care if I join?"

He laughed. "Knock yourself out."

The two made three laps around the wall, and she could finally see the back side of the meadow. The trees wrapped around it in an almost perfect circle.

He outran her, which came as no surprise, but when Elliott told her he wanted to get back in shape she'd assumed he was out of shape to begin with. She tried her hardest to match his pace, but she'd never been much of a runner.

After their run, they went straight into exercises which again left her quite displeased with herself. She collapsed after their final set of pushups.

"How well are you able to defend yourself?"

She took in a shaky breath. "At the moment?"

Elliott laughed. "In general."

Kiuno sat up wiping the sweat from her eyes. "I never really thought about it." She'd like to think she'd be able to handle herself, but after being attacked for a piece of fish it was doubtful.

"Do you want to learn?"

"It's not like I'm doing much else."

They started with the basics, and she quickly realized her lack of knowledge. They spent time on how to throw a simple punch then moved into reading an opponent. It made her wonder if this whole experience was part of some life lesson to not take things for granted.

Every morning thereafter she worked with Elliott, only to regret it when Kikyo came for her. Both men seemed inclined to turn her into a fighting machine.

"So where are you from?" She tried for the third day in a row. Kikyo always ignored her questions and pointed to the target, much to her disappointment.

"Georgia."

He speaks.

"Anywhere close to Savannah?" She'd been there occasionally on family vacations.

He pointed to the target again when she turned to him. "No, I've never been to the coast."

"You lived that close and never visited?"

"My father wasn't fond of it."

"Do you still live with him?"

He nodded, and she fired another arrow. It struck too low.

"He taught me everything I know. My brother left for college last year."

"What about your mom?"

He fell silent which made her turn to look at him again.

"She's been gone a long time."

Kiuno's heart clenched. "I'm so—"

He cut her short. "I worried about him being on his own."

"Is he in good health?"

Kikyo nodded and let out a small laugh. "He'd scold me if he knew the reason I stayed."

She let a few more arrows loose and hit the target though they were still off center.

"You're getting better, but I can see your arms shaking from here."

"I worked out with Elliott again this morning. He's teaching me to defend myself."

"Good. You could use it."

Kiuno glared at him before remembering his cheek, and her face flushed. "I never asked you to intervene for me back then."

"You expect me to let a group of men beat up a defenseless girl?"

"No, but if you're going to be chivalrous then don't blame the victim."

He smiled. "Fair enough."

They took a separate route on the way back, and she wondered if Kikyo were mapping the area or looking for new hunting grounds. He appeared comfortable among the trees and moved as if he were one with the forest. She made so much noise in comparison.

Watching the ground, Kiuno tried to mimic his steps. She avoided dead debris and sticks, but still felt as if the ground resisted every movement.

"Close your eyes."

Just as her head rose, Kiuno was spun around and almost tripped before Kikyo pulled her into his chest. She raised both hands to put space between them, and disappointment flooded her core. That wasn't the way Elliott showed her to react. Maybe knowing it was Kikyo prevented her from striking him. When did he move behind her anyway?

"Ki—"

"Be quiet," he whispered.

Alarm bells went off. His body was too close, but that wasn't what had her worried. His breathing came out in rapid gasps, and through his shirt she could feel his heart pounding.

Kiuno stilled, and a scent like the forest overwhelmed her senses. She couldn't think or wrap her mind around what he might be staring at. She tried to steel herself and push against him again, but he tightened his grip.

"Let go."

"Be still." His voice shook. So unlike Kikyo. He'd been angry when they first arrived not afraid. She tried to listen. His head shifted from side to side, and his grip tightened even though she hadn't moved. He was much stronger than she expected.

"What's going on?"

"We need to get back, but you have to keep your eyes closed."

"Why?" The unknown was paralyzing as her mind envisioned the worst of scenarios.

"Just trust me."

Though reluctant she nodded once, and he tentatively released his hold. One hand pushed at the center of her back while the other wrapped around her wrist.

"Are you going to tell me wh—"

"Step," he ordered. She did so, and he pushed her forward ignoring the rest of her questions. When she tripped Kikyo wrapped his arm around her waist to hold her steady. It felt like forever before he gave her permission to open her eyes again.

The forest had thinned, telling her they were almost to the meadow, but nothing seemed out of place. Kiuno tried to look behind her, but he pushed her forward.

Once they broke from the trees Kikyo pulled her into a sprint until they reached the gate. A million questions burned in her mind as she followed him until they found Elliott. He appeared to be in deep conversation, but Kikyo interrupted.

"I need to talk to you." Elliott looked him over, his merriment shifting to something darker. He excused himself and followed Kikyo, with Kiuno tagging along.

"What happened?" Elliott asked, his eyes darting between them.

Kikyo looked at her once then back to Elliott. "I found them."

"Found who?" Understanding set over his features even as the question fell from his lips.

"They were…in pieces. Scattered." She'd never seen Kikyo's face so pale. "It's fresh."

Elliott didn't hesitate. "Close the gate."

CHRONOPOINT

REALM: 1
DAY: 39

Rain clattered on the roof above as Kiuno sat with her back against the wall. Night had long since fallen. The wind howled between rickety buildings, pulling at the wooden planks. Thunder shook the ground as cracks of lightning shot across the sky. She wondered if this torrent would ever end.

Most stayed inside the safety of the houses, but she opted to remain outside, the air too thick among the crowd. Small droplets hit her occasionally from the leaking roof and caused her to shudder. That, amongst other things.

A week had passed since Kikyo discovered the bodies, and she silently thanked him for sparing her the sight. He'd been distant, and Elliott spent a lot of time consoling him. She guessed from his experience in the military he understood the shock. It left her feeling lost.

Elliott followed Kikyo back to the site the following day and dragged the bodies back in bags. He informed everyone about the tragedy and fear spread.

Forced to stay behind she watched their sulking figures enter the forest and return soon after. Elliott stacked the bags on top of one another and placed wood between them. The stench from the fire sent several retreating to what they claimed as home. She stayed and watched as the flames consumed the bodies and tried not to gag.

A figure running through the dark brought Kiuno from her reverie. Elliott sought shelter beneath the same roof and shook droplets from his arms and hair. He sighed sinking to the ground.

"Rough day?" she asked. They'd all been feeling worn since the discovery.

"Not any more than usual." Silence fell as they listened to the rain and rhythm of the storm.

Elliott ran his fingers through his hair. She couldn't see them now, but she envisioned the dark circles that had formed under his eyes in the passing days.

"Hard to believe it's been a month," she said.

He didn't comment at first. "Too long."

She tilted her head to look at him, but his gaze went far beyond the gate. Perhaps far beyond things she could imagine.

"You should sleep. Nothing is going to brave this storm."

He seemed to examine the area once again before laying back and folding his arms. "Wake me if anything happens."

MIDAFTERNOON, KIUNO busied herself cleaning fish when the boy on watch sprinted to Elliott. She watched their frantic exchange and jumped up to follow when both dashed to the gate.

Kikyo sat perched atop the wall, bow in hand. The sight worried her.

"What's going on?" She came to stand beside Elliott but didn't need to wait on his response. Riding toward them were twelve people on horseback.

Her heart skipped.

A month of waiting, a month of worry, yet it wasn't relief that flooded her now.

Were these men responsible? Could they have killed in such a horrible fashion? What if they were the people who'd put them here to begin with?

"What do you make of it?" she asked, her eyes darting between them.

Elliott was silent, studying, the apprehension on his face painfully obvious. "I'm not sure yet."

Each kept their gaze fixed, the small group getting closer by the second. Elliott turned to the three boys standing beside him. "Get everyone inside, block the doors and keep quiet. Kiuno, go up top and take your bow."

Her blood raced. "You think they're coming to—"

"I'm not taking chances." His stern voice silenced her.

The three ran off as instructed, and she watched confused people slowly obey. Elliott's gaze never left the men. After a moment, he turned to her. "Up." She nodded and grabbed a bow before climbing the wooden ladder, an eerie silence settling around them.

Seconds ticked by.

Kiuno glanced at Kikyo and envied his readiness. He knelt with an arrow prepared, the string just taut enough so it wouldn't slip and one foot forward to shift at a moment's notice.

Kikyo. The epitome of calm. Able to take in each moment as it came to him. Only once had she seen his countenance falter.

He sat ready, poised.

Kiuno clenched her hands to stop the shaking. They had the advantage. They could shoot without—she paused and shook the thought from her mind. Killing wasn't an option but injuring, she could manage that. Force them to run if things got out of hand. She wasn't a murderer and wasn't about to let this place turn her into one. Glancing at Kikyo, she wondered if he felt the same.

As the thunder of hooves slowed, she could make out the newcomers, but it did little to ease her fears. They looked almost barbaric wearing leather and having swords fastened to their belts.

Swords. Could they have hacked other human beings to pieces?

All eyes turned to the archers. Threats to be considered. If they had any idea how much her hands were shaking, they'd laugh.

Kikyo rested his hand over hers, and she startled. His gaze didn't shift. His warmth was a welcome comfort that told her everything would be fine. She took a deep breath. Kikyo's steady hands returned to his arrow, and they waited.

Two men dismounted and handed the reins to their companions. The one closest to them nodded to her and Kikyo before turning to Elliott. "Greetings. My name is Eldridge, and this is Tyler." Kikyo shifted when the male stepped closer to the gate and extended his hand.

"Elliott." He eyed the two but stepped forward anyway. Her heart clenched.

Tyler leaned in, whispering something to his companion, but Eldridge waved him off. The way he and Kikyo glared at one another was unnerving.

"What can I do for you?" Elliott asked.

"We might be able to shed some light on your situation if you're open to listen. We're not here to cause anyone harm."

"Then why are you so armed?" Elliott's tone made her hair stand on end.

"Because it's dangerous out here. We've traveled a long way, and this is necessary to survive. Things aren't quite as bad in this realm, but I assure you some parts warrant our attire."

Realm?

Elliott remained silent.

"We aren't the ones who put you here." Eldridge rolled up his right sleeve to reveal a light gray stone. From where Kiuno sat it resembled the one around Elliott's wrist. Tyler did the same. "We were abandoned just the same."

How was that possible? They had horses and weapons. What prevented them from going home?

"Please, I know things have been rough for you, but I promise we're here to help."

She glanced at Kikyo when Elliott nodded and opened the gate.

They entered and dismounted one at a time. She tried to watch their movements but chewed her lip. Was getting information worth it? It wasn't as if anyone else had come for them.

The gate closed, and the horses were let loose. One man in particular caught her attention. He appeared much older and didn't carry a weapon. Instead, he pulled a bag from the animal and looked around pensively before heading to the corner with the others, the exact corner where she slept.

Tired of staring, Kiuno set her bow on the wall and tucked her knife in her shoe. Kikyo grabbed her arm, a warning in his gaze.

"I'll be careful." He would be watching. As would Elliott. There wasn't much to worry about with those two around. Kikyo nodded and released his hold, walking down the wall where the strangers had gathered.

Elliott acknowledged her presence with a nod when she stood next to him.

Stay vigilant.

Rather than jumping to an explanation, Eldridge asked for a tour and Kiuno followed. People poked their heads out, and she clicked her tongue in frustration. So much for staying hidden.

He wanted to know how they survived, where they found water and who oversaw organization. The conversation felt forced to her ears, but she understood. He was trying to build trust. The way Elliott kept his hand around his dagger told her it would take a lot more than cheap talk.

After their short walk, Eldridge appeared impressed. Elliott granted him the opportunity to speak with a few people before they started back in eager silence. None so much as turned to look at her.

She desperately wanted to know what Eldridge had to say, but kept quiet following Elliott's lead. Kiuno was sure he had a plan.

There was a large blanket spread across the grass with the older man seated in the center. Eldridge welcomed Elliott to have a seat, but Tyler almost knocked her over as he stood to block the path. She prayed Kikyo didn't put an arrow through him right there.

"Can we help you little girl?" She glared at him and the way he spat 'little girl'.

"She's with me," Elliott said. He walked over, placing a hand on her shoulder.

Eldridge raised one brow. "Really? Has she helped you establish all this?"

"She's played a role in it." Elliott gave her a reassuring smile. She got the message and took a breath.

"Interesting." The three seated themselves around the blanket. Eldridge spoke again, seeming to whisper to himself. "Where should I begin?"

"Wherever you feel is best," Elliott replied.

Eldridge straightened and cleared his throat. "This might be a little overwhelming so bear with me. Have you connected your given names to anything?"

Elliott shook his head. "Nothing specific."

"They're names used in a game."

"Chronopoint?" she asked, unable to contain the question.

Eldridge nodded once. "Everyone who came in contact with that game is here." He waved one hand over the area.

"So, there are other villages like this one." Elliott confirmed.

"More than you can imagine, we've been moving from place to place recruiting those left behind."

"Recruiting for what?" Elliott gave him a confused look.

"To go home."

Silence fell between them.

"Do you know where we are?" she asked.

Eldridge let out another long sigh. "I do..."

She could feel the tension growing as Elliott tried to keep his patience. "We've been here over a month, people have died, and we haven't heard a word from anyone outside. I'm willing to accept just about any explanation."

The way Eldridge looked at them made her wonder what kind of horror his next words would hold. "All right then." He straightened and said, "We're in a world that has been completely fabricated by someone with extreme intelligence and a sadistic nature."

Silence.

"What do you mean fabricated?" she asked.

"I mean, it isn't real."

"That doesn't make sense, if it isn't real, then how are we here?"

"This world is virtual, created by a computer system. Someone with more knowledge on how technology works could explain the finer details. We're still mapping the realms to determine how large it is. We haven't come across the reason either, but it seems we've been placed in a world similar to the game we once played."

They waited for him to laugh, to tell them they'd seen the smoke in the distance and were sent on a rescue mission, but Eldridge stayed silent, shifting his eyes between her and Elliott.

Kiuno opened her mouth once and closed it again. "What you're saying is, you don't know how to get home."

His expression softened. "Not the exact path, but we're working on it."

"But this is crazy," she exclaimed, "How could someone take random people and transport them to some virtual world? That just isn't possible!"

"It *is* possible, and unfortunately we're among the first to see it happen. It was difficult for everyone when they first heard the news. A new age of technology is being developed, but no one knew it already existed to this magnitude."

"If this is just a virtual world, shouldn't we be able to wake up or something?" she asked.

"I wish it were that simple. We aren't sleeping. What you see are our real bodies. It took me seeing the portals to begin understanding. Somehow, we were broken into particles before being reconstructed here. It's been tested with inanimate objects, but no one imagined it would be tried with humans. At least not yet. The sad part, was the experimenting involved during the initial stages."

"What do you mean by experimenting?" She shuddered.

"I mean, not everyone made it entirely intact. It wasn't a pretty scene." He grimaced.

Kiuno felt as though her heart would beat from her chest. This wasn't real.

Elliott interrupted. "How many people are we talking?"

"Dead?" Eldridge clarified.

"No, how many are here?"

"Seems like thousands, tens of thousands maybe. I don't know how many played. We meet more every day."

Kiuno saw the worry on Elliott's face. "Every *single* person who played is here?"

"It seems that way, though we don't exactly have a record to go by."

She let out a shaky breath, her stomach feeling as though a lead weight had been dropped in it. If everyone who played was here…her husband, her friends…where had they ended up? Were they safe, did they even make it through the transport process?

A month.

Her thoughts raced. They should have explored sooner. They should have found someone—

But they tried…

Those people were torn apart. What if her husband—

Her mouth went dry, and she clenched her fists.

"How do you know all this?" She could hear the accusation in Elliott's words.

"A book. They're in random towns and give a vague explanation."

"What does it say?"

"There are ten realms, and a portal connects each. To keep it simple, if you reach the tenth you get to go home."

"That's a far cry from Chronopoint's game play."

Eldridge chuckled. "You should be thankful. If this was Chronopoint we'd all be killing one another."

Silence fell over them again, and she tried to steady her mind.

"You've seen these portals?" Elliott asked.

"We're already in the fourth realm and headed to the fifth soon."

Elliott paused, and she could feel his eyes on her before he continued. "Why do you say this world is dangerous?"

"It goes beyond basic survival. There are beasts that wander the wilderness, no doubt created from the demented imagination of a lunatic. Naturally, they create a problem."

"And you're recruiting to minimize casualties?"

Eldridge nodded.

"What about those unable to fight?"

"They're kept safe behind walls sturdier than this. There are other groups at the front as well, each with their own leader in place."

"Are these groups based on previous friendships?"

Eldridge nodded. "Several are. It's what has spurred us forward. With trust established, leadership fell into place naturally."

Kiuno remembered laughing at the idea of the game's involvement. It seemed so ridiculous at the time. What kind of crisis would they be facing back home with so many missing? Could anyone get them out? Did they even know where to start?

She tried to fight the tears. People were sacrificed, used as test subjects for the creator to get things right. How many died for nothing?

Everyone...they'd be going by their gaming names. Not only had her name been cleared from her memory, but all others had as well.

Her husband would be Elite. That one was easy, and her cousin went by Silver. Then there was Scorpios, Maltack, and Blue. They'd all been dear friends and the originals to their alliance. Then there were the other leaders like K.J. and Reece. So many that could be anywhere...or already gone.

"How did you come by your clothing and weapons?" Elliott asked.

"Fortune smiled on us, and they were already in the villages when we arrived. Oddly enough, some know how to craft them as well. I suppose their talents were once hobbies."

"And your group's primary focus is getting out of this place?"

"Of course. I'm hoping the fifth realm will have been found before we get back. I'll admit we've made mistakes and lost people from our ambition, but it's opened our eyes."

Eldridge continued. "We may not have a list of people who got dragged into this mess, but we're working on a record of those within the ranks. It's not a perfect system, but if you know anyone, we'd be willing to look."

Kiuno glanced at Eldridge and then to the older man who'd been silent throughout the conversation. She swallowed to relieve the lump that had formed in her throat. "Elite."

He pulled a large book from his pack and opened it toward the middle. Lines crossed out several names, and she couldn't help but assume the worse.

He flipped through several pages before shaking his head.

"Scorpios?"

Again, the same process ensued with another disappointment. Kiuno gave him a handful of names, but not one turned up.

What were the chances they'd bypassed Eldridge's group? Probably good if this place was as big as they claimed.

"Don't be discouraged. We're only one group living in the fourth realm. There are dozens out recruiting. They could have arrived in the time we've been gone."

Kiuno could feel Elliott's eyes on her but couldn't bring herself to meet them.

"Do we have a choice?" Elliott asked.

Her blood ran cold, but to her relief Eldridge let out a small laugh. "There's always a choice. We didn't come here to force anyone, though we do encourage them to stay together. I can promise that if you come with us, there will be no shortage of food, and we live fairly comfortable, all things considered."

"We'd be foolish to refuse, but let me run it by the others. I can't decide for them."

"I understand. Shall I join you?"

Elliott nodded before turning to her. "Are you all right?"

She waved for him to go.

The three men headed toward the waiting crowd, and she stood and started back to the wall. She didn't feel up to entertaining the older man's questioning gaze.

Kiuno found one of the beige horses and touched the soft muzzle wondering if it'd been transported or was just another fabrication of this waking nightmare.

FIRE BURNS

REALM: 1
DAY: 40

Kiuno sat atop the stone wall with her legs crossed, watching as the sun set over this fictitious expanse of land. The tree's shadows grew toward her, stretching across the meadow like fingers trying to pull her into their world. The sun painted the sky with calming hues, a mixture of pale orange and pink.

Someone had created all this, had placed every tree. It all felt so real. It *still* felt real. The idea of it being fake…

It was the reason they'd been dumped in the middle of nowhere. They were at the mercy of some lunatic's creation.

Kiuno ran her thumb over the little blue stone. Eldridge had a stone, as did the others with him. They weren't the people who put them here. Their eyes looked worn and homesick. Many of the same feelings she shared.

Family, friends…they were all here. Everyone she'd grown close to in that two-year time span. Their names weren't in the book. Did that mean they'd joined with another group? It was a possibility and better than—she choked, fighting back tears.

Her husband would search for her once he got the news, she knew him well enough. Maybe it was in her best interest to go with Eldridge's group, she would be safer and then—Kiuno paused. Then what? Wait? Go between the separate groups in search of Elite every day?

She shook her head. They wouldn't allow that. If she ate their food and slept under their roofs, she would be obligated to contribute. Running back and forth would just make her useless.

A slight noise was the only thing that alerted her to his presence. "What do you think of them?" Kikyo asked, sitting beside her.

"I assume you were listening?"

"Would you assume otherwise?" His response made her smile if only a little.

"I'm not sure I trust them," she admitted. They were strangers. Who knew if they were telling the truth.

"And you shouldn't."

His tone caught her by surprise. "You think they're lying?"

"It's not that. With groups like this, you have to understand your place. They'll present themselves as having your best interests at heart, but all they want is what you can give in return. In this case, the goal is escaping and while that's our goal as well, I feel they're willing to sacrifice more to reach it."

"I'm aware."

"Is it safe to assume you won't be joining them then?" He sounded hopeful, as if he'd already decided he wouldn't be going. Where would that leave them? Two people out on their own in the middle of some dangerous world?

"I don't know."

He turned to her, but she didn't meet his gaze. "Something else is bothering you."

Silence followed.

He was observant as usual, but she couldn't bring herself to speak. She'd been working to keep her composure and couldn't risk voicing her mind's chaos without spilling her feelings with it.

"Maybe," she managed.

The two of them watched the final bit of light fade before Kikyo stood. "I'm going to see what else I can find out."

"Be careful."

"Always am." He slid down the ladder, disappearing into the shadows. His calm appearance made her wonder if he had anyone to worry about like she did.

Hours passed.

Kiuno's body felt stiff from sitting on the hard stone, but it was the safest place with their new friends around. She trusted Kikyo's instincts. Her own were screaming or had been. Right now, she just felt numb.

Eldridge had a lot to offer them, not the least of which included protection. It was good to know she wasn't the only one opposed to joining them. She had family to find.

Kiuno turned as Elliott made his way up the creaking ladder. "I've yet to figure out why you kids enjoy sitting up here." She gave him a small smile.

He sat beside her, looking over the meadow. "Are you doing all right?"

Kiuno clenched her fists, her body trembling.

Am I?

Thoughts from earlier raced through her mind. She was scared but not for herself.

She was scared for everyone she'd ever loved. Scared to find out what might have happened, to get that news. She didn't want to say their names and watch someone's eyes divert as they tried to find words.

Kiuno longed for home like she'd never done before, to lie in bed with his arms around her and pretend this was all a bad dream. She wanted to look forward to a Friday night with friends instead of their next meal. She wanted the experiments to be a lie.

"Kiuno?" She clenched her jaw to fight them, but the tears spilled over. Elliott wrapped one arm around her shoulders and pulled her into him. She cried. Hard. The composure she'd held onto this entire month falling onto his shoulder. The only hope she clung to had been shattered, torn to tiny hopeless shards.

Elliott held her in silence and waited for her to take a few shaky breaths before speaking. "I know you're scared, but we'll figure this out."

Kiuno shook her head. "He's out there somewhere and I—" Her voice cracked.

"Elite is your husband?"

She nodded. "It's bad enough I'm here, but why them too? I don't even know if they…" She clenched her jaw again.

The experiments tore at her the most. She knew they could survive, provided they were given a chance. The people she called friends were more like family. She'd do anything for them. The thought of them being hurt made her heart ache like nothing she'd ever felt before.

Elliott stayed silent for a time. "If your husband were given the same opportunity, what would he do?"

There was no question. "He'd look elsewhere."

"You're sure?"

She nodded. "If my name wasn't in that book he wouldn't leave me behind."

"Then you've already decided not to go?"

"I have to find them, and if it means going out by myself then that's what I'll do."

He chuckled. "You think I or Kikyo would just let you wander on your own?"

"Kikyo doesn't want to go either, but I can't ask you. Too many people rely on you."

"And now they have help." She sat up, trying to see his face in the darkness. "I can't let you have all the fun. Someone has to keep an eye on you kids."

She smiled as more tears threatened. "Thank you."

"No more waterworks. There's no reason to lose hope yet. How many of your friends are we looking for?"

"A lot."

"And what exactly constitutes a lot?"

"I was a leader in that game."

"Regardless, we'll help you find them." She smiled again before laying her head on his shoulder. Even here, she'd made good friends.

TYLER PACED the tent, his adrenaline racing as he rubbed his palms together. "You saw it, didn't you?" His voice shook with excitement.

"I did, but we need to be patient, and let them come willing. She'll be a better asset that way." Eldridge flipped through another page as if he were trying to find some secret they'd missed.

Tyler's face flushed as his temper rose. "I will not pass on this opportunity. We've traveled too far and lost too many to let it go. I'll take full responsibility if things go south, but the girl is coming with us."

His far too passive companion sighed. "Just let me handle things. It's unlikely anyone has figured out what they're capable of, especially her. The people are afraid, and fear is something easily manipulated. I'm confident we can convince her to come. We simply have to tread carefully, a few seem protective over her."

He snorted. "A couple of boys aren't going to stop us."

"Tyler please, try to stay collected for once." Eldridge rubbed his temple.

"Fine, try it your way."

"Thank you." He respected Eldridge, but sometimes his methods didn't get the job done. Either way they would get what they needed and then escape this wretched place.

WITH DAWN breaking the pair climbed down the ladder and started toward the twelve, her decision final.

Her only worry now lay with Kikyo, but it was short lived. She found him perched on the opposite side of the wall, moving to stand as they approached, but his expression made her pensive. He didn't smile and held his bow at the ready, shifting his gaze from her to their guests.

Kiuno nudged Elliott, but Eldridge greeted them before she could speak. "I trust you slept well?" Eldridge exchanged a glance with Tyler, and she looked at Kikyo again.

"We did," Elliott lied. After staying up, trying to absorb yesterday's news her eyes burned, and her body felt exhausted.

"After you left, I stayed to talk with some of the villagers. They agreed to leave this morning. I hope you don't mind. We've been away for a while."

"This is your last stop?" Elliott asked.

"We have one more, but rumors tell us there's not much left." His voice seemed full of regret.

"If you can promise their safety, whatever decision they make is fine with me."

Eldridge said, "You have my word, they'll be fine. Once we enter the third realm there will be an escort. We don't travel through that land on our own."

"Good." The silence settled over them like a thick blanket of unanswered questions.

Eldridge cleared his throat. "I'm eager for you to meet our leader. I'm sure there will be a fitting job for your expertise."

Elliott glanced at her. "I think three of us will be traveling on our own from here."

"Why?" Eldridge looked between them.

"Kiuno has concerns about her family's whereabouts."

Eldridge's expression shifted. "I know you were disappointed, but that doesn't mean they aren't there."

"They're not," she stated.

"How are you so sure?"

"Because I know my husband."

She watched several emotions play across his face until resistance won. "I'd like to argue the point, but you'd know him best. Will you join us once you've found him?"

"I think I'd like that."

"Eldridge," Tyler said with a hiss. "Our discussion?" The man's eyes were wide and wild.

Eldridge sighed. "We can't force someone against their will, it'll only create problems."

Force?

"She has what we've been searching for!" Tyler exclaimed and lunged forward, gripping her wrist.

"Tyler, we can't ju—"

"We are under orders to bring anyone like her home. If you have any complaints, then take it up with our leader."

With a jerk, she stumbled forward, and her foot caught the ground. A sharp pain shot through her wrist, and his fingers dug into her skin. Elliott pulled his knife, and two men positioned themselves before him, drawing their swords. Kikyo ran until he stood above the gate and pulled back an arrow.

Time froze.

Elliott, armed with nothing more than a small dagger, faced the two men with larger blades. Behind him stood another, bow in hand, arrow notched and gaze directed at Kikyo.

What could she have that they wanted?

Eldridge's commands floated through the air. Villagers murmured amongst one another, but none moved to help, just like the time she was attacked. Cowards remained cowards.

Fear shot through her as the arrow drew back, Kikyo oblivious to the danger. She needed to warn him. What could he have heard? What didn't she know? Their plan was obvious. Take her captive and kill those that resisted.

Like hell.

Kiuno planted her feet and yanked against his hold with every ounce of strength she possessed. Tyler stumbled, but his grip only tightened. Tears sprang to her eyes as she pulled again.

A foreign sensation stirred deep in her gut and flames spiraled down her arm, bursting around her wrist. Tyler cried, and they both fell to the ground. Kiuno rolled, but the fire chased her as if determined to keep her within its grasp. She struggled in a panic, trying to put it out until realizing it didn't burn.

Kiuno paused her frantic flailing and looked at the flames that encircled her arm. The flicker mesmerizing. Tyler still sat on the ground, clutching his hand.

The flames didn't dissipate. She wasn't sure whether to be afraid or fascinated. Kiuno twisted her hand back and forth. Not one spot of marred skin.

Eldridge stepped forward with both hands raised. "This has all been a huge misunderstanding."

"That's an understatement," Elliott said.

Eldridge placed himself between his men and Elliott. "Help Tyler onto his horse, and take him outside the gate. We'll be there soon." The male cast a final glance her way, then sheathed his sword. Tyler didn't object.

Eldridge continued, "As for the rest of you, there is no need for violence. Put your weapons away and help the villagers prepare for travel."

Kiuno looked at the people. A familiar fear in their eyes, but most of it was directed her way. Perhaps it was a good thing she wouldn't be joining them.

Elliott sheathed his knife, but Kikyo refused to move. His gaze still swept the area as if they might attack any moment.

Eldridge turned to her and his expression softened. "This is the first time?"

She nodded.

"The fire will continue to feed from your energy until you've calmed down."

Calm down? How was she supposed to calm down? The thought sent another wave of adrenaline through her body, and the flames responded. They crawled further up her arm, almost at the shoulder now. Her friends had come so close to dying.

"It can stay," she spat.

Eldridge nodded and headed back to the gate.

There was a current. Something that flowed wild through her body and spun out of control. She tried to grasp it, but the flow eluded her, like an older child playing a game with their sibling, one they'd never win.

Kiuno distanced herself upon hearing the whispers. She started down the center road toward the water basin and stayed on the well beaten path. It wouldn't do any good to light the entire meadow on fire.

Kikyo joined her shortly after but kept his distance. He leaned against the nearest house, bow still in hand. Maybe he thought someone would come after them. She looked at the flames again. It wasn't likely.

The villagers exchanged packs and sorted through items to make traveling easier. There wasn't a lot to take. They had leftover meat that would feed them for a few days and some extra animal hides to keep warm. A pang of longing washed over her as she watched. Despite her anger toward Tyler she hoped they were telling the truth.

Once her heart slowed, the flames died until there was nothing left but their warmth against her skin. She ran her fingers over the area.

Eldridge approached with Elliott on his heels. He stopped, several yards out, when Kikyo leaned forward and pulled on the arrow. Eldridge nodded to him. "There's still a lot unknown about the magic of this world."

"Magic?" she asked.

"We can teach you. I hope you can forgive Tyler's actions. We've been searching for someone with the color stone you possess. He got carried away."

"What does a stone have to do with any of this? Is such a trivial thing so important that you'd be willing to kill my friends?" Kiuno fought against the flames that threatened to burst forth again. This so-called magic was going to be a problem.

"The color generally marks the element one is able to use. Red signifies fire, deep blues are that of water, green for wind, and tan for earth. The common steel color you see indicates no magical talent at all. Most of us have that one, but a lucky few have been blessed with gifts beyond imagination. To be honest, I'm impressed with how naturally it presented itself."

Compliments would not quell her anger nor distract her from the question at hand. "I thought you said red represented fire."

"I did, there are different variations depending on the person."

Kiuno sighed in annoyance and held up her wrist. "Does this look red to you?"

He shook his head.

"So, tell me why this rock is so damn important."

He shuffled his feet. "Honestly, we don't know. The book shows a picture of that stone with the caption 'Fire from the Sky' and claims it to be the most powerful magic. Only catch is it's uncontrollable as well."

"And you feel this power will help kill monsters, thus sparing your men." Elliott finished.

"Exactly."

Kiuno scoffed. "How can it help if you can't control it?"

He shifted again. "I'm not sure. We were given orders."

"Maybe you need a new leader," she said. Elliott smirked.

"I apologize, perhaps you'll consider joining us when we have more information?"

"Perhaps." Elliott's tone was dismissive and Eldridge nodded and turned. She watched Elliott get people situated, shifting larger packs to the horses. As least the men weren't too proud to walk.

Several villagers hugged Elliott and he bid them farewell. None bothered to speak with her. She was forgotten. Nothing more than a firework that had fizzled.

At least they had something to look forward to. Something to keep them safe. They weren't fighters and would function well in a larger community, as long as it existed.

The three watched until the small crowd disappeared beyond the trees, and exhaustion hit her full force. The world spun and Kikyo's hands wrapped around her shoulders as she tilted back.

"You all right?"

She nodded and used the gate to steady herself. "I think I'm just tired." Both kept a careful eye on her for the rest of the afternoon. Once he was sure she wouldn't faint, Kikyo's expression turned somber, and his distance increased.

"I'm not going to spontaneously combust." Both laughed, but neither commented, the fatigue hitting them all.

They settled in the center of town around the large fire that had since turned to coals. Its only purpose had been to light the darkness. Smoke no longer mattered, no one was coming to their rescue.

She tried to organize the events of the day but felt as though it'd dragged on longer than possible. Then she remembered they hadn't slept.

Dread swept over her when she thought about how things could have ended. If not for the magic she would be tied to a horse right now and the two beside her would be dead or dying.

If people sought the stone, then she needed to be careful and keep it hidden.

Stars came out to play, perfectly placed just as those from the real world. She wondered if this was how the sky looked beyond city lights or if it was enhanced for the sake of this place.

Everything had changed.

Beyond the gate lay a dangerous world, and those she loved were in the middle of it. She tried not to imagine everything that could have happened. They were strong, they would survive.

She looked at Kikyo who lay with his arms folded behind his head, seemingly asleep. What color was his stone? The sleeves of his shirt hid it from view and she'd never given it much thought. She'd seen the cool gray of Elliott's the first night.

Kikyo maintained his distance all afternoon. Even now, he slept farther away than necessary. Had he been afraid of her, or was it the concept of magic in general? Elliott acted as though he didn't mind, if anything, he seemed intrigued.

She tried pulling for the magic again, but it was so foreign she wasn't even sure it'd happened. Kiuno smiled at her own foolishness and turned her attention back to the stars.

"What's on your mind?" Elliott asked.

She raised her arm. "Everything."

His gaze fell on the stone.

"I didn't mean to burn him," she admitted.

"Even more reason to learn how to control it," Kikyo said. She thought he'd fallen asleep, but a firm voice told her otherwise. "If we end up in another confrontation and you have an outburst like that who's to say we won't be caught in the crossfire?"

"No need to worry her," Elliott said.

"He's right though, I was just trying to escape."

"He'll reconsider grabbing someone like that in the future. You instilled a good lesson in him." Kiuno laughed. "Now get some sleep."

Stars shot across the sky and she fell into a restless slumber that mixed with burning fire and dreams of home.

AIR BREATHES

REALM: 1
DAY: 42

Kiuno woke to the smell of food and the sun beating down on her. Elliott cooked while Kikyo sat in silence. None opted for conversation.

She rolled her sore wrist. Kiuno was sure Tyler had pulled something in it, but all that remained were the bruised fingerprints on her skin. Kikyo caught her looking at the marks, and she put her arm down to hide them. He clenched his jaw, but kept quiet.

The empty town held an eerie air. The silence almost deafening. She'd become accustomed to seeing everyone running about and laughing with those they'd grown close to. She looked at Elliott and wondered if it'd been hard to let them go. He seemed fond of several amongst the group.

Each building sat empty, the rotting planks more apparent now that people didn't give them life. Small animals scurried through the grass, reminding her of the twisted creatures her nightmares tried to conjure. She was eager to leave.

Elliott stood. "I'm going to see if there's anything left. I'll leave the snares to you."

Kikyo rose and she followed, grabbing her bow. There had been no incidents since the search parties, but that didn't ease her fears. Perhaps she should have considered that occurrence before Eldridge left.

An uneasy silence settled over them as she and Kikyo entered the forest. His sidelong glances did nothing to ease her discomfort.

"Kikyo?" He stopped, turning to acknowledge her question. "What's wrong?"

"You need to learn to control it."

That again. He'd mentioned it last night. She knew what could happen.

"I know, I—"

"I can help you." Instead of explaining, Kikyo pushed up his right sleeve, revealing a translucent, green stone, his name etched perfectly across the surface.

"Wind?" she asked. He nodded. "And you know how to control it?" As if answering her question, a slight breeze made its way through the trees, ruffling her hair and then faded just as quickly. "Why haven't you ever said anything?"

"It was confusing at the time. I thought it wise to keep such information to myself. Now that things have been explained and you've shown signs of a more dangerous element, I felt the need to tell you." He stared into her eyes, his gaze unnerving. "The air is gentle and practice with it doesn't leave much room for error, but with fire...even a single spark could spell disaster."

The urgency in his voice was unsettling. Kikyo was usually calm, collected. The last time he lost his composure people had died. Why did this bother him so much?

"Are you afraid of it?" she asked. He stared at her as if she'd just asked an impossible question and turned away. There was a long pause before he turned back and lifted his left pant leg.

Her breath hitched.

"When I was ten, our house caught fire." He looked off in the distance. "I was trapped inside. I didn't escape entirely unscathed and my mother, well, she didn't escape at all. We lost many things that night."

"I'm so sorry…" Her eyes misted as she allowed the image of a scared young boy sink into her mind.

"Don't be, it was a long time ago." That was the reason he'd been keeping his distance. He wasn't scared of her, but the flames they knew nothing about. Despite that fear, he was offering his help.

"What do I need to do?"

He indicated for her to sit then joined her, crossing his legs. Kikyo brought both palms forward and she mimicked the action.

"Feel for it, dig deep for that pool in your core. It's like a rush. A spark that must be held onto and brought to the surface. Yesterday was ideal with your adrenaline going. It'll be much harder to recreate that same feeling."

Kiuno watched the air shift in his palm to form a small tornado, tiny particles of dirt making it visible to the naked eye. "Concentrate the energy in your palm. When you pulled back from Tyler you were focused on your hand."

She looked at her palm but felt foolish. It was alien, something unreal, fabricated. Kiuno reminded herself where she was and looked at the small whirlwind again, but the fire from yesterday seemed like a far-off dream.

Taking a breath, she searched for the sensation, anything that would match what she felt before. It was hard to search for something you knew nothing about. There was nothing like the adrenaline rush except the rush itself. Sitting in a forest wasn't going to create that blood racing sensation.

She let her hands fall. "I don't know where to start."

Kikyo studied her for a minute. "Keep feeling for it, if you find anything, let me know." She nodded. "And if you don't mind, I'd like to keep this between us."

Kiuno gave him a puzzled look. "You don't want Elliott to know?"

"Not yet. I trust Elliott, we all know he's done far more than could have ever been expected. Just call it a backup plan." She nodded again, it wasn't as if his secret would hurt anything.

Her mind floated back to the arrow pointed at Kikyo's chest, and she wondered if he'd seen. Perhaps he wasn't quite as vulnerable as she'd first thought.

THE SNARES gave her and Kikyo a few rabbits, and they were back in the village before the sun hit its peak.

Kikyo skinned while Elliott cooked. She was pretty much useless for such things, but they didn't complain. It wasn't for her lack of trying.

Each ate in silence, snuffed out the fire, and Elliott wrapped a single bag around his shoulder. Whatever he'd found hadn't been much.

At the gate she turned, taking a final glance over what she'd called home the past few weeks. It appeared as though people had never inhabited it. Grass still covered the area, the wooden structures still looked like rotting shacks and now the fire had been smothered. It was lonely and desolate.

"Come on." They followed Elliott to the river. Eldridge was kind enough to give directions that would lead them straight to the portal. Would this world feel more real once she saw it?

That night they ate leftovers, and Elliott stoked a fire. Kiuno leaned her head against a tree wondering how long it would be before she heard from Elite, from everyone. Would the next town hold any answers? What about the one after that?

"How far are we from the portal?" she asked, her focus shifting to the treetops.

"We'll be there tomorrow."

"Maybe we should have gone with them," she whispered. Her eyes traced through the trees, wondering if anything was stalking them, watching.

"No," Kikyo said. "After he grabbed you—" he cut himself short. Elliott nodded in agreement. "We'll be fine."

Each made themselves comfortable and she thought back to the arrow Kikyo had pointed at Tyler. Would he kill for her? Both men's actions indicated there was no question, but she'd like to never truly know that answer.

VOID

REALM: 1
DAY: 43

She woke to Kikyo's gentle shake, the sun's light just visible through the trees. "What are you doing?"

"Come with me." She stretched and rose, following a few steps before stopping to glance back at Elliott's sleeping form.

"Shouldn't we wake him?"

"Let him sleep, we won't be far." Though reluctant, she followed.

They sat as before, and Kikyo went over his magic again, trying to detailedly instruct how his own flowed. She felt for it, searching for the foreign substance that resided somewhere in her body.

Kiuno tried forcing her heart to race, but it only resulted in Kikyo reminding her to breathe. She tried to replay the events with Tyler, envisioning his tight grip around her bruised wrist but nothing came of it.

"This isn't going to work," she sighed, throwing her hands in her lap.

"I didn't think you were one to quit."

She glared at him and remembered the doubt he had when they first met. She'd proven him wrong once. "I'm not, this just feels ridiculous."

He let his hands drop. "Don't rush it, you'll see progress eventually."

She knew he was right, but it didn't help. She didn't like to be out of control, especially after what he'd been through. The thought of hurting him was painful. After a few more attempts they headed back, and Elliott woke, oblivious to their absence.

Come evening, the trees opened to another meadow, but this one wasn't lush and green as she expected. The land spread before them was barren, the grass and trees dead, and the air held an electric charge that made her hair stand on end. In the center was the cause of such desolation.

The portal.

It arched like a doorway, the area around the center shifting and shimmering as if it weren't part of this dimension. The sight reminded her of steam that rose from asphalt on a hot summer day. Purple mist poured from a blackened core, tendrils reaching like hands for any life that dared venture too close.

"What is that?" she whispered.

"Our way to the second realm," Elliott answered.

"I didn't think it would look...so eerie." Her skin crawled. Everything about it brought reality crashing down. The reality of the monsters and experiments.

"Eldridge told me the travel is fast. You won't be there long, though it can make you light headed."

Won't be where long? Her mouth went dry as her heart sped up.

Kiuno held her breath when Kikyo approached the mysterious void. His feet disturbed the purple vapor that hovered over the ground like mist on a cool morning. He stretched one hand forward, testing the void and disappeared.

"You're next." She crept forward with Elliott's guidance, every fiber in her body telling her to run. The air turned cooler with each step, almost suffocating. Mimicking Kikyo, she tested the blackened core, but Elliott pushed her through.

An icy current shocked her body. Her limbs took on a ghostly feel, as if she were being stretched too thin. Everything twisted in spiraling grays, but before she could fear being stuck, Kiuno felt solid earth collide with her knees. She remained kneeling, eyes clamped as the world spun, cool air spilling at her back.

"Kiuno?" Elliott's voice arrived a second later.

"I might be sick." He stepped back when her stomach heaved.

"Are you all right?" Kikyo asked. She nodded and used him as a support to stand. Kiuno took a few steps to separate herself from the cold air. She'd be okay with waiting awhile before passing through another.

A thinner forest surrounded them with a straight path cut through its center. There were more pines in this wood than the last. Seeing the footprints on the ground and how many had passed this way renewed her spirits.

"This will take us to a town?" she asked, still looking down the path. It was put there purposefully. Another part of the game. Not a single tree or plant grew past the invisible line that marked the trail.

"Eldridge said it should only take a few days."

"All forest?" Kikyo asked.

"It'll open into prairie."

"Hunting will be more difficult."

"We'll get enough to hold us over, but I think it's best to stop here for the night."

Kiuno looked back at the portal. "As long as we're away from that thing." They smirked, but all agreed.

"We should continue training, especially in light of the creatures Eldridge mentioned," Elliott said. She hated to think about it. About the monsters from her nightmares being alive, stalking their every move.

He continued, "Beyond the third realm, people have become hostile." She remembered Eldridge mentioning that they didn't travel alone through the third realm, but she'd assumed it was because of the monsters.

"Why?"

"There's no governing force. No law. What's to stop them? They can take what they want. Do as they please."

She'd always wondered how the world would be without law, but this wasn't the answer she'd hoped for.

"What's the plan for dinner?" Kikyo asked.

"I'll leave that to you, however, Kiuno will not be getting off so easily."

She groaned. "Why does Kikyo get to go?"

"Because I'll actually bring something back." They snickered when she made a face. She still needed practice with the bow, lots of it.

Back in their small town, she'd only sparred with Elliott on occasion and even then, it was nothing compared to what he did now. He pushed her beyond limits, his fists colliding with her body as she struggled to react. Elliott wanted her able take a strike, to prepare her for the worst.

WITH MORNING, they continued and met miles of tall grass by noon. Looking at the footprints, Kiuno prayed she'd find some information on Elite. If this many people had passed by then surely someone had heard of him.

Seems like thousands, tens of thousands maybe. She shook her head trying to fight Eldridge's words.

When evening came, they sparred together. Elliott went over movements she struggled with, and Kiuno became more confident. At least until she faced Kikyo. If she'd ever doubted he'd be able to defend himself, she didn't now.

Kikyo launched at her with more ferocity than Elliott ever had, leaving her to look foolish as she struggled to match his pace. He never held back, and she had the bruises to prove it. Blue was becoming her new favorite color.

As the outlines of a distant structure came into view, the group picked up their pace. It was early evening before they were close enough to see the wooden wall. It towered as tall as the stone one in the first realm. She wondered if they'd built it or if it'd been there when everyone arrived. Kiuno looked at the dark clouds in the distance, at least they had shelter tonight.

It was clear now. They were meant to survive. Whatever psychopath put them here did so with a purpose, even if it was just for entertainment.

Were they monitored or did the captors wait on a grand exit? The thought was unsettling, but if they weren't monitored then the monsters wouldn't serve a purpose. A shiver ran down her spine—someone was watching.

As they walked through the gate, several armed guards greeted them. Archers sat perched on platforms that'd been built into the wall, support beams stretching to the ground on the inside. She suspected they were guarding against some*thing* rather than some*one*. Gruesome creatures with claws and dripping fangs flashed across her mind.

An overwhelming buzz greeted them as they entered the main stretch. Various people lined the dirt pathway while others rushed from one building to the next. They were driven. This wasn't a timid group that feared for their lives, it was a determined one. People that knew how to survive and flourish.

Children played in the street, chasing one another in a game she knew nothing about. A smile tugged at the corner of her mouth, though a grim thought passed shortly after. She wondered if they'd misjudged how long they'd been here. Could people adapt this fast?

Elliott interrupted her thoughts. "There should be an inn around here, I'll see if they have any room." He turned to them. "Have a look around, see if there's anything useful."

A pang of nervousness shot through her at the thought of them separating, but an assuring smile from Elliott eased those fears. It wasn't as if the villagers would attack them. Or at least that's what she hoped.

Kiuno took in the people. Their smiles, though few, were there. Sturdy walls stood around them, the horizontal slats carrying a smooth finish. Stone foundations stood strong, ready for the brewing storm.

Weapons were scarce with swords and staffs being the most prevalent. So medieval. Is this what the creator wanted? To throw them back in time? The small knife in her belt suddenly didn't feel ideal.

As they rounded another corner, they came to a section that seemed to contain mostly houses. It extended back and hadn't been visible from the entrance. Kikyo pulled her in a different direction, apparently deciding they'd done enough exploring. He asked those in passing where to find the inn.

A stone foundation rose from the ground to surround the bottom floor, and wooden planks finished the second story. A sign swayed in the cool breeze, and smoke poured from the chimney.

As they pushed the door open, an onslaught of voices met their ears. Laughter, sweat and—Kiuno paused…alcohol?

She took a second look to be sure her nose wasn't fooling her. Half of them were drunk. She stood there awestruck. In a place like this? What purpose did that serve?

Elliott sat perched on a stool by the far wall with a mug in hand. He spoke to two younger men behind the counter and appeared as though he'd been drawn into their drunken madness.

She cast a worried glance to Kikyo.

They fought their way through the scattered tables and chairs until Elliott waved them over. He exchanged a few words with his newfound friends, and one of them pointed to a staircase on their left.

Elliott shook one man's hand, and they followed him through the throng of people.

At the top was a long hall. They entered the last room on the left. Kiuno closed the door and leaned against it to take a deep breath. She'd forgotten how loud a crowd could be.

"What did you find?" Kikyo asked, giving him an odd look.

"We won't have to worry about payment, though he mentioned anything done for the community was appreciated. I offered your hunting skills. It's been crowded lately with people passing into the third realm."

"I thought you were drunk," Kikyo stated, crossing his arms.

Elliott laughed. "It takes a bit more than the weak crap they have to accomplish that. Drinking is simply a way to get information. I suggest we stay a few days, get as much information as we can from the passerby's. They close the gates in the evening, so if you want to head out early just ask. There are predators that have caused some trouble."

"What kind of predators?" Her heart skipped.

"Didn't mention specifics, but they recommended hunting with a group."

"I prefer us alone. Kiuno and I can handle ourselves."

"Figured you might say that, just be sure you two watch one another."

"We always do," she said.

Elliott nodded. "All right, now onto the good news."

"You mean other than an actual bed?" She'd been eyeing it since they walked through the door.

"There's a tub of warm water waiting in that little room." He pointed to what she'd assumed to be a closet and noticed the droplets on the floor. "I'm sure it's more inviting than a bed."

Kiuno paused. "You mean a bath?"

"A *warm* bath. I figured the lady should go first." He winked at her, and she turned to find Kikyo nodding in agreement. She wasted no time and closed the door behind her.

The room was small and steamy, just big enough for her and a little round wash tub in the corner. A cover kept the heat trapped within. Kiuno ran her hand along the walls, feeling the smooth finish before peeling her dirty clothes off and dipping a foot into the warm liquid.

She sunk into the water, drawing in her knees and relished in the way it made her muscles relax. She hadn't been in a warm bath since they'd arrived. It was a luxury none took the time for. Whenever she'd bathed before, it'd been done in the river with Kikyo standing guard. He was the only one she trusted to keep her dignity.

Using the liquid in a small dish, Kiuno washed the filth from her body, dousing herself in the fragrance of a sweet flower. She leaned back, temporarily forgetting the worries of this world. Though she would have loved to stay there all night, she knew the boys would appreciate the warm water as well.

Kiuno dried herself with a rough towel and grabbed her old clothes before noticing a fresh set on a corner stool. This had to be heaven. A few more sat beneath her own and though it was a little big, she wouldn't complain about clean clothes.

"I expected you to be longer." Elliott said as she used the towel to tousle her hair.

She shrugged. "I didn't want the water getting cold." She couldn't fathom the work it took to heat and imagined people carrying buckets up the stairs.

"Fair enough, Kikyo, you can go next." He stood, and she was briefly embarrassed that he'd be using the same bath water. Considering the situation, it was the least of her worries. Normality had changed.

She sat on the edge of the bed, soft fur acting as blankets. Despite it being made of straw, it was the most comfortable thing she'd laid on in a month. Kiuno braided her hair to the side and was out as soon as her head hit the pillow.

PREDATOR

REALM: 2
DAY: 45

When her eyes opened, the light had dimmed and shadows danced on the walls of their own accord. It took a moment for the fog to clear and realize a fire was going. Kiuno rolled over to find Elliott seated before the flames, his hands clasped under his chin in thought. Kikyo lay fast asleep on the far side of the bed. She rose slowly and tiptoed to the fireplace.

"You're awake." He'd changed his clothes and looked different now that dirt wasn't smudged across his face.

"You clean up nice," she said.

"Not too bad yourself." She listened to the quiet, the murmurs of those below no longer echoing through the floor. Rain clattered on the rooftop drowning the sounds of the night, but none leaked through the boards. It was nice to be dry for a change.

"How long have I been out?"

"A few hours."

"You didn't sleep?"

He glanced at the door. "I wanted to stay up for a bit."

She followed his gaze, realizing he didn't want to leave them completely vulnerable. After all Eldridge had informed him of, she understood his worry.

"Why don't you get some sleep, I'll be up," she offered.

"All right." Elliott took her place in the bed and she sat on the stool returning her gaze to the fire. If she could learn to start one, it would make Elliott's life easier. Kikyo made it look so simple, maybe their energies flowed differently.

Would anyone she knew be able to manipulate magic as well? She hoped so. Anything that would help them survive.

The rain ebbed and started again as the night wore on, the clatter causing her to doze. She fought it until the sun crept over the horizon.

Kikyo woke first. She'd never been much of a morning person, but his time clock seemed to be set with the sun. He stood by the fire for a moment in silence.

"Ready?"

"Shouldn't we wait for Elliott?"

Kikyo grabbed his bow. "He'll be all right."

"Does he know we're leaving?"

"I told him after you fell asleep."

The guards were reluctant to open the gate and told them of a four-legged beast that stalked the plains, but Kikyo insisted they'd be all right. At least one of them had some confidence. They had an advantage with magic but still. How was he so calm after seeing those from the first village torn apart?

Several paths cut through the grass, some wider than others with puddles filling in the tracks left behind. They veered from the wider path cutting down a narrow trail where the grass grabbed at her pants, dampening the bottoms.

The sun only gave them a bit of light, but the crisp morning air was refreshing. The grass had started to shift to a golden color, and it seemed the days were growing shorter. Autumn. What would they do once winter arrived? Kiuno glanced back at the wall and wondered if every town would be as airtight. She hated the cold.

Kikyo interrupted her thoughts and indicated for her to sit as he stomped the wet grass surrounding them.

He went through the details of his magic again, speaking of a flow that ebbed from the center of his body. She felt for it, trying to focus on the rush, but it'd been so long since Tyler that she struggled with the specifics. Another disappointing morning wasn't what she needed.

"Breathe Kiuno." She let out the breath she'd been holding and forced her shoulders down. Kiuno released her stomach and let the tension roll from her body as she stopped fighting a battle she would never win. She let her mind wander from her hand and up through her arm until—

A spark.

It was small. A pulse. Not quite the rush she'd been expecting. Kiuno focused on that feeling, reviving it before it could fade. The more she concentrated, the stronger it grew, pulsing along unseen currents.

"I can feel it," she whispered. Kiuno kept her eyes closed, afraid any movement would make the feeling vanish.

Kikyo took her hand and tilted it palm up, placing his own beneath hers. "Focus that energy here." She let the heat from his hand guide her as she pushed the warm sensation through her body. She glided it up through her sternum, across her shoulder and down through her arm. It fought and wavered like a small flame fighting for oxygen. She continued until the feeling was in her fingertips and opened her eyes.

A small spark sent her excitement soaring before it fizzled. "Did you see it?"

"Yes, now again." Kiuno took a shaky breath and calmed her racing heart to find the pulse once again. She pushed it down the same path, and once it reached her fingertips she shoved. Heat wafted them both in the face making Kikyo grimace, but he didn't move his hand.

"Good, pull back a little."

Though it had fought to be released, she now struggled to contain it, like a dam finally breaking free. Kiuno remembered how effortless it'd been with Tyler. The struggle had her sweating. Eldridge mentioned her magic being uncontrollable. What had he meant by that?

"How does it feel?"

"Difficult," she said.

"In what way?"

"To restrain."

"You've managed the hardest part. The rest will come with practice."

She followed his eyes to the spark and watched the flame shift, spinning to become one with magic of his own. A small fiery tornado whirled in her palm, dancing between the two of them. She marveled at how easily he could manipulate it and then looked up to see his previous fear dissipated. Perfect control.

They stayed still, silent, watching the miniature display until he removed his hand and the flame faded in a wisp of smoke.

"That was amazing." Their eyes met, but he didn't comment. Kikyo stood and helped her up. Her heart pounded when he didn't step back, the deep scent of a forest overwhelming her senses. His hand lingered and the look in his eye caused her breath to catch.

Kiuno shifted her feet, but both turned to the chilling growl that echoed behind them.

Three red eyes stared back, the rest of its body blending almost perfectly with its surroundings. Thick curled horns grew from its head with flattened ears resting against them. It resembled a large feline. A hunter stalking its prey.

No. Not prey. Predators invading another's territory.

Kikyo inched for his bow, but it lunged before he could reach it. His hand clamped around her wrist, dragging her to the ground as an invisible force flipped the creature over them. It landed gracefully, turning to bare its fangs. In the open, Kiuno could see a set of tails and lean muscles that promised a deadly encounter.

They should have listened.

"Kiuno, get behind me." She did as commanded, cursing herself for not bringing another weapon. Her little knife would hardly be a threat. Anything that would prevent those jaws from clamping around their throats.

The air tore at her clothes when the creature lunged again, and she ducked as it soared over their heads. A frustrated growl rippled from its throat, and it circled. Kikyo kept his eyes locked with the creature's, trying to predict the next move.

"Are you doing that?" she asked.

"Yes," he replied, his breathing labored. "I'm shifting the air into a vortex, but it's extremely difficult." He appeared calm, but his shaky voice told her otherwise. The magic was draining him. Her heart beat faster. If his magic faltered...

In a desperate attempt to help, Kiuno fumbled for her bow. Kikyo stood in the wake of danger. Her hands shook. Why couldn't she just—

The feline jumped, the arrow missed, and Kikyo shoved her to the side. Panic shot through her as his cry of pain echoed across the field. She spun on the wet ground to find jaws clamped around his arm and blood dripping. Claws dug into the surrounding dirt. One shake of its head...

Kiuno screamed his name, trying to get the creature's attention as fire spun down her arm and exploded around the beast. It howled in rage and turned to face her.

Her body shook as she struggled to pull and release a second arrow. It imbedded itself in the creature's front leg, but the animal barely flinched. Ignoring Kikyo it circled her, searching for a way around the flames. Now, she just needed a plan.

It lunged again. Kiuno shielded her face, but the fire reacted against her will, erupting around her body, and the creature roared again. Three arrows flew in rapid succession filling the air with a gargled yelp.

She took a moment to process that Kikyo had shot them. Fear shown through all three eyes and the top one moved unnaturally. She held her breath when it whimpered and took a few steps back, disappearing into the grass.

She stood in silence, her body trembling from exertion as the magic pulsed like fire in her veins. A few sparks were running wild through the grass. Kikyo shuffled to his feet and followed her gaze. Each flame turned into puffs of smoke, smothered as he stole the oxygen.

Blood dripped from his fingertips.

She started toward him, but he took a step back and raised one hand. Kiuno paused, realizing the flames still flickered around her arm. She tried taking a deep breath, but they didn't recede.

The sight of his blood made her pulse race. She forced the magic into submission which took far longer than she would have liked. Even with them gone, the heat lingered at the surface, trying to claw for an escape.

"How bad is it?" she asked.

He winced and examined the area before responding. "Not great, but I'll live."

Kiuno peeled away his sleeve to reveal several deep puncture wounds along his forearm. She ripped the bottom of her shirt to tie a bandage around the deepest of them.

"Are you okay to walk?"

"It didn't attack my leg," he said, his voice heavy with sarcasm.

She sighed. "I can see that." Even in this situation he could still make her feel foolish, but she could tell he was just as exhausted. Maybe more so.

Kiuno slung both bows over her shoulder before he spoke again. "We should get moving, he won't go far."

"What are you talking about?"

"It'll die with the shots I took."

"You're bleeding," she said bewildered. "We need to get back t—"

"I'm fine, we came out here to hunt, there's no reason to return empty handed."

The stubbornness in his gaze told her he wouldn't be persuaded. Wasn't a wound like that supposed to be treated as soon as possible? Did a bite need stitches, was infection an issue? She continued to stare as questions raced through her mind, but his gaze didn't falter.

"Fine."

"Are *you* hurt?" His question almost made her laugh. She wasn't the one bleeding.

"No, the fire prevented it from getting close enough." The only wounds she could claim were a few scrapes on her hands from hitting the ground.

"You controlled it well."

She hesitated. "It wasn't intentional."

"I know."

"You do?"

He nodded. "That's the second time you've used it under these circumstances. I assume the adrenaline helps you focus. It's good enough for now." She couldn't say she agreed, but if not for her magic, both situations might have turned out much worse.

The two followed a path of broken, bloody grass until they found the creature lying on its side, its breathing labored. Kikyo put another arrow in it, and they waited for death to take its course. Kikyo took the bag from around her shoulder and pulled out his leather tarp. He'd made it back at the first village and used it to drag his kills home.

The feline was heavier than any deer they'd ever caught, and she struggled to move the limp body. Thick claws and sharp teeth were much larger up close, and the third eye lay open slightly. It sent another shiver down her spine. Who would create such a thing?

"Are you sure you're going to be able to pull this?" she asked, glancing at his arm.

"Stop worrying, I'll be fine."

"Just tell me if you get tired."

The weight of the creature slowed them considerably, the two only managing a few feet at a time. Kiuno knew he didn't want to go back to the village empty handed, but she worried for his health.

Less than an hour later, Kikyo collapsed. "This is taking too long." Sweat beaded on his forehead, and his breathing was more labored than before. "Go get some help."

"I can't just leave you here."

"We took care of the threat."

"What if there's more?"

"Then there's more, but I can't help you drag this back and I'm not leaving it." She'd never viewed Kikyo as overly prideful, but right now she was considering punching him in the face and dragging him. "Kiuno."

She sighed, feeling the pent-up frustration take its toll. "Can you still shoot with that arm?"

"I took this down, didn't I?"

She paused, still considering the option of dragging him. "All right." She placed both bows beside him and he leaned against the dead animal as she took off. Her legs felt like lead weight, but she pushed herself into a hard sprint. Rest would come when Kikyo was safe.

The guards regarded her oddly when she reached them. Kiuno bent over to catch her breath and explained the situation. One man informed another to send a wagon.

Four laid down anything unnecessary and jogged back with her. The thought of leaving Kikyo alone any longer than necessary left her anxious, and the men showed no objection to her urgency. They knew what was out there.

When the beast came into view, Kikyo moved to sit up and relief flooded through her core. He was fine, seated in the exact spot she'd left him.

"You took *that* down?" They stared in awe, each glancing between the two. Kiuno wondered if they thought she'd been exaggerating. Typical.

"Barely." Kikyo gripped his arm tighter. The adrenaline must have worn off, giving rise to pain. He didn't object when she helped him, wrapping one arm behind his back to keep him steady. Between magic, adrenaline, and pain, it was enough to make anyone a little unstable. The group of six waited until the cart arrived.

The approaching horses jerked their heads and pawed the ground when they smelled the predator. Kiuno envied their instincts.

Kikyo rode in the cart with her beside him as they made their way back. The men that ran with her spoke in hushed tones, but she could see the smile behind their eyes.

Elliott paced the gate when they arrived. Maybe someone told him what was happening, or maybe he saw the commotion and overheard. Either way, she could see the worried lines in his face and the relief when he saw them alive.

"Are you hurt?" His eyes swept over them before she could respond.

"We'll live. Kikyo probably needs to see someone though." Blood had soaked through the cloth around his arm, and Elliott's eyes lingered in the wagon, the animal clearly visible.

He gaped slightly, but shook his head. "I'll hear about it later, there's a medical building just down from the inn."

They followed him and watched relief spread across the faces of each who peered into the wagon, and a hard truth settled over her. Without magic, they'd be dead.

REALITY

REALM: 2
DAY: 45

A doctor. She couldn't believe how fortunate they were.

When the woman saw the two stagger in, she pushed those in her office out the door and set to work on Kikyo's arm. She poured water over the wound to wash away the blood which revealed several puncture marks and a small tear. He needed stitches.

With little to stop the pain, Kikyo had to endure the process. Kiuno stayed for moral support. His arm had turned various shades of blue from bruising, but overall the woman declared him lucky. The creature could have easily removed it.

The doctor, Maria, wanted to watch his injury for the next week or two. Though he had been fortunate, there was still a risk of infection which would complicate matters. After stitching, Maria lightly wrapped his arm and placed it in a sling, giving him strict instructions to rest and keep the area clean.

If she'd been a second later...

"Sorry Kiuno, I guess we're staying longer than intended."

"Don't worry about it. I'm just glad you're alive. We'd be dead without your quick thinking."

"I could say the same, it wasn't my magic that prevented that thing from tearing my arm off." He paused. "Thank you."

Heat rose to her cheeks. "You're welcome." He lingered a moment, making it seem as though he wanted to say more, but he turned instead, and they started back to the inn.

"I find it strange how you've been able to control the flames in unstable situations. I would have thought the rush would cause a loss in focus."

She shrugged. "Maybe my brain is wired wrong." At that he stopped, causing her pause. She stared at the strange way his face scrunched before he burst into a fit of laughter, something she had yet to see. Maybe it was a build up from the stress or perhaps what she said had indeed been funny, she wasn't sure. Kiuno couldn't resist the contagion of the act, however, and laughed along with him.

He tried to collect himself as they entered the inn. It was humming with people. The crowd appeared calmer today, but most already had drinks in their hands. Several pointed to them, raising their glasses in turn. The two acknowledged the gesture, waving back before escaping up the staircase where Elliott sat waiting.

"I cannot believe the amount of trouble you two manage. I let you out of my sight for one day."

"Trouble?" she said. It wasn't as if they'd intended to get attacked.

"While you were being treated, I asked around trying to get information, but no one will talk about anything except that beast you took down. It's been killing hunting parties for weeks." He leaned closer. "How'd you do it?"

She turned to Kikyo for an answer. His magic was a secret, but telling Elliott she'd killed something like that on her own didn't seem plausible.

Kikyo sighed. "I suppose I can't hide it forever." He pulled back the cloth around his wrist.

Elliott furrowed his brow. "So, all the times you've been out with Kiuno?"

"You knew?"

"Of course I knew, I just thought—well, you probably don't want to know what I thought."

"Elliott!" she screamed, her face heating. "You know I'm married."

"Yes, I'm aware." She stared at him in disbelief then back at Kikyo who refused to meet her eyes. "Anyway." He cleared his throat. "Tell me the details."

"Well, Kikyo can control the wind, so he threw it, kind of." She looked to him for help.

"You can throw things with air?"

"Somewhat, it's difficult. I'd never tried it before, and it took more energy than I expected which resulted in this." Kikyo lifted his arm.

"I see, so what happened next?"

"When the beast clamped down on me, Kiuno lost control, or rather, gained control over her magic. Honestly, it was perfect timing. She distracted it long enough for me to put a few arrows in."

"I'm glad you two are all right, you didn't get hurt Kiuno?" Elliott tried looking her over again.

"Just a few scrapes, the flames seemed to react faster than I could think."

He nodded. "I thought you might like to know, I asked a few people about your husband."

"Did you find anything?"

"Not much, they said two men were asking about you, but the villagers couldn't remember what they looked like. They only remembered your name due to its uniqueness."

"How long ago?"

"Over a week. The two were moving on to the third realm. The portal isn't far off."

"So, they *are* moving without her?" Kikyo said.

She took a moment to ponder. "They must think I've already gone ahead."

"Are you known to be that reckless?"

"Well, we are out traveling on our own, so I would say yes," Elliott said, laughing. "Once Kikyo is healed, we'll just continue to the next realm, we're bound to run into them eventually."

She smiled. They were alive, still far away from her, yes, but alive. That was enough for now. She only hoped it was her husband, perhaps the other man was a traveling companion he'd run into, or someone they both knew like Scorpios.

"I'll be fine. We can leave whenever you want."

Kiuno glared at him. "And what happens if we get into trouble, what if I can't use my magic and you can't wield your weapon? It's too risky, as much as I want to find them, I can't risk either of you to do so."

Elliott agreed. "She's right, and we'll be able to gather information from those returning from the third realm as well."

"Returning?" she asked.

"They trade. This group is set up to welcome anyone from the first or second realm and prepare them for the third. They'll join eventually but want to be sure no one is left behind."

"Any more information on the creatures there?"

"Just stories, most probably fed by their own fear. They're dangerous, which is why so many are still sitting here. Some have gone over, only to come back. They said it wasn't worth it."

Kikyo sighed. "We have to avoid the road because of people and the wilderness because of monsters. Is there anything good to look forward to?"

"Actually, yes," Elliott said. "Since you kindly took out the creature causing a problem, the people here have decided to throw a little celebration in your honor." Kikyo turned a few shades paler.

"Why, it's not as if we did anything but get lucky," she said.

"Times are uncertain, any cause for celebration is a good one. It helps lift their spirits. I believe the beast is already over a fire as we speak.

THEY WERE forced to stay inside and rest until nightfall. Elliott returned, leading them to the town center where things had taken quite a shift. Tables and logs lined several blazing fires, and it looked as though everyone in town had come to celebrate. This wasn't just about taking down a beast, it was a memorial for those who'd lost their lives.

In a world where they'd been fighting for their survival, the celebration was a pleasant shift. People were dancing, singing and laughing as if this were part of their normal lives.

As honorary guests, they were seated and offered drinks, to which both declined. Neither felt safe enough to allow the indulgence, though Elliott didn't seem to mind. He ran off with a group his own age, probably sharing stories from days long past.

They had to recount the details of their heroic deed, and Kikyo tied a cloth around her wrist to hide the stone. With all the commotion, he must have thought it necessary. She didn't object.

A group of young women giggling in a corner drew her attention. It took her a minute to follow their darting eyes, the girls shifting focus whenever she looked their way. She almost burst out laughing to see them fawning over Kikyo.

Kiuno stood, instructing her oblivious friend to remain where he was and made her way toward them. They shifted uncomfortably when she leaned against their table.

"He's a sight for the eyes, isn't he?" Two of the girls blushed, making her laugh. Kikyo eyed her, comprehension sweeping over his features, she returned a wicked grin to his shaking head.

"He's single if you're curious." The three looked at one another and then back at her.

"Aren't you two a thing?" the brunette asked.

"No, no, we're only friends. I'm actually married." She waved her hand. "Why don't you go talk to him?"

"Can we?" Seeing the way their eyes glinted almost had her feeling sorry for her friend...almost. She laughed, ushering them forward.

When they approached, he searched for an escape, but one didn't come quick enough. They sat beside him, probably asking how he took out such a vicious creature. She giggled as he struggled to stay out of their reach, pulling his arm from their hands.

Kiuno watched for a few minutes before deciding she needed a quieter space. He'd be entertained for a while.

The noise faded to a blissful night as she walked between buildings. The dirt street was empty except for the few guards that sat on top of the wall. She wondered if they got to enjoy themselves, but perhaps they were like Kikyo and preferred it this way. None turned as she walked beneath them.

Without a destination, Kiuno watched the stars until she came upon the line of houses they'd skipped yesterday. The street was empty, and she followed it to satisfy her curiosity.

A low wooden fence drew her attention. It sat at the end of the road and was only a few feet tall. She thought perhaps the villagers had planted a garden.

Then she saw them.

Crosses dotted the area with several bracelets hanging from each, the night breeze moving through them as if afraid to disturb the dead. Her heart skipped as reality hit her.

Not everyone had made it.

Her legs moved forward automatically, needing to know, yet not wanting to find out. With shaking fingers, she picked up the first gray stone, turning it so she could read the name.

It wasn't one she recognized. Her throat went dry as she turned over the second.

Another unfamiliar name.

Had they known one another? Is that why they hung on the same cross, or maybe there simply wasn't enough room.

Crawling between each cross, she turned the stones to read the names, her heart pounding the whole while. She thought back to the record book and the names that were crossed out. She knew people had been lost, or maybe she'd been denying it this whole time. How many had died before anyone figured out what was happening? This was only the second realm—

A soft hand rested on her shoulder making her start. "I didn't expect you to find this on your own."

"Kikyo?" His gaze swept over the area. A grim expression on his face.

"Elliott told me about it. We were going to look through them before—"

"You mean for Elite." She choked, a burning sensation forming in her throat.

He nodded, and she gazed back over the crosses. Some graves were still fresh, and flowers had been planted along the fence line, but the center was barren.

"I'll start at the other end." Kikyo knelt at the back, taking his time to turn over each stone. Kiuno was torn between watching him for signs of recognition and looking through her own.

Someone was searching for her, but how did she know if it was Elite? It could be anyone. What if he never left this place?

Kiuno shook her head, trying to rid the thought from her mind. That wasn't possible, they were stronger than that, stronger than her. If she could survive, so could they.

She lingered on the colored stones, wondering if the people had discovered their abilities and whether the knowledge could have saved them. Maybe groups like Eldridge had been too late.

Kikyo met her in the center, allowing her to look over the last few names.

"He's not here." Relief flooded her body, but she couldn't stop yet. It wasn't just Elite, there were so many others...

He didn't complain as she made her way through. Did every town have something like this? What about the towns they'd passed up? What if he were sitting in some unmarked grave and she was left to—

Her heart skipped and knees buckled.

Not her.

Rena.

She wasn't a big part of their alliance, but she was part of it nonetheless. She was too young. Maybe not much older than fourteen if Kiuno remembered right.

"Kiuno?"

Tears spilled over as she gazed at the name. Rena had magic. She had a way to defend herself yet not even that had saved her. What happened? Did she suffer? Did the creature they took down kill her?

"I knew her," she whispered. Did she want to look at the rest of the names if this was the heartache she'd feel? What did it matter if there was nothing she could do about it? Kiuno didn't even know the girl's real name or where she lived. It wasn't as if she could tell her parents when they got back to the real world.

With aching slowness, Kiuno made her way through the rest and was thankful to come up empty.

"I'm sorry," Kikyo said. She didn't respond. There was nothing to say. Even if she'd found Rena sooner, she couldn't be sure the situation would have turned out different. They couldn't be sure of anything.

Kiuno followed him back to the inn, but her mind wandered beyond the walls. Beyond this world and what her life should have been like.

When they got back the room was empty. Kikyo lit the fire, and she curled into bed, her mind exhausted. She didn't want to think, she just wanted to fade away and wake up from this nightmare.

WITH MORNING, Kiuno found herself surprised to have slept soundly. Perhaps yesterday's encounter had been enough to force her body to rest. Rolling over, she found Kikyo staring at the ceiling. "Didn't sleep?"

"I did, just not well."

"Why?"

He shrugged. "I rested a little after he came in." She looked over Kikyo to find Elliott sprawled across the floor.

"Was he out long?"

"He staggered in about two hours after you fell asleep. Sank to the floor without a word."

She smiled. "I'm sure he had fun."

Kikyo suddenly turned to her, his face mere inches away. "Speaking of, don't think you're getting away with what you did."

She feigned innocence. "I'm not sure what you're talking about."

"They almost drove me to the brink of insanity."

"Don't act like it was bad, you got away fine."

He glared. "It was horrible, and if you ever do anything of the sort again I will make you shoot at a target until you're able to hit the exact mark with Every. Single. Shot." She cringed, knowing it would take a lifetime to shoot as he did.

"Sorry, I thought you might enjoy the entertainment. Most guys would love that kind of attention."

"And most guys are idiots."

Kiuno covered her mouth, trying to stifle her laughter for Elliott's sake.

TRAINING

REALM: 2
DAY: 47

W"here are we going?" Kiuno asked as she tried to keep up with Elliott's pace.

"After what I've heard about the third realm, we need a better way to defend ourselves."

"Kikyo isn't joining us?" He was already gone when she woke, but Elliott pushed her out the door before she could ask.

"He'll be here in a bit. I told him to see the doctor. Check on that arm. It's been causing some pain. Better to be sure there's nothing to worry about." She chewed her lip. If he got an infection, things could take a turn for the worst.

"What are we learning?" Kiuno asked as a means of distraction.

"Swordsmanship."

She groaned. "We've fallen back a few centuries."

Elliott laughed. "In a sense we have, but it's all we have to work with. With any luck, we won't be forced to stay here long enough to develop any further."

She followed in silence until a question she'd been burning to ask couldn't be held back. "You and Kikyo. Isn't there anyone you're worried about?"

He paused. "I didn't play long, so I don't remember anyone. As far as Kikyo goes, I couldn't say, but given his personality I doubt he connected much." He turned to her. "Honestly, we're the lucky ones. I wouldn't want my daughter in a place like this."

No, he wouldn't. But it explained why he was so protective of her. She was someone's daughter. What was her family thinking now? Maybe with so many people missing in the real world, her fate was obvious.

"We're meeting a guy named Hodge. He's with a group at the front."

"Why'd he come back?"

"Wanted a break and to help others prepare for the coming realms."

"And he just happens to know how to use a sword?" she asked. What person in the modern age had that kind of knowledge?

"I imagine he has a background in martial arts. Doesn't matter, as long as it's practical."

Groups of people stood huddled at the back wall. Some held weapons, while others practiced hand to hand combat.

"You must be Elliott." They turned to the male voice. Someone much younger than she'd been expecting.

"I am. Nice to meet you. This is Kiuno." She gave a small wave. "Kikyo will join us shortly."

"I heard what happened. Glad everything turned out well." Hodge carried a bright smile, but his eyes looked worn. Dark circles clung above his cheeks, and a scar ran behind one ear. She swallowed the lump in her throat.

"So am I." Elliott glanced at her. "We'll be better prepared should something like that come up again."

"And it will." His tone. How many battles had he fought? How many had he—

"I heard you can manipulate fire?" Hodge interrupted her thoughts. She nodded.

"They welcome people like you at the front. You've no idea how much magic is respected there." He turned back to Elliott. "I have two weeks with you, right?"

"Is that enough time?" Elliott asked.

"To learn yes, but practice is necessary to perfect any skill."

Hodge turned to pick up three sheathed swords and handed one to her. It was heavier than she expected. "Go ahead and get a feel for the weight. That might be a bit heavy for you Kiuno, but it's the small-est we have. I can teach you the basics, but I wouldn't recommend combat until we find something lighter."

She pulled the long weapon from its sheath, the sound of steel against steel making her teeth grind. It was heavy. Foreign. Something that didn't belong in her hands.

They mimicked the way Hodge held the blade and followed his instruction. Avoid your opponent's swing. Strike when there was an opening. Never collide with someone stronger than yourself.

She listened. Moved. Swung. But it wasn't right. The weapon felt off.

"What have I missed?" She turned to Kikyo's voice, his arm still bandaged but no longer in a sling.

"What did she say?" Kiuno asked.

"No infection, just some irritation, it's normal. I'm free to move around as long as I continue to take it easy."

She smiled, relieved.

Hodge took the sword from her and replaced it with a stick a bit taller than herself. "We call it a staff. It might be more your style. At least until we find a sword suited for your stature."

Kiuno ran her fingers down the wooden shaft. It felt more natural but— "How is this going to help me?"

Wood against steel?

He smirked. "Allow me to show you."

That night she crawled into bed with an aching body. Kiuno loved the weapon. It was designed to disable your opponent rather than kill them. When she questioned its effectiveness, Hodge showed no mercy.

Kikyo went through the motions, but they took care to watch his arm. The bruising made the marks look worse than they were.

Two weeks flew by.

It felt as though time had its own agenda. They spent every morning either training or hunting. During the evening hours they asked those in passing if they'd heard about her husband. Whoever was looking for her had to be far ahead by now. She hated waiting, but Kikyo needed time to heal. She wouldn't risk his life to catch up.

Kikyo, like herself, preferred the staff. It was a light weapon and enabled them to move around their opponents with an elegance the sword lacked. She still practiced with the sword, but everything about the staff felt better. The balance. The fluidity.

That afternoon they sat in the small room at the inn, impatiently awaiting Elliott's return. It was time to move on. Time to see what progress had been made. Kiuno hoped they were almost to the final realm. They both turned when the door opened. "Finally," she huffed.

Elliott's arms were full of an array of items. He'd made them stay, saying he had things to take care of. She imagined his 'things' were probably friends. Elliott was sacrificing so much. Would he be moving forward if she'd never met him?

"Sorry, took longer than I thought. I got some dried food for the road and warmer clothes. The third realm is a great deal cooler."

"Do the realms have varying weather patterns?"

"They don't know." Autumn had set in, but it still felt too early for winter. As if they needed things to be any more difficult.

"What are those?" She pointed to the long, wrapped packages.

"A small token of appreciation." He pulled two sheathed blades from under the cloth, a third already attached to his waist. Elliott handed her one, and she drew the weapon. It was almost light enough to wield with one hand.

"Where did you get them?" she asked.

"Hodge found them, said they'd be put to better use in our hands. I think he was just looking out for you."

"They're wonderful."

"I'd rather not use them unless absolutely necessary," Elliott added.

Even if they were thieves, or bandits, or whatever people wanted to refer to them as, the thought of killing someone still felt wrong. She doubted she'd be able to. If they came across another monster, however, Kiuno welcomed the use of a blade.

Elliott handed them a new set of clothes, and she moved into the smaller room to change. The shirt had long sleeves and squared at the neck, hanging loose around her center. She used the wide belt to hold it in place. The pants were made of thick leather and tied at the sides, lacing all the way down her leg.

Kiuno braided her hair to one side and looked herself over. Despite trying to escape this world, she felt as though it was transforming her. A heavy cloak was the only thing left, but she simply draped it across her arm and walked out.

"Is this necessary?" Kikyo asked.

Kiuno couldn't suppress her giggle. "It looks good on you Kikyo. You look like a bad-ass elf. Even have the skills to match."

He cringed. "Kiuno just referred to me as a mystical creature. I'm changing."

Elliott chuckled. "We needed new clothes, and this is the best they can do. Most will be wearing something similar before we reach where we're headed so don't worry too much. They'll keep us warm."

Kikyo sighed and put the last bit of dried food into his pack before slinging it over his shoulder. She did the same, tying the sword to her belt as Elliott demonstrated.

After being among them so long, a small crowd gathered to bid them farewell. This included Kikyo's fangirls, and Kiuno couldn't help but laugh when they started crying. Kikyo's embarrassment was worth the repercussions she'd face later.

When the noise faded, she felt back in her element. The air shifted through the grass in a silent greeting, and she noted the cool touch it brought over her skin. The breeze didn't warrant the heavy cloak, but it was clear winter was headed their way.

They only walked a few hours before the spinning vortex came into view, the icy air taunting her. Dead trees lined the area around the grass, and she wondered why it had such a negative impact on the environment. Perhaps it wasn't in their best interest to go through, but it wasn't as if they had much of a choice.

Kikyo stepped through first, but she didn't hesitate this time. Better to get it done and over with. Only eight more to go.

Outside the icy prison it was much cooler, and she thanked Elliott for getting them new clothes. Just as before, it took her mind a few minutes to stop spinning, and Elliott helped her to her feet.

"Seems they were right about the weather." She wasn't the only one pulling her cloak from the bag.

Elliott made a face. "We won't be able to avoid a fire at night." They'd planned to stay hidden, afraid bandits might ambush them, but without a fire the group might very well freeze to death.

"Are we staying on the road?" Kikyo asked and looked between her and Elliott.

Elliott pulled a piece of paper from his inside pocket and examined it. "The nearest town is empty. From there the path follows along the mountains and turns westward before the next portal. If we did, we'd be wasting time."

"So, we'll just travel this way and cut through," Kiuno said, pointing at the map.

Elliott agreed.

Slippery rock formations surrounded them. Trees grew at the edges of cliffs with their roots dangling down and cutting into the rock. The air was humid, and water seemed to trickle over every surface. Ferns grew in abundance, their feathery leaves hiding the roots as they climbed from one platform to the next. Seldom did the ground settle enough for an easy trip.

At sunset, they followed Elliott down a ravine and settled for the night, laying their packs and weapons against a boulder. Their clothes were damp and cold, but being down in the valley would help protect against the wind. They gathered firewood in the waning light and piled it beside the small stream.

Both men stared at her.

"What?"

"You're the one with the fire," Elliott said.

"Fire I can't control."

"It's just like we practiced." Kiuno looked at Kikyo then back at the wood. What practice? She had done nothing with the magic in two weeks.

Taking a deep breath, Kiuno fought the cold to search for that small spark that would lead her to the flow of energy. She imagined microscopic tunnels running through her veins until she felt the shift.

Kiuno grabbed it and shoved the sensation through her arm. The flame, though a little too big, was instant. She pushed the fire that trailed up her elbow down through her wrist and into the palm, touching her hand to the wood. It was a mystery that the fire never seemed to scorch her clothes.

"Such amazing talent," Elliott whispered.

"I have a good teacher." She looked at Kikyo who seated himself against the rock. It was too early for sleep, but the three were content to warm their damp bodies by the fire. With winter coming, days were sure to be shorter and it would take extra planning to be sure they'd survive each night.

There were storms coming. Bandits, monsters, cold.

Yes. A storm was coming, and Kiuno questioned whether they'd have the strength to break through.

DESTRUCTION

REALM: 3
DAY: 61

The trio fell asleep after a long talk about home. It seemed food was the first thing on everyone's mind. Elliott wanted a steak smothered in butter while Kikyo said he'd kill for a cheeseburger. Kiuno was going after something sweet, just thinking about it made her mouth water.

One thing she hadn't been happy about was Elliott's prediction. He reasoned they might be in this place a few more months. The thought was daunting, but it was much better than Kikyo's guess of them being stuck in this hell over a year. That was, of course, if they made it out at all.

Days passed as they climbed over slippery rocks, doing their best to maintain a straight path. The terrain proved treacherous, and Kikyo prevented Kiuno's fall more than once. She'd never been a fan of heights and this was testing that fear. The only positive aspect was an abundant supply of water.

Kikyo grabbed her arm and pulled her up the final ledge where she collapsed and steadied her racing heart. Barren land spread before them. It might have been a meadow once, but the cold had killed everything green. It left hard clumps of dead grass that tried to trip them as they continued.

In the distance, a steady stream of smoke rose to the sky. A town. Finally.

The sun was beginning to dip below the horizon when they reached the bottom of the hill. Over the top resided what she hoped to be another prosperous village, but the scent in the air was rancid, almost familiar. Whatever they were burning clouded her lungs and made her gag.

Kiuno ran ahead, leaving the two behind to discuss their sleeping arrangements, should this place have no room. It didn't matter, they hadn't come across anyone in days. She just wanted information. Maybe someone could update them on the realms. Would this town be larger than the last or—

Kiuno froze.

"What do you see?" Kikyo called, but she couldn't respond, she couldn't move as she gazed over the burnt land in horror.

Skeletal remnants stood where buildings once did, ash covering everything in the vicinity. Small flickers fought to stay alive between the mounds of bodies. They were thrown across the ground as if part of the rubble. Charred. Contorted.

Her stomach twisted from the scent lingering through the air as weak legs carried her forward. Had anyone survived? Should they bury—

"It's best we go around." Elliott's gentle hand wrapped around her shoulder.

How could someone be so cruel? They were warned of bandits… but not this.

"The fires will finish what they started." Elliott pulled her a little harder this time, but she resisted. What if Elite…

Both men followed her in silence.

How many were dead? For what purpose? It was impossible to tell male from female, but the small bodies were easy to distinguish. No mercy.

A glint of silver caught her eye and she bent to touch the familiar band that wrapped around a blackened wrist, the material unmarred. It wasn't a name she recognized.

How many?

"We shouldn't linger." Elliott tried again. From her peripheral she could see Kikyo searching the bracelets, no doubt for her husband, but her feet stayed glued to the ground.

"Elliott." They both turned to Kikyo and her heart leapt into her throat. Elliott eyed her before investigating Kikyo's find.

Please no...

Kiuno wanted to run, but her body wouldn't obey. She couldn't tear her eyes away from the scene. Is this why Kikyo protected her back in the forest? Is this how he'd felt?

Elliott grabbed her arm and turned her back to the hill. "Let's go."

"Elite," she whispered. He'd understand.

His jaw clenched. "He's not here."

"How do you know?" He couldn't convince her by simply saying Elite was strong, that he wouldn't succumb to something like this. It didn't matter how strong a person was. To survive such a massacre would be nothing short of a miracle.

"Because," his voice shook, "Kikyo found Eldridge."

A FEW days later, the first snowflake fell from a gray sky.

Kiuno sat curled into her companions, all of them fighting for warmth. After seeing Eldridge's group butchered, Elliott kept their fires low. Tonight, they'd been lucky enough to stumble across a cave, but the mouth of it had a wide entrance, allowing the chilling breeze to flow through.

Nightmares plagued her mind as she fumbled with a reason for such cruelty, knowing there were murders and no one to stop them. They could be anywhere. Do anything they pleased without consequence.

Rena. Now Eldridge and everyone from the village. Who would be next? Kiuno curled tighter into her companions.

The following afternoon they were climbing across rocky slopes once again. It led them to another cliff-side where they looked out onto barren grassland. Scattered pines were the only bit of life, save a small village at the base of the rocks, a fire burning in its core.

None spoke. She wasn't the only one hesitant. If this group had been the cause of such pain…

Her blood boiled. Strange how one encounter could open your eyes to hidden danger.

They backed away from the edge and set up for the night. The structure that stood twenty feet below them paled in comparison to the few they'd seen. The walls were made from tree trunks tied together, and it had spikes that jutted from the ground around the perimeter. She assumed this was meant to ward off predators. Two silhouettes stood at the gate, but no one guarded the top or rear.

"What do you want to do?" Elliott asked.

Despite the danger, she was torn. Skipping this village contradicted their search, but she didn't want to risk their lives either. What would make the next village safer than this one? The appearance?

"We watch them tonight and decide in the morning," Kikyo said.

Elliott waited on her answer. "That sounds good."

Both had been worrying over her since finding Eldridge's group. She'd been quiet. Light hearted conversation didn't feel right, not yet.

They hid themselves behind a rock that protruded from the ground like a guardian statue and avoided a fire for fear of disclosing their location. Each wrapped themselves in blankets and huddled together. She hoped it wouldn't snow.

Elliott offered first watch, but it was no secret they'd all struggle with sleep anyway. With the biting wind and no fire, it was all they could do to keep warm.

Kiuno drifted, her mind waking when she needed more warmth. Her teeth clattered, and Kikyo had enough mercy to drape one arm around her. She didn't care what it looked like. The night lingered beyond what she felt it should until the first rays of light peered over the horizon.

She jolted at dawn. "You didn't give me a shift?"

"There wasn't any need," Elliott said.

"Why not, does it look okay to go down?"

"Hardly." Venom dripped from Kikyo's voice. His hostility put her on edge, but Elliott interrupted before he could explain.

"Here comes another." She inched up beside them and watched the silhouette of six figures walking toward the camp. Rope tied the rear three together. Horrified, Kiuno watched as they were led past the gate, their motives clear.

"Wait…they're taking them?"

Slaves? First brutality and now this?

Elliott turned away, his fists clenched. "There's nothing we can do."

"We can't just leave them here!"

"What choice do we have? Three people can't take on an entire camp."

No, but there had to be a way around it. Were they not going to consider a plan? Sure, it'd be difficult, but that didn't mean impossible.

"I'm not leaving." She clenched her jaw and glared at those below. She couldn't.

Elliott sighed. "Kikyo, what are your thoughts?"

Blue eyes scanned the area again. "They were fairly inactive last night, most likely indulging in—" He paused, glancing at Kiuno before skipping his sentence. "One of us could sneak in, see how the area is laid out, but the risk—" He shook his head. "If we're caught, that's it."

Elliott nodded. "I agree, there're too many. We can let the next group we come across know about this and hope they have the manpower. It would be suicide if we went in. They'll just kill us and take Kiuno for themselves."

Kiuno gritted her teeth. She just needed to sneak down, release them and escape without notice—Could she do it?

"Kiuno?"

She turned away and rolled her blanket without speaking.

Kiuno trailed behind as they walked along the cliff side, her gaze drawn to the structure below. The cliff turned into a steep hill, tapering with every step. By the time they were level, the town would be long gone, and those people forgotten.

She could see it perfectly, the unguarded rear. It would be easy. How much were those people suffering, what kind of evils had been done to them? What if one of her friends was down there?

She looked at the two in front. Both silent. They knew she was unhappy. They were too. Being helpless was humiliating. They only wanted to keep her safe, to ensure she survived until the end, but what was the point if others were sacrificed?

Adrenaline coursed through her veins as she threw her pack to the ground and did a full turn to slide down the cliff. Both men called from behind in frantic voices, but she didn't turn. She couldn't. Kiuno ducked between the trees and raced forward until she pressed her back against the wooden wall.

The tiny spark she usually had to fight for raged through the currents, begging for release. She'd grant it. Fire sparked around her arms, catching the dry wood. She kept her palm against the wall as she ran, leaving a trail of flames in her wake.

"Kiuno." His harsh whisper made her turn. Elliott looked to be sure the guards hadn't caught sight of them. "If we're going to do this, we need to be very careful. The fire is a clever trick, but we don't know how many are waiting behind those walls. Kikyo and I will take out the front two. Once we're inside, stay hidden, the smoke will create a distraction. Meanwhile, I want you to burn every building we pass once we're sure it's empty. We'll find the prisoners and slip out."

She nodded, her mind set.

"Kiuno." His voice shifted, almost hesitant. "I need you to realize what you're doing before we jump into this." She stared at him, wondering what he meant, but the smoke in the sky caught her attention. He drew it back. "If we're exposed, which is likely, we'll have to fight. You'll have to fight. Do you understand what that means?"

"I do." If he was trying to scare her, it wasn't going to work.

He didn't appear convinced. "I hope so."

He nodded to Kikyo, who moved to the vantage point. They could hear commotion inside, and it drew in one of the guards. An arrow buried itself into the neck of the other. Elliott wasted no time. He ran forward and dragged the man away from the entrance, ensuring he was dead before they moved on.

They peeked around the corner before running in, the younger two trailing behind. They found it difficult to maneuver with the buildings crammed against the wall. Hopefully they wouldn't be forced to fight within the confined space.

Elliott peeked into the window of the first house, confirming it was empty before she set it afire. She looked at Kikyo, wondering how he would handle all this, but he maintained a calm appearance. The small tornado with flames shifting through its core came to mind. Perhaps he planned to do the same here.

At the second house, Kiuno peered around the corner, checking on those that were attempting to drown the flames she'd started minutes prior. Smoke replaced the fire, and it wouldn't take them long to notice the next. Without a distraction, they'd be discovered.

Elliott hissed as she ran into another building alone. Empty. She set to work, lighting the bed on fire before hiding in a corner as men ran toward the crackling wood.

Risking a glance around the door, four men stood closer than she would have liked, while others ran for water. With a moment's opportunity, she snuck around the other side, seeing both men and women being hauled out of houses with bound hands and gagged mouths.

Fire burned in her core, but she fought the surge for now. They needed to stay hidden for the plan to work.

Kiuno ducked and ran around three more buildings in search of her companions only to find them across the center road. Elliott caught her eye, looked around the building he was leaning against and waved her through. She ran her hand along the wall as she went, a trail of fire following.

The smoke filled her lungs and her eyes watered. Panic swept through the men as they continued to run, searching for a reason for such spontaneous outbursts.

Elliott pointed toward the center, and she followed his finger to a slanted door buried halfway in the ground. Fingers wrapped around the bars and reached for the latch. She cursed. They were keeping them in an underground cellar. This complicated things.

"Stay here," Elliott commanded. They watched him run toward the door and kneel, pulling on the iron bars. She glanced around, her heart hammering through her chest. He was exposed, how long before someone spotted him?

Elliott used the hilt of his sword to break the lock and set the weapon down before lifting desperate people from the hole they'd been trapped in.

Kiuno looked to the other side of the street as a man emerged carrying a pot of water. His eyes locked on Elliott's back, and an arrow buried itself in his chest as the warning rang out. He fell to his knees, clutching the shaft of the weapon that caused his life to spill across the ground.

She looked behind, searching for Kikyo, but he'd already made his way to the roof and pulled another arrow. Several men closed in on Elliott, each of them carrying swords and daggers. A metallic ring filled the air.

What should she do?

Elliott turned his attention to them, picking up his sword as he positioned himself between the enemy and victims.

Kikyo released two more arrows, and the men scattered. Elliott used the distraction to pull the last few prisoners up, and most of the men turned to find Kikyo. He seemed to be a greater threat, but that put her in the center of attention. She wouldn't be able to hide, it was time to use what Elliott taught her.

Kiuno pulled the sword from her belt. She'd left the staff. Speed would be her greatest asset. All she needed to do was keep moving and let Kikyo pick them off.

Arrows flew.

At least three men on the far side pointed their bows at Kikyo. Fear gripped her heart as she turned, unable to warn him, but a violent wind tore through the air and the arrows fell aside.

She smirked. *Not vulnerable in the least.*

Kiuno ran forward, the first male colliding with her despite the flames that still raged around her body. She ducked at his swing and used her momentum to slam her shoulder into his ribcage. He fell back, and she turned to the second, bursting her flames forth. The man shrunk back, but a third surprised her from behind, and the tip of his blade caught her upper arm. She turned with the swing, avoiding the worst of it.

He swung again, and it was all she could do to avoid the sharp blade. Her lessons with Hodge came back.

Your sword isn't a shield.

She ducked again and thrust, driving her weapon into his gut and twisted. Pain swept over his face as she stepped back. His knees hit the ground, blood soaking his shirt, and his eyes rolled back.

Her heart skipped, breath coming in shallow gasps. It was necessary. Right? Her hands trembled as she struggled to hold the blade, blood dripping from its tip.

You'll have to fight, do you understand?

Motionless. One mistake and they'd all end up the same.

"Kiuno!" She turned to Elliott's frantic call. A sword was over her, coming down fast. Fear raced down her spine, but an invisible force threw her back, skidding her against the ground.

"Focus!" Kikyo screamed. There wasn't time to think. She had to survive.

Kiuno plunged her sword through the second man's throat and looked away as the blood gushed over her hand. The feeling twisted her gut, but she couldn't afford to stop. It was her life or theirs.

The flames surged again. They curled around her as if they had a life of their own. Three looked at their fallen comrades and ran toward her. Two arrows whizzed past, dropping their targets, and she let the flames consume the last. He writhed on the ground, begging as he fought for an escape.

It reminded her of the contorted figures from days before. Dead men, woman, children…

This power. It was different. The warmth of the blaze acting like a shield. They'd survive. She'd ensure it.

Checking on Elliott, Kiuno turned to see another young man helping on the other side, pulling people from a second cell. She gripped her sword tighter. Just how many had they held hostage? How long had they suffered?

Elliott lifted a small child, and rage ripped through her core.

"Kiuno." She followed Elliott's gaze and her heart skipped.

Thirty men stood at the gate. Some sat on horses while others dismounted. They drew their weapons, and she looked at her friends, each of them breathing heavily. Elliott stood to her right. Kikyo drew his sword. Had she sentenced them to death?

The clash of steel rang in her ears as she hit time and time again, spinning around blades that grazed her arms and shoulders. One hit. Just one and they'd fall.

A sharp kick sent her sprawling to the ground. Her assailant stood over her, but a man in rags tackled him, stabbing repeatedly with a sharpened piece of wood. Blood splattered over his face, and the violent rage left her speechless.

The male was young, probably only in his twenties, but his eyes were wild, body covered in dirt and blood. "We can help." She nodded, what pain had they suffered to warrant such malice?

With the young man's guidance, more of the victims picked up weapons. They were willing to fight for their freedom.

Flames still crawled along the wall and most every building was on fire. The smoke created a dense fog. They needed to get out of here. The fire wouldn't harm her, but it would kill the others.

Kikyo… His sword sliced another throat. The captives unable to fight stood away from the chaos, and several men closed in on them.

Kiuno broke from Elliott's group and placed herself between the vulnerable and their pursuers. Eight stood strong, each of them examining the flames that still flickered around her body. Their smiles mocked her effort.

The last man on horseback jumped down, and fire wrapped his body as he drew a heavy sword. Kiuno took a step back. She'd never fought against magic before, they'd never practiced. Why hadn't they considered it a possibility?

Her body shook from exertion. Would she have the strength to fight him? Kiuno tried to steel herself. She couldn't falter. Not before taking care of him. If she died, everyone died.

With a smug expression, he charged, the opposing flames reaching forward like claws ready to tear her apart. She met his resolve, and magic burst forth in a magnitude of sparks. The two pushed against one another, both fighting for dominance. She flinched from the heat and barely blocked his sword as it came down over her head.

Kiuno jumped back, but he pressed forward, hitting her with blow after blow. She couldn't take much more of this. His size alone was enough to overpower her and trying to concentrate on keeping both blade and magic at bay was sapping the last of her strength.

She moved to his right, causing him to stumble, his side wide open. Stars shot across her vision as his hilt busted against the back of her head. Kiuno hit the ground, ears ringing. The world faltered, and the heat grew closer. She fumbled for the blade as his shadow loomed over her. Tears sprang to her eyes. Kikyo needed her—

A thunderous howl filled the air, and the man's sword clattered to the ground. She turned to see the blurry image of an arrow buried in his bicep.

"Kill them all!" he roared. Her heart clenched as seven others approached the defenseless. Pleas of mercy echoed through the air.

A young woman, about her age, ran forward and fell to her knees. She begged for mercy, but a sword plunged through her throat. She garbled unintelligible words and fell to the ground when he pulled the blade out. The one still standing over her smirked.

She stared at the woman, her mouth gaping. That could have been her. If she'd never met Elliott, if she'd been the one captured... A child screamed, echoes of pain continuing through the air.

Kiuno clenched her sword as the power surged once more. It took every ounce of strength to stand on shaking legs. Their leader took a step back, hoping to avoid the hungry flames, but his efforts were in vain.

Her magic clashed with his again, but this time he faltered, the fear in his eyes palpable. She screamed, her battle cry echoing as he was snuffed out like a candle. Something insignificant compared to her magnificence.

He rolled across the ground in agony, suffering like he'd made so many others suffer. She extended her arms, the flames rushing to collide with the wall and form a ring around the innocent. They wouldn't hurt any longer. Those threatening to end their lives met the same fate as their leader, choking on their last breath.

She locked eyes with Elliott and motioned to the exit. He nodded and pulled Kikyo toward the fire. Kiuno pushed against the heavy flames, forming a path that would lead them out of harm's way. It felt as though she were in perfect control, yet the flames consumed everything they touched and spread like wildfire.

She chased down those that tried to escape, dancing with the raging inferno in perfect unison.

Sound faded.

Screams turned to crackling fire.

Stillness.

They'd done it.

Together they'd survived against the odds, but she still had to get out. Kiuno couldn't be sure she wouldn't burn if she fainted.

Her mind faltered. Each aching step taking her closer to the exit, and everything faded when her feet hit the dull grass.

REPERCUSSIONS

REALM: 3
DAY: 66

Heavy eyes fluttered open, a blurry mixture of blue and green. She tried to move, but winced, her body far heavier than she remembered.

"Kiuno?" Kikyo's image hovered above her.

"Hey," her voice cracked, throat raw. The coughing fit that followed added to her pain. She took a few breaths and tried to close her eyes to ease the pounding headache.

"How are you feeling?"

"Not so good." She imagined she didn't look very well either. Elliott was there a moment later and sat her up, though she would have rather stayed still. Kiuno's vision swam, and Kikyo handed her a flask, the cool liquid relieving to her parched throat.

"That was some display back there, kiddo."

She gave him a weak smile. "If this is the price I have to pay, I'm never doing it again."

"Is she ok?" Kiuno didn't recognize the woman's voice, but Elliott responded after placing his hand over her forehead.

"She'll be fine. Just expended too much energy." That was an understatement.

"I'm glad to hear it." Kiuno glanced up to see the frail woman staring. The clothing around her body torn and in disarray.

"So, is it over?" she asked.

Elliott chuckled. "Considering you burnt the entire place to the ground, I would say yes." Her mind started to refocus as she looked up to see billowing clouds and then out across the dead plains. There were so many people, all those they'd set free.

Small fires still burned within, but they only fed on the remains of charred rubble. Those seeking to cause them harm were dead.

"We're grateful." Two males approached, and she caught sight of the scorched ground beneath her fingertips. Kiuno ran her hand through the ashes. How long had the fire lingered around her? She looked to Kikyo, but he turned away.

"We took the liberty of telling them this was all your crazy idea," Elliott explained. She took them all in again, a small smile creeping to her lips. They were tired but would live to escape this place. At least that was her hope. The two thanked them again and left the trio to themselves.

"What do we do now?" she asked.

"Didn't think that far ahead did you?" Kikyo's change in tone had her turning to find his blue glare directed her way. She knew he had every right to be angry. She could have killed them all.

"Don't worry," Elliott assured. "A few of the men say there's a town not too far north. We'll follow them and rest a while." She was glad they had a destination, but Kikyo's anger worried her.

"Maybe we'll get another party." She tried to lighten his mood, but he was having none of it.

J.E. REED

"If you ever do anything like that again—" He clenched his fists, unable to finish the threat. He'd been worried about her; she was sure both had. Kikyo walked away after that, leaving her to believe he was too angry to be in her presence. Perhaps she'd crossed a line with him, but he returned a few minutes later with a horse in tow.

"It's one of the few that didn't take off," he said. Elliott helped her stand, but didn't let go as she staggered back.

"You're riding so don't argue," Kikyo stated. She shrunk from his command. Elliott hoisted her up, but she tottered, and he had to steady her again.

"Are you going to be all right up there?" Elliott held her arm. Her first reaction would have been to say yes, but she wasn't sure. Her mind continued to tilt. Walking seemed an issue, let alone riding.

The saddle shifted, and someone took the reins. "I've got her." Kikyo sat behind her, reins in one hand, the other wrapping her waist.

"I can just try to walk…" she trailed off. Her cheeks flushed from his proximity.

"Don't make things weird, I'm only up here for your safety, if you weren't such an idiot, you wouldn't be in this situation."

They started north, led by those who knew the way. Awkward silence filled the space between them, but despite Kikyo's anger, she was happy. They'd rescued these people from unknown amounts of torture at the hands of those despicable men. Simply seeing the few children smiling about their freedom was enough to lift her spirits.

The sway of the horse turned her stomach, and Kikyo held her when she retched over the side. She couldn't count how many times they asked if she were all right. Kiuno nodded and told them to keep going.

After an hour, her vision cleared a little, but the throbbing pain in her head wouldn't subside. She finally allowed herself to relax and leaned into Kikyo. The warmth of his body helped fight the chill creeping in.

They were determined to reach the town by nightfall and placed several children on the remaining horses so they wouldn't have to stop. After what they'd been through she understood the urgency.

The ride was long, and her body ached with every minute that passed. It wasn't until the sun started to set that wooden walls came into view.

Many ran ahead and greeted those at the gate. She wondered if they would be hesitant to welcome such a large group, but none were turned away.

An older man approached Elliott. "Are you the leader of this group?"

"No, we helped them escape an unpleasant situation, but they're the ones who guided us here."

The man glanced at the others, seeming to take in the magnitude of their condition before turning back. "What happened?"

"I'm sure they'll be happy to recount the details, however," Elliott turned to her, "we'd like if our companion could find a place to rest first."

The man looked at her, and she wondered just how bad she appeared. "Of course, please come this way."

They followed him into a bustling town, the noise making her head pound all over again. It pulsed with life, just as the previous one had. She tried closing her eyes, to drown the stimulation that added to her pain.

Elliott wrapped his arms beneath her own and helped her down. He kept a firm hold on her as a violent chill raked her form. She missed Kikyo's body heat.

A woman led them through the crowd with Elliott practically carrying her. Too much was happening for her to keep track. The most she could focus on was not throwing up again.

"Two rooms?" Kikyo questioned.

"Yes, one for the girl and another for you men." She peeked her head up to find an older woman giving her a sympathetic smile.

"We'll just take one," Elliott said.

The woman looked ready to protest, but Kikyo's menacing glare silenced her. It wasn't fair for him to do that to everyone.

Elliott carried her up the stairs and through a door. She'd never been happier to see a pair of beds. A small wooden table sat between them, and there was a fireplace in the corner.

"You have doctors here?" Kikyo asked before she could leave.

"They've been sent for."

"Thank you." She nodded and left with Elliott in tow.

Kiuno sighed. She hated doctors. It wasn't as if Kikyo couldn't take care of her.

"Why did you ask for one?"

"Because you're injured."

"You realize I'll have to explain my magic."

He scoffed. "With your display this morning I seriously doubt anyone in this town won't know before tomorrow."

Hatred still lingered in his voice. Had Kikyo been afraid of the flames? Is that why he was so agitated? Had he gotten hurt? She couldn't tell. They were all covered in dirt and blood. Hopefully more of the enemy's than their own.

"Hey Kikyo?"

"Hmm?"

"Um, will you stay?"

He seemed perplexed, but didn't protest. "Lie down, I'll wake you when they get here." Kiuno glanced at him once more, but he averted his face. Time must have passed, but it seemed only seconds later he shook her.

In the doorway stood a tall man with short brown hair and a bag slung over one shoulder. She sat up, and Kikyo moved from the bedside to make room.

"So, this is the fire girl?" She cringed and Kikyo gave her a knowing look.

"It's just Kiuno."

"A pleasure to meet you, seems you're already a celebrity here. What hurts?"

What doesn't?

"I'll be fine; I think I just need some rest—"

"She's dizzy, her head is throbbing, and she's thrown up several times. I don't know how serious her other injuries might be."

"I see, may I?"

Kiuno nodded. His fingers felt around her head, neck and ribs, cold and unwelcoming. She winced when his hands went over places she hadn't even realized hurt. She had several shallow cuts but none he deemed serious. He had her follow his finger and do some other odd things before stepping back.

"You have a few bruised ribs, something you'll feel more of in the morning, but nothing is fractured or broken. That bump on your head and your symptoms indicate you might have a concussion, but that could be the magic's fault as well. We've come to learn that when working with magic, the body can get overtaxed. We're unsure why this is as we lack the use of modern medical equipment. From what I've been told you created quite a stir, so it might be best to refrain from it for a bit. Let your body recuperate."

"You've experienced this with others?" Kikyo asked.

"A few times, especially with those that have been with us from the start. They're always taking things too far."

"There are others here that can use magic?" Her excitement grew. Kikyo had been the only one she'd encountered that could use magic, aside from the man back at the camp. Maybe they could learn a few things.

"Yes, in fact, they're quite fascinating. You seem to possess a natural talent as well, just be careful not to overdo it." He gathered his things and left, closing the door behind him. They sat still for a few minutes, neither speaking

"I'm going to go check on Elliott, I'll let you know if we find anything useful." He turned to leave.

She didn't know what to do. She didn't want him angry with her, she didn't want to look back and regret, not after what they'd just been through.

"Kikyo, do you hate me?" He paused with his hand on the knob and for a moment she thought he might just walk out. Had she really pushed him that far? Had she ended their friendship? Silence lingered, but he remained still.

"Kik—"

"I thought you were going to die," he whispered. "I watched a man raise his blade over you and wasn't sure I could make it."

"You did and I'm thankful—"

He spun, voice raising. "What happens when I'm not there next time you do something so reckless? What would you have done if you'd been captured or Elliott and I killed? Don't you think about the consequences your actions could have held? You almost died."

She stared, eyes wide. He never yelled, not like this. He was right of course, she'd acted on a whim, hoping her actions would turn out.

"And the fire," he continued. "It burned so strong around you that we couldn't get close. Had you not followed us out," he paused, shaking his head. She tried to fight the tears as her thoughts flowed to his mother.

"I'm sorry." She looked away, afraid to see that anger or fear. Kiuno wasn't sure which was worse.

"You're not allowed to cry." She didn't realize the tears were slipping down her cheek. "And I don't hate you, I could never hate you Kiuno. Elliott is pissed too; he just won't show it."

"I didn't mean to cause so much trouble."

Kikyo smirked. "I can only imagine what Elite goes through with you. I think if I were him, I'd be out searching as well."

She risked a glance to see sorrow behind the anger and worry, things he normally kept hidden.

"Now lay down and get some rest, we won't be far."

SQUARE ONE

REALM: 3
DAY: 67

When her eyes opened, Kiuno was glad to see solid outlines rather than blurry figures. Her body protested each movement, but the raging headache had finally passed. She remembered the inn and turned her neck to see dim coals flickering in the fireplace. The moon shone in the room through a small window. She supposed she'd been out a few hours.

In the bed parallel to her own slept Elliott, his larger figure giving him away even in the darkness. A quick spike of panic flew through her, but she relaxed seconds later seeing Kikyo silhouetted at the foot of her bed. He sat on the floor, his back leaning against the frame, head down and arms crossed. Despite the anger they had regarding her actions, both still cared for her deeply.

Elliott stirred. "You're finally awake." Kikyo moved at the sound of his voice.

"How long have I been out?" Her body was stiff, and she still felt drained.

"A little over twenty-four hours."

She'd slept an entire day? Was this a side effect of the magic?

"How are you feeling?" Kikyo asked, sitting beside her.

"Better, but I'm really thirsty."

Elliott stood. "Hold on, I'll go grab you something."

Silence filled the room and Kikyo placed a hand on her forehead. "You started a fever while you were sleeping," he explained. "It appears to be gone now."

Her heart ached. She hated to worry him. "Sorry."

"There's no need to keep apologizing. What's done is done. I'm just glad you're better." He smiled, and she relaxed.

"You said it was the middle of the night?"

He looked to the window before responding. "Probably closer to morning now."

"Then how is Elliott getting something?" She assumed they'd lock the place up.

"The doctor has been here a few times to check on you. The people who run this place offered anything we needed once you woke." She had hoped to avoid the attention of too many, but it seemed everyone would know her before she even introduced herself.

Elliott was back minutes later, carrying soup and bread. It didn't matter at this point if it were cold. She was famished. They waited for her to finish.

"We've discovered some interesting things while you were out," Elliott said.

"Like what?"

"The people here are teaching others how to use their magic properly."

"Really?"

"There are several who have mastered their elements. As least as far as their knowledge goes."

"What have they told you?"

It was Kikyo who answered. "It's more complex than I thought. The color of our stones only indicates the element we are most apt to use, if you look at the underlying shades, more are possible. Everything varies of course."

"Is it possible someone could use all of them?"

"Everyone has their strengths and weaknesses, however most can only manipulate one element effectively. More interesting than that is their method of creating a barrier."

"What do you mean?"

"Those able to use an element can create a shield against it. Again, this differs based on their abilities. If one weren't very good with fire, for instance, they wouldn't be able to guard against it."

"That's amazing."

"It is. Most using magic have moved toward the front lines or rotate in and out. Having the ability to fight and defend from a distance is a great asset."

He was right, there would be less casualties that way, but did it drain them as it did her?

"They can shield and use magic at the same time?" she asked.

"Sort of. It takes a great deal of concentration to block an attack."

"I'd like to meet some of them."

"You will, they've been asking about you. They want to see what you're capable of." Kiuno wasn't sure how she felt about that. None would get a display like before.

Elliott added. "I've also heard rumors of those able to heal injuries, though I'm not sure to what extent." He paused. "Something else you might want to consider is hiding your stone. I asked around, and no one has seen one like it, but they're looking."

"Don't you think they might be able to tell me what it means?" she asked.

Elliott sighed. "It's possible, but if they react as Tyler did they might be desperate enough to force you where you don't want to go."

Kikyo smirked. "I'd like to see them try."

Kiuno's pride swelled. She wasn't helpless anymore but still. She wasn't excited about the possibility of things turning sour. People were looking for a way to survive. They were desperate.

"Maybe there's something wrong with me. Whatever happened back at the camp clearly had nothing to do with fire from any sky. Plus, it left me knocked out cold."

Elliott chuckled. "No maybe about it. There is definitely something wrong with you. You went after a camp full of men and burnt it to the ground. Most would call that suicide."

"It worked out all right."

A warning flashed through his eyes. "We got lucky, nothing more. Had Kikyo not been watching your back, you'd be dead. Without that crazy magic you possess, it wouldn't have been possible at all. It's critical you realize your decision was a foolish one."

Kiuno remembered Kikyo mentioning Elliott's anger. She had been stupid. Even so, she couldn't bring herself to regret it and couldn't promise it wouldn't happen again.

The memories came flooding back. Each scene replaying in her mind. Every swing. Luck. That's all it was. Kikyo saved her more than once, and it'd slipped her mind until now.

How many people had fallen? How many had she killed? She looked at her trembling hands and clenched her teeth as she remembered that first sickening blow. The blade pierced cleanly. So many bodies. All of them motionless.

"Kiuno?"

She looked into soft, brown eyes and wondered how such a kind person could have fought in a war.

"I killed them," she whispered. She'd only hesitated once. Thereafter the fire burned without remorse. Their screams echoed in her mind. Was there another option? Could a larger group have forced them to surrender? Would the captives have lasted that long?

Elliott sighed. "It's not something I wanted you to experience. Most aren't proud of it. The act of killing takes part of your soul." He placed a hand over hers. "Don't linger on their faces. Those men had no honor. Be glad you had the strength to come out alive."

Tears fell, and Elliott held her. She wasn't sure why she cried now. Maybe it was the act of killing. Maybe it was how close she'd come to messing everything up. Or maybe it was how close she'd come to death.

ONCE SHE'D calmed down and the three ate breakfast, Kiuno followed them into the icy air. Kikyo ensured the cloth covered her wrist, but she doubted anyone would see it with how tightly she held the cloak.

It was freezing.

People rushed by them, eager to do their chores and return to a warm fire. She wondered if they were happy with their new lives or pretended for the sake of their sanity.

Once through the main gate they followed a trail that led to the rear of the village. Frozen grass crunched beneath her feet as they neared a group of people, the spectacle they created leaving her in awe.

Despite the cold, plants grew all around them, the vines rising to capture their opponents, snaking up their legs. Water formed as if drawn from thin air. It flowed around the manipulator with little to no form and shifted to jagged spikes of ice that crashed into tiny shards.

Fire burst out and around the arms of those controlling it and burned as if the user were its breath of life. Wind ripped through the area, lifting people off the ground and forcing other elements to do its bidding.

It was beyond words.

People sparred using both blade and magic alike, but no harm came to any of them.

Kikyo pointed to the sideline. "They're blocking the magic. Each focuses on an individual. It lets them practice without hurting one another."

"You know," Elliott said, "we could stay for a bit, let you two pick up a few tricks. They've already offered."

Kikyo scoffed. "They just want to see Kiuno's fire."

His uncaring attitude didn't fool her. Curious eyes darted from one person to the next, wanting to ask a million questions, yet refraining. After their recent encounter, maybe it wouldn't be a bad idea. She had strength but with no control or skill, it did little good.

"I think that's a good idea." She dreaded wasting more time, but this was something important. Their survival was important.

Elliott engaged in conversation while she continued to look at everything around them. It wasn't long before she was handed a wooden sword and told to position herself. Though her body still hurt, Kiuno obeyed.

Kikyo eyed her. "Are you up to this?"

"I can't let you outdo me."

He smirked. "Good."

Kikyo lunged at her, but when the blunt wood should have collided with her side, he pulled the attack. Both were handed a shield and though it felt awkward, it was nice to have something to hide behind.

She pushed Kikyo's blow back and knocked him off balance.

He wasn't having it again.

As usual, she appeared clumsy compared to Kikyo's elegance.

After an hour Elliott called it quits and moved to the more interesting subject. Magic always seemed to fascinate him, and she wondered if he were a bit jealous about not having the ability.

"Kiuno, why don't you sit and rest for a while," Elliott offered.

She would have loved to join, but remembered the doctor telling her to take things easy. She didn't want to relive the symptoms of yesterday.

The instructor, who was an entire head shorter than Kikyo, could also manipulate the wind. She had a hard time following them at first, but once tiny particles of debris joined the twirling air, she fixated her gaze on Kikyo. His grace and precision unmatched.

In the span of a few hours Kikyo was correlating the movement of wind with his staff. He turned and pivoted with the element as if they were one. Was there ever going to be something he couldn't do?

That night, she saw the bandages. Elliott's were worse. He carried a large gash over the left hip, and she scolded them for not telling her. She wasn't the only one that should be resting.

Kikyo hid his pain, but she could see his face scrunch with small movements. She felt it too. Now that the excitement was over, her ribs ached with every breath. The small cuts across her arms itched, and the blisters on her hands burned.

Four days crawled by before she attempted to use her magic again. Thinking about the aftermath made her nervous, but she had to try.

Rumor of her participation must have spread fast. A large crowd, pretending to be occupied, cast glances her way. The short instructor from days ago stood before her. She'd finally learned his name was Jose.

Several sat on the sideline ready to block her magic. They described the feeling as pushing against a heavy wall. She'd felt something similar while facing the leader of the slave camp. Being able to do it without creating actual flames saved energy.

"All right, let's start with something small to be sure you're feeling all right." She nodded and the people surrounding them took a few steps back. If they expected a grand display they were going to be disappointed.

Kiuno took a breath. All was silent. She searched her core for the spark buried beneath layers of her subconscious. It still felt distant, but was becoming more familiar.

Minutes passed, and her frustration grew.

Nothing.

"It's gone," she whispered.

"What's gone?" Jose asked.

"The spark. I can't find it."

"No need to worry," he assured. "It happens all the time. Your body is still recovering."

"That's normal?" Kikyo asked.

He nodded. "You expended a great deal of energy, and your body is just protecting itself."

"How long will that last?"

"Could be a few days or weeks. Just keep resting. It'll come back when you're ready."

Weeks?

Kiuno sighed. It seemed Elliott would be lighting his own fires for a while.

DESOLATION

REALM: 4
DAY: 82

They stayed a week and a half before Elliott thought it better to move on. Kiuno practiced several times a day, but she'd come no closer to accessing her magic, leaving her in constant disappointment.

Truthfully, she hadn't learned much. No one seemed to have trouble summoning their elements. To them, the current was clear, and they could pull it forth at a second's notice.

Kikyo, on the other hand, picked up a lot. He practiced as they traveled by blocking the harsh winds. She remembered how worn he'd been after fighting the feline. That seemed like such a long time ago.

The villagers pointed them toward the fourth realm and the weather grew colder every day. Thin scattered pines did nothing to block the breeze. Kiuno wondered if they would have to settle in one place until the worst of winter blew over. She wasn't sure how they would fare trudging through a blizzard.

So many things had changed since they first arrived, her fear being one of them. The twisted creatures of the land once occupied the forefront of her mind. Now she thought more about the people who thrived on violence.

Through experience, they'd learned to be more careful, but there was always the possibility of running across hostility.

Her mind wandered to Eldridge. Had they stumbled upon a village of bandits or were they attacked while they rested? What happened to the escort that was supposed to protect them? Would she be a lifeless body left forgotten if she had gone with them?

Kiuno glanced at her wrist, the blue stone hidden beneath thin fabric. People sought it as a means for hope, yet it was a mystery shrouded in danger. What purpose could it serve if no one knew what it meant? Maybe it didn't have a point at all...

She ducked, feeling the wind from his staff brush against her face. Elliott had almost taken her head off with that last swing.

"Pay attention," Elliott chided. She moved back into her stance, shoving the thoughts aside. A wandering mind wasn't the best of things while sparring. They'd moved into the fourth realm a few days ago and made time for training every day since. With her magic absent, it was her only defense.

Pines littered the area, but they were too far apart, leaving the trio vulnerable. Anyone within half a mile could see their fire.

Despite what they'd been told, Kiuno felt her body had shut off the magic altogether. Kikyo worked with her like he used to, trying to dig for any sign of the spark or current, but she was back to square one.

She parried Elliott's staff, and the impact left a sting in her palms. A shadow flashed to her right. She shoved Elliott forward, spinning the staff to block Kikyo's attack and struggled to remain upright. He never went easy.

"You're improving." Elliott smiled and offered his hand.

An odd game developed where one would surprise the other in a mocked ambush. She'd been the victim of too many strikes. They kept her on edge and conspired against her. Kiuno's ribs were more bruised now than ever. It seemed her body would never lose its bluish color while in this place.

"You aren't too bad yourself, old man."

Elliott's contagious laughter filled the air. "Your youth will catch me eventually. I have a hard-enough time keeping up with Kikyo." She looked at their friend, knowing full well what he meant.

They set their staffs aside and Elliott started on dinner. She didn't like camping in the open, but it was too cold to go without. The sun fell on another day, casting an orange glow over the land. Elliott yawned and pulled his blanket from their pack. Maybe tomorrow they'd stumble across something more interesting and preferably warmer.

A thin layer of snow covered the ground and she knew the next village they ran into might very well be their home for a while. Unless the wi—a rush of air flew across her cheek. Behind her an arrow protruded from the tree.

It'd barely missed.

Kiuno whipped her head back and ducked as more flew.

Where had it come from?

Kikyo ducked down close to her and painful seconds ticked by as she scanned the trees, her mind racing.

Where was—

"Elliott?" His knees hit the ground, and she jumped the few feet to close the distance. His hands gripped her arm painfully as she looked him over.

Four arrows protruded from his back, each buried deep. Frantic, she turned to Kikyo, but he remained still, eyes scanning.

Did he know? Could he see them? Why weren't they firing anymore?

She couldn't speak, couldn't breathe. Another arrow buried itself in Elliott's back and he let out a hissing breath. Her fingers trembled as red soaked through his shirt. She needed to move. They needed to escape.

She turned to Kikyo and her heart faltered.

Fear.

The one person she relied on to keep his composure. He looked at her and then back to the trees. If he didn't know what to do, if he were scared—An arrow buried itself straight through the top of Kikyo's shoulder. He cured, breaking the tip and cast the offending object aside.

This wasn't real. It was all just a bad dream. Fingers dug into her shoulders and she turned to desperate eyes. Elliott needed help. She had to pull the arrows out, but he stilled her movement by gripping tighter.

"Run."

Kikyo slammed her down and she watched Elliott's head collide with the hard ground, his body limp. She screamed, reaching, barely recognizing her own voice. She had to protect him, but Kikyo was too strong, pinning her in place.

Tears streamed down her face as she stared at Elliott and the blood dripping from the corner of his mouth.

Kikyo stood and the sound of scraping metal sent chills down her spine. Several men surrounded them, their weapons drawn. Kiuno finally got the mind to stand and draw her own.

If Kikyo was going to fight, then she would fight too. Her eyes drifted to Elliott despite the approaching danger.

Run.

He could guide them. He could tell them what to do.

Stand up Elliott.

They tackled Kikyo, trying to wrestle him to the ground. His lips moved, but it was as if the audio had been turned off to her world. He slammed his fist into one man's face and kneed another in the gut before they restrained his hands.

She should help, she needed to help, but everything happened in a blur. She couldn't breathe, and something collided with her head, causing the nightmare to shift to darkness.

WHEN KIUNO'S eyes opened, the first thing she noticed was the throbbing pain in the back of her head. Her vision swam as she tried to focus in the dim lighting. Had she passed out again or was she dead? No, the pain told her otherwise. She now lay on a wooden floor, arms bound behind her back.

Hadn't those last events been a nightmare?

Turning, she caught sight of anxious blue eyes staring into her own. Her friend sat bound and gagged. Defenseless. Beside him sat another, crimson staining his frozen form. When she looked back at Kikyo, he shook his head.

Elliott was gone. After all they'd done…he wasn't even given the chance to fight.

She watched Kikyo's eyes shift from mourning to cold hatred as a man's heavy footfalls approached. A calloused hand hauled her up, making her head spin. She was sure it'd been split open.

Kiuno counted thirteen men.

They were nothing, she could take them out with ease, that was, if she still had her magic. In her current state, it wasn't likely. If Kikyo hadn't been able to overpower them, what chance did she stand?

Kiuno looked at Kikyo, wondering if his magic were strong enough to fight them off. He must have been waiting for her to wake up. It'd be hard to run carrying dead weight.

The man wrapped his fingers in her hair. "What's wrong boy, want your girlfriend?" He let out a mocking laugh in response to Kikyo's scowl. "Don't worry, we'll give her back. Might even be nice enough to let you live."

"Don't go making promises." Another warned. He appeared disinterested. Maybe she could talk her way out of this.

"Don't spoil my fun." His hot breath against her neck and nipping teeth sent chills down her spine. Kiuno clamped her eyes shut. This wasn't happening. This couldn't happen. Not after—

"Let her go!" Kikyo's thunderous voice caused the men to start, all eyes turning. Somehow, he'd removed the cloth from his mouth.

"And if I refuse? You plan on doing something about it?"

He twisted her to face Kikyo, sliding his hands down her wrists as if mocking what Kikyo would never have. He slammed her against a nearby table. Kiuno reared up, spun around and spat in his face. He slammed her against the table again, and stars shot across her vision.

"Get your filthy hands off her!" Her captor flew across the room, hitting the wall with enough force to rattle the small cabin.

All men got to their feet as a furious current blew through the space. Kikyo stood at the core, eyes darting between each of them. His arms remained bound, but that simple mishap wouldn't hinder the magic.

"The boy is one of the magic wielders. Kill him."

Kiuno reached for the fire, but nothing happened. Surely this warranted its return. Thinking fast, she used her feet to trip those closest and sat back on the table to slam her legs into another.

Kiuno tucked her legs and pulled her arms forward, but a harsh kick sent her sprawling to the ground. Kikyo's howling fury shoved three of them away from her. It seemed as if the air itself carried his ferocity.

She should've learned not to doubt him, not after everything he'd learned. They might just be able to pull this off.

Kiuno needed to act as the distraction. Allow Kikyo to take them out one by one. As long as she didn't get held down—

Something plunged into her right side. At first Kiuno thought she'd been punched. It wasn't until she saw his wicked grin that she noticed the knife. Her blood ran cold as she looked down to find a small slit in her shirt.

She stepped back as a piece of wood shot through his head. He fell, and she clutched her wound. How deep was it? Would she bleed to death?

A blade flew and impaled another to her left. Kikyo was protecting her.

Kiuno turned to find three men slamming him to the ground. Each struggled against the fury that twisted around his body. She jumped to her feet.

They were breaking his concentration.

She was breaking his concentration.

With bound hands, Kiuno dove for a dagger on the floor, but someone grabbed her ankle and her face slammed into the hardwood. The man crawled over her, pinning her with his weight.

She watched the nightmare unfold.

One man climbed over Kikyo and pulled a knife from his belt. It was against his throat before she had time to plea, but she cried out anyway, begging for a miracle, for someone to save him.

Dragging it across, the blade cleanly cut his skin and crimson spilled along the wooden floor.

KIKYO

REALM: 4
DAY: 82

Kikyo was always told, when death came, he'd watch his life flash before his eyes. Instead, he heard one thing.

Her voice.

Do you hate me?

The words stung as much as the first time she'd uttered them. They echoed in his mind as he watched her struggle. It didn't hit him that this was the end until he hit the ground. From then, he knew, there were only seconds left.

Instead of blissful memories with his mother baking pie or his brother teasing him in the yard, he heard her voice.

Instead of all the times his father had taken him in the woods to track wild game, that small whisper echoed in his mind.

Couldn't it at least have been something more pleasant?

Do you hate me?

She couldn't see the little smirk back then. Despite his anger, he couldn't believe she would ask something so ridiculous, like a child seeking affection, a child afraid of being rejected.

It was her fault...back when she first arrived, it was because of her he'd been struck in the face. He knew, from that moment, she was trouble. Bringing food into a group of starving people...how stupid. He and Elliott saved her from being mauled that day. Even after the fact, they still wanted to see if she had anything in her pockets. Honestly, the girl didn't even have a pack, where did they expect her to hide it?

Kiuno was better at things than she gave herself credit for. Too humble for her own good. She didn't want to outdo anyone, but he forced her. For her own sake, to be able to defend herself, she needed to be pushed to the limit. Past those limits even. She didn't hold back with him, and he was proud of that. Proud to see her fighting just as hard now.

He wasn't in pain, he hoped she knew that, but the anguish on her face told him otherwise. She would hurt. For a long time, she would suffer, blaming herself for things she couldn't control.

He would have given her a playful smile if he were able. Something to remember. Something to drown out the gruesome site that would follow in mere seconds.

The cold blade pressed against his neck, but her fire was spreading.

She'd survive. That inferno couldn't be quenched, he'd seen it before. She was the strongest of them, though she didn't know it yet.

Do you hate me?

I could never hate you.

There was so much more to be said, so many things he could have told her, but he didn't dare.

Hate you? Never, if anything Kiuno, I...

FAILURE

REALM: 4
DAY: 82

W*hy?*
She laid there in shock, heart constricting as his head collided with the floor and blue eyes glazed over.

Her world shifted, cheeks already soaked from memories as she willed him to stand. Willed herself to wake up.

Her entire body shook, but she pushed to her knees, never taking her eyes off him. The flames surged in a torrent, their warmth filling the cabin.

Why now? Why, when it no longer mattered? Why did the fire crave the freedom to consume those around her, raging as their own inferno?

The rope melted from her hands as she crawled to his body, lifeless eyes still upon her.

The screams seemed like something in the distance. Echoes begging for their lives.

Kiuno reached out to wipe a tear only to watch his skin scorch from her touch. She recoiled, trembling hands clenching to fists.

It wasn't enough that he was gone, but she couldn't touch him either? She wouldn't be able to pull his body from this fiery grave? Why couldn't she do this simple thing for him?

Pale green caught her eye, the wrist guard removed, no doubt by the men who did this. The green was in stark contrast to the puddle of red it lay in.

Though her fingertips burned his skin, she pulled the bracelet from his wrist. It didn't resist. Nor did it burn. Could they only be removed after death?

Her gaze fell to Elliott, and she forced herself to crawl to him. She lifted his cold wrist, and a sob racked her body as she slid it over his hand. His eyes were closed, body frozen. What were his last thoughts?

Run.

Her shoulders shook. Why didn't she listen, why did—part of the ceiling crashed beside her, and she jumped back.

A spark caught Kikyo's leg. The same leg that carried the scars of his past.

Another beam fell, and splinters flew in her face. Fear and grief pulled her in different directions until self-preservation won over. She staggered to her feet, and ran out, the structure collapsing seconds later.

Frigid air burnt her skin as she fell to her knees, the smoke carrying all their dreams far away.

Three months…three months of planning, preparing and bonding. They were her family in the absence of her real one. They helped her, followed her, despite being given better options. Neither had a thought toward their own goal and she'd never even asked them why.

Why push her? Why care?

Kiuno clenched her fists, her body trembling between sobs. Why couldn't she protect them, why had her powers waited, why had she frozen like a coward? Elliott told her to run, Kikyo might have survived if she had listened.

Her breathing shifted to rapid gasps, and she struggled against the burn in her lungs.

What was the purpose if they were all going to die? Was that the intention? To take pleasure in their misery?

They weren't going home. Not now. Elliott would never see his daughter. Kikyo would never be reunited with his brother. The worst part was she didn't even know their real names. She'd never be able to find their families, no one would ever know about the men who'd given her everything.

Kiuno laced her fingers through her hair, pulling, grasping for some piece of reality before letting out an ear-piercing scream.

It didn't matter if anyone heard, she couldn't stop this pain, she couldn't bear the hollow eyes playing in her mind over and over again.

"I'm sorry… I'm so sorry…"

THE SUN crept over the horizon, but it did little for her numb body.

She'd nestled against a tree, clutching her throbbing side as she watched the flames shrink to burning coals. Sleep wasn't an option. Not with the resting place of her friends right before her. She clutched the bracelets, having nothing else to remind her of their existence. Nothing but memories.

Kiuno played the scenario in her mind time and time again. There were so many choices, so many possibilities that might have prevented this. If she would have just found a group or stayed in the last village until winter passed. If only she hadn't rushed them to move forward.

Cold droplets fell from the gray expanse above. She'd been stripped of her cloak and weapons, everything lost in the fire. A shirt with ripped sleeves and torn pants were all that kept her warm.

Her hand shook when she looked at the bloody palm. Whether from pain or trauma she couldn't be sure, perhaps a mixture of both. She needed help, but—maybe she should just lie there, die in that very spot and be with her friends again.

Kikyo's scowl entered her mind and her body quivered, struggling for breath between the tears.

No. He died for her, at the very least, she wouldn't let that be in vain.

She slid both bracelets on her left wrist and used the tree trunk to lift herself, screaming from the pain. She looked at the ash one last time before turning away.

Rain poured down, each icy drop sending a tremor through her body. Instinct told her to stay dry, but she'd gone all night with an open wound. She knew nothing about medicine and wasn't even sure she'd survive.

Her body threatened to collapse with every step.

She was so tired.

If they were gone what chance did anyone else stand? How long before she'd have to feel this heavy pain again? What if she were the only one left?

Kiuno staggered along. She couldn't do this on her own, and she didn't want to. They guided her. They gave her direction. She needed their teachings, their encouragement.

Was she wrong to dream everything would work out?

She failed, and who was to say she wouldn't fail again? Who would be next? Scorpios, Maltack…Elite? Would she lose her reason for existing?

Time faded as she trudged through the mud. She didn't know whether to cry or be thankful when a town came into view. They'd been so close…

Heavy feet pushed her forward, one step at a time. Those at the gate ran to meet her, but not as fast as the ground. Her head collided with the earth, and she stayed there, unable to lift herself anymore. Strangers pulled her up, people she didn't know. Why did they help her?

Muffled voices floated through the rain. Their grip firm, yet gentle. Had they seen her wound?

A door creaked open, and the heat of a fire burned against her skin. Droplets fell from her hair onto the floor.

Someone lifted her shirt and ran outside, his voice echoed, but she couldn't make it out.

Her consciousness faded then emerged, like waves in an ocean.

There was a boy and an older man. She could discern that much. The older male knelt and placed his hand over her wound. Stabbing pain caused her to cry out, and she gripped his arm.

Stop. Just stop.

Warmth flooded through her side as the room faded. Was she still alive?

"What happened to you?" Young, concerned eyes looked her over. He was only a boy of maybe twelve.

She couldn't answer.

They helped her change, wrapped her in fur and laid her before the fire.

Exhaustion hit hard, and her mind faded with a whisper.

"Sleep now Kiuno, I'll take watch."

SORROW

REALM: 4
DAY: 83

Jolting with every thunder crack, Kiuno found it impossible to sleep. The raging storm coinciding with nightmares of a bloody blade. Each time the scene shifted. She'd move, she'd be brave, but no matter how hard she tried, it always ended the same.

The boy was attentive and tried to console her. His eyes were young, kind…but they weren't the blue she longed for. Kiuno curled into herself, seeking sleep, yet fighting against it. Nothing could stop the nightmare that had become her reality.

The storm slowed as night fell and she gazed into the flames, letting their flicker take her deeper, to a place beyond the room.

She'd killed those men with the fire, but the magic eluded her now. Maybe it'd only ever work when *it* decided. Maybe she didn't have a say in the matter. She choked on a sob. Only a few seconds sooner and Kikyo—

Her body trembled.

Powerless.

"You should try eating something." His voice shook. She wondered if he was afraid she might lash out. Even so, he never left her side. The only thing she could offer was the shake of her head.

"What's your name?" She looked at the bracelet on her wrist, then drifted to the pale green and gray that rested against the other. Why did the name matter when it wasn't her own?

"Kiuno." Her voice cracked, and another wave of tears consumed her. The boy fell silent and sat the food on a nearby table.

Fire. Death. Freedom. They'd saved complete strangers and she'd been proud of it. Yet it was the very reason she couldn't save Kikyo. If she had to do it all again, would she walk away?

Kiuno clenched her fists. How was she supposed to feel? Angry? Maybe at herself.

Vengeful? Those that'd caused the pain were already dead. She let her hands fall into her lap and ran her finger over the stones for the hundredth time.

Lost. Lost to her purpose. She had friends. Her family was out there. Elite was out there. But what if she couldn't save them either?

VOICES OUTSIDE woke her. Morning. The rain had stopped, and the door creaked open. "Kiuno?" He paused when she didn't turn. "Will you come with me? I want you to meet someone."

She didn't want to move, but she owed this kid her life. If not for him, Kikyo's sacrifice would have been—

The wound.

Kiuno lifted her shirt to see a thin, pink line along her side. It was raw, but the skin had been knit together.

He fidgeted and wrung his hands when she looked at him. Was he the one responsible? Is that why adults had left her with a child?

Shedding all but one blanket, she stood, her body still numb to the world, almost as if she were on auto pilot. He opened the door and led them into the cold. Thin air hit her lungs like a dagger.

Outside, ice had frozen everything. Large icicles hung from the roofs and dangled from every shelf. The few people that braved the slippery world kept their gaze on the ground, focusing on their footing. She did the same, though it was mostly to hide her face. If she looked half as bad as she felt, people might stare.

The cold seeped into her bones. Somehow, it found every hole and crept through, causing her to shake violently. Most were dressed in heavy cloaks with fur that lined the hoods.

Were they afraid?

Kiuno bumped into the kid, not realizing he'd stopped. A cart passed, they crossed the street and rounded a wooden fence. This wasn't the main wall. It only stood about a foot taller than herself. A small section squared off from prying eyes.

They entered a narrow gate, though it could hardly be called such. It was just part of the wall on a hinge. Inside, a cottage sat nestled in the farthest corner with a thin stream of smoke rising from the chimney. Pottery lined the walls and ice clung to everything with a ledge, it was difficult to tell what might rest beneath the layers of frozen water.

An older man, at least in his sixties, opened the little wooden door. He paused as if confused but greeted the boy with a smile. "This is her?"

The boy nodded.

"You look better than you did yesterday." His eyes ran up her frame, evaluating. She met his gaze.

His strong shoulders spoke of authority, but a sense of tranquility also radiated from his presence. Why she wanted him to see her pain, she couldn't grasp. Maybe she just needed someone to know, to understand if they could.

He stepped back inside for a moment, and she followed the young one to the porch where they awaited his return. The older returned carrying two staffs. "Please, indulge me."

Kiuno looked at the weapon and back at the older male. She clenched the blanket tighter. Memories of countless exercises, the bruises and their laughter flooded her mind. They prepared. Planned. Their goal was to keep one another safe.

It had all been for nothing.

She'd thought Tyler and his companions were dangerous and insisted navigating this dangerous world with only the two of them. They could have traveled with a group in the next town over. She could have been more patient and maybe—

"The callouses on your hands tell me you've used a weapon. Is the sword more your preference?"

Punishment. Was that the reason? Was she being punished for the lives she'd taken? Had she been the cause of another's pain and thus brought this upon herself?

Tears fell. Blood. Fear. It all clouded her vision as everything replayed in her mind. Elliott's lifeless body. Kikyo's hollow eyes. She wished she could hear them tell her to position her feet wider just one more time.

"I apologize. Please, come inside." His hand lightly rested on her back, and she fought the urge to swat it. Inside, a comforting fire greeted them. She sat on a flat pillow, and a long silence filled the air.

"My name is Vincent. I have a second bedroom that you're welcome to."

"Why?" she asked.

He poked a stick into the fire and folded his legs beneath him. "Do you have anywhere else to go?" She didn't speak. "That's what I thought." He added another log. "How is your side?"

"Better."

"May I see?"

Slowly, she let the blanket fall. His icy fingers lifted the hem of her shirt and he pressed on the scar, a light glow emitting from his fingertips. Elliott's words came back to her.

I've heard rumors of those able to heal injuries.

"You weren't coherent enough for me to ask yesterday, but are you hurt anywhere else?"

Kiuno indicated her pounding head, and he wrapped his fingers around her temple, the relief instantaneous. "Thank you," she whispered.

He returned to tend the fire. "I want to ask what happened, but I can see recent events have caused you pain beyond physical injury." He glanced at her as if waiting for a response before continuing. "We're staying until spring, you can come with us to the next realm then."

"Will there be a spring?" It seemed so far off and who knew if the game wouldn't shift. Maybe they'd be locked inside an endless winter.

"Let's hope so."

She could hear Vincent whispering to the boy in hushed tones and thought she heard her name, but she didn't bother to ask. He was a child. It was natural to be curious. Instead of food, Vincent handed her a warm cup of tea, and she nodded her thanks.

Elite. If she wanted anyone right now, it was him. He always knew how to ease her pain, always found a way to make her laugh, even when things were at their worst.

I need you.

Her body was more tired than she'd ever felt in her life. She craved rest, but it never came. Nightmares plagued her mind at night and memories haunted her during the day. How long would it take for this ache to subside?

The boy left as the sun went down, and Vincent handed her another cup of tea. She took it, grateful, and let the warmth sink into her body.

"Despite how you might feel, not everything is lost." He gazed into the fire. "We'll always face hardships, that's just how things are, but you have to pick yourself up no matter how hard the fall." He turned to her. "You can't blame yourself for whatever happened out there."

She looked away. Couldn't blame herself? Couldn't forgive herself more like.

They remained sitting for what seemed like another hour, and he showed her the spare room. It was small, with a single bed crammed in the quarters. A dark curtain hung where a door should have been. Kiuno crawled beneath the soft furs and curled into a ball.

Dark shadows loomed over her companions as she ran, screaming their names. No matter how much she tried, neither would turn. Neither one of them could hear her. The shadows crept closer and closer, baring their teeth. Fangs pierced flesh, bodies ripped to pieces. She could do nothing as they reached for her, hollow eyes making her gut twist.

Vincent stood in the doorway when she bolted up screaming. The pull in her side made her yelp and gasp for breath. At first, she didn't recognize the room, but soon it came back, and she dropped her face into her hands and wept. He brought more tea, leaving it on the bedside without question.

As the sun crawled over the horizon, Kiuno rose and made her way through the curtain to find Vincent already seated before the fire. She cringed, wondering if he'd been up all night. Perhaps he wouldn't be as willing to have her here if he were going to lose sleep.

He gave her a small smile and handed her a large chunk of bread. "You need to eat, that should be easy enough on your stomach." It churned as she nibbled on the piece.

Once finished, Vincent left her with the noise of the fire again, but the solitude was going to drive her crazy. Finding an extra cloak, she wrapped it around herself and opened the door.

Sharp air made her recoil, and the blinding white caused her to squint, but she found Vincent in the far corner trying to pry something out of the icy confines. He wasn't surprised when she approached and simply handed her an ice-covered container. He pried off another and they headed inside.

Several jars later, she figured out his role. An herbalist. His ability to heal suddenly made sense.

"Why didn't you bring them in before the storm?" she asked.

"I was careless."

They spent the next few days melting and sorting. She'd researched nothing on plants and found his information helpful. They were dried, which prevented her from knowing what they'd look like in the wild, but at least she'd have a bit of knowledge should she ever need it. Yarrow, for example, helped with fever but could also be used on an open wound.

Vincent made a blend that afternoon, sending an array of aromas floating through the air, a mixture to ease her anxiety. Lavender was about the only familiar smell she could distinguish. The brew seemed to help as the twisted knot in her stomach finally eased.

"I don't wish to pry, but how recent were the events that led you here?"

Kiuno looked at her hands. "Three days, I think."

"Right as we found you then."

She was thankful for the knock at their door. The child she'd originally stayed with peered in with curious eyes. He hadn't visited since that first night. Vincent sighed, excused himself and ushered the boy out the door. When they didn't return right away, she followed.

Outside, in the cold air, the two faced one another, staffs in hand. Teacher and student. It reminded her of those first days with Elliott. She sat near the pile of logs beside the door and watched.

Vincent danced around the boy with a grace that surprised her, though the young one wasn't bad either. They exchanged quick blows, Vincent would give him some advice and then they'd begin again.

Blissful memories floated through her mind with every crack and groan. It felt as though life before this world never existed.

She stayed seated long after they were finished and watched the stars stake their claim in the sky. It seemed clearer in the cold. Perhaps the air made one feel how much darkness overshadowed the light.

Vincent joined her, passing a bowl of broth. "Eat." There was no room for argument.

"What's his name?" she asked.

"Liam."

She took a few sips and felt the warmth seep through her body. "You two seem close."

"Is that so? He's only been here a few weeks. Boy bothered me day and night until I agreed to teach him."

"He's not bad."

"His balance is a problem."

She might have smiled, but being able to use a weapon was the difference between life and death. He'd eventually have to fight.

How many have to die?

ASHES

REALM: 4
DAY: 99

For the next two weeks Vincent saw to her care. He monitored her wound, which must have been more severe than she realized. If not for him…she shook her head. That shadow of death had passed.

With all the herbs melted, the cottage carried a pungent aroma that comprised various herbs Vincent used in his medicine. New visitors were rare, but people still fell ill, and he saw to their care.

The weather shifted as with any winter she remembered. Small flakes always fell from the gray sky. Vincent offered short words of wisdom when he found the time, and she suspected he was the reason Liam hadn't bombarded her with questions. Solitude gave her time to think. To process and begin healing.

Nightmares still plagued her subconscious, but after the first week, Kiuno found herself able to sleep through the night. With rest, her mind cleared. She couldn't give up on everything. Not after Kikyo's sacrifice. She took a while to come to terms with Elliott's death. That it hadn't been her fault. But Kikyo… He'd given his life to protect her.

She'd never viewed herself so weak, but grief had a way of sinking its clutches down to anyone's surest convictions. That time had passed. She had to find Elite and the others. She wouldn't let herself be weak again, not until they were safe.

"Kiuno." She leaned down, saw Vincent gesturing from the porch, and she jumped from the roof. She followed him into the cabin, and they both sat before the fire, trying to warm numb fingers.

He stirred the soup that hung over the flames in a black pot. "How have you been doing?"

She glanced at him and then away. "I'm surviving." It was the best she could offer.

"That's acceptable." He sat back and took a drink of tea. "I want to know what happened out there."

Pain. One moment of happiness turned to complete anguish. Elliott struck down instantly. The men taunting. Kikyo fighting so hard only to have his life stolen. Why did he need to know?

"With that being said," he continued, "I will share mine first." Relief and surprise mixed as she watched him. His expression shifted. Emotion, normally kept hidden, now displayed across his face unchecked. His feelings of shame, guilt and heartache. The desire to comfort him swept across her consciousness, but what did she have to offer?

"Everyone arrived in this world the same way. My story is no different. I wandered around, seeking shelter. I found the first realm to be self-sufficient. Everyone had a place to go, people they could rely on. I arrived at one of those places and naturally bonded with the people there.

"When it became apparent no one was coming, I set out on my own. Most were too afraid to leave, save one boy. He begged to tag along, but I refused. I thought leaving him there was the safest course of action. He promised to fill my role until I returned.

"I packed for a long trip, but the next village wasn't far off. They'd gotten information about a larger civilization just a few days north and

I headed that direction. Once there, I learned the truth and returned to that second village to fill them in. They packed and move on while I returned to the first."

Vincent paused and clenched his jaw. "I'll never forget the black smoke reaching toward the sky that day. It sent my heart racing, and I prayed for a miracle, but it was too late. Bodies lay scattered across the ground. At first, I couldn't understand the horror of how people could do something so violent, then I saw the tracks. Foot prints of a creature larger than any I'd ever seen. None survived.

"It took me three days to dig their graves. I struggled with whether I could have made a difference. Perhaps I would have simply been another victim." Kiuno stared at him, lost for words, then he gave an unexpected smile.

"But I didn't give up there. I traveled back to that third village intending to contribute to the civilization I wanted those lost to be part of. With my knowledge in herbalism I could help the sick. It wasn't much later that I discovered my abilities." He sat forward, pouring two bowls of stew and she stayed silent.

"I can't go back and fix what happened. Part of me wishes I would have taken the boy, that he would still be alive, but it wouldn't change the fate of the others, and the guilt would remain. It's difficult to accept, but if we linger in those dark places too long, that darkness will consume us."

Silence settled between them as they waited for the food to cool. He knew pain, even if it differed from her own. He waited patiently, but where was she supposed to begin?

"We were attacked," she tried, the words barely a whisper.

"How many?"

"Thirteen."

"And you ran?" he offered.

"No." She shook her head. "I would never run."

He sat back and waited for her to continue. "Elliott," her voice cracked, "died quickly. Five arrows hit him before we knew what happened, but Kikyo…he fought to protect me."

"One person?"

"He had abilities."

"Ah, a magic user."

"But…I couldn't do anything, I froze, all I could see was Elliott." She took a breath as the tears fell and struggled to speak. "I was knocked unconscious shortly after, waking to find myself bound. Kikyo was still alive." Hatred burned through her. "Those disgusting men sought to—do things. Kikyo became angry and used his magic. Once they saw that—"

"They killed him," he finished. Silence echoed in the room as he stirred the bowl. "You were outnumbered, you can't blame yourself with those odds."

"I wasn't strong enough."

He sat his food down and looked at her. "Ki—"

"I can use magic too," she interrupted, "but it's difficult and I couldn't reach it, not until it was too late."

"That's how you escaped?"

"I didn't escape." Their eyes locked. "I killed all of them." She clenched her fists. "But I wasn't able to get their bodies out." More silence followed as they listened to the crackling fire, the noise trying to take her back to a darker place.

"Your friends had the burial of kings, it's an honor." She cried, and they were quiet again until her tears ebbed. "Why couldn't you use your magic?"

"I don't know." She wiped her eyes.

"You've always had trouble with it?"

She nodded. "Kikyo worked with me, but it's always been difficult. The only time it came easy was if the situation called for it."

"What do you mean?"

"We got into trouble a few times, and it was like a switch had been flipped."

"Forgive me, but how was *that* situation different?"

Kiuno allowed a smile to spread across her lips. It felt so long ago that they'd saved those people from being slaves. The pain of killing back then paled in comparison to what she felt now.

"Weeks before, we stumbled across a small village that was using people for their own…pleasures. We rescued them."

"Just the three of you?" he asked, surprised.

"I was a bit impulsive. When the men were taken care of, I passed out and haven't been able to reach the magic since. Not willingly anyway."

"I see." He stood and gestured for her to follow. Vincent grabbed two staffs from the corner before opening the door, and Kiuno draped a cloak over her shoulders.

At the center of the yard he turned and threw a staff in her direction. She caught it on reflex and swung. Memories of a fonder time rushed through her mind.

Vincent had been keeping her from doing much due to the wound, afraid any small tear could lead to internal bleeding. Nothing felt restricted now. Excitement pulsed through her veins as she looked at her opponent, almost as though her body craved the movement. Kiuno smiled. Despite their deaths, their memories would live on. Her training would live on.

Kiuno took her stance and shifted the weapon. Vincent sprung first, his movement quick and precise. She spun around him with ease. His speed didn't match Kikyo's and the hits weren't as powerful as Elliott's, but he carried an elegance she'd not previously encountered.

"You've been trained well." She smirked. All those grueling routines with Elliott weren't for naught. They continued, each testing the other as they pushed back and forth. Her body remembered the counters, remembered the advances. It wasn't a fight to determine a victor, but to remind her what she was capable. He didn't want to break her, he wanted to set her free.

It was late when they stopped. Vincent held up one hand struggling for breath. "I'm used to sparring a twelve-year-old. I'm afraid I might be getting a bit rusty." Sweat poured down her face, the cold wind almost painful against it, but she didn't want to stop. There was still daylight and for the first time in weeks, she felt exhilarated.

"Sorry, I'm used to being pushed."

"I can tell." He took another breath before rising to his feet. "I'm going inside to warm up, care to join me?"

Kiuno looked at the staff. "I think I'll stay out here." He gave her a curious look, but nodded and went inside the cabin.

In the silence, she took a deep breath, letting the frigid air rush through her lungs. The gate in the corner drew her attention, and she wondered if anyone would stop her should she choose to leave. It wasn't as if she were a prisoner.

The gate creaked when she pushed it open and a snow-covered path led to the main road. A few people turned when she looked both ways, but no one made a fuss. She walked down the center path, finally able to take in the town. The men that stood at the main gate glanced at her when she paused, but none attempted to stop her. If they remembered dragging her through the mud a few weeks ago, they didn't mention it.

White covered everything as far as the eye could see. Footprints were the only thing that indicated a path existed. Kiuno walked a few paces before setting off at a dead run.

Cool air stung her face and her lungs cried out, but she pushed, running as fast as her body would allow. Her movements slowed when she veered into deeper snow, but she kept going. She needed this, after all the nightmares, after allowing it to fester with no way out, she needed to feel the pain, feel the burn, feel she was still alive.

Her heart skipped when she came across the familiar site. The cabin. Had they really been so close? It sat in a small pile, covered with snow, but she recognized the tree she'd sat beneath.

Kiuno crept forward, kneeling before the fallen structure. She ran her hand over the snow, a few pieces of wood jutting from the white. If she overturned those pieces, would she find those eyes staring back?

She looked up to the gray clouds and let her body fall back into the snow. It melted around her skin, sending shivers through her body, but she remained still. Naked branches swayed in the wind, appearing as skeletal fingers reaching toward a barren sky. Come spring they would be full of life and maybe their final resting place wouldn't look so desolate.

A twig broke, and she rolled, reaching for the knife in her shoe. She cursed, having forgotten it. "Sorry, I didn't mean to scare you." Liam stood with a cloak across his arm and a worried expression on his face.

"What are you doing here?" she asked, her tone too aggressive.

"I just...I saw you take off. I didn't know if you were okay." She studied him, watching his feet shift, and she took a breath to calm her racing heart.

"I'm fine." She glanced back at the structure before moving to a log where she brushed the snow aside and sat.

"Are you coming back?" His innocent worry reminded her of her friend, Maltack. Though Mal was at least eighteen by now, she still thought of him as a kid. He was smart for his age and she hoped he'd found a way to survive. Maybe he'd run into a few of the others.

"Yes, I just needed..." she trailed off.

"To run?"

Kiuno smiled. "Yes, to run." He came over and sat beside her, handing her the cloak. She wrapped it around her shoulders. "How did you meet Vincent?" She already knew, but starting conversation was better than silence.

"When the group I was traveling with passed through, I saw him training and wanted to learn."

"Why?"

"Because I want to fight on the front lines and help get us home." His answer startled her. This innocent boy wanted to fight at the front?

"What would make you want to do a thing like that?" she asked.

"Why wouldn't I? We can't get home if we don't fight."

"What happens if you die?" The words were out before she could stop them, but he was right. If no one fought, then no one would see home again.

"I won't die," he said, not bothered by her statement.

"I've heard others say the same." Perhaps she shouldn't have said that either, but he was young, he needed to understand.

"You've lost someone important to you huh?" She looked away, had Vincent said something? No, he didn't seem like one to tell another's private affairs, perhaps Liam could see it written across her face.

"Yes," she whispered.

"I have too, I think everyone has."

"And knowing people have died, when we've only come this far, makes you still want to fight?"

"Yes, because they wanted the same thing." She understood. Despite his age, this kid was well versed in the hardships of this wretched place. She didn't know what he'd seen or what he'd been through, but he was right about one thing. By now, almost everyone had suffered for one reason or another.

"Kiuno?" She turned back to him. "Don't give up, they wouldn't want you to." A smile tugged at the corner of her lips, and she looked back to the burnt cabin.

No, they wouldn't.

GIVE ME A REASON

REALM: 4
DAY: 189

Eternal darkness surrounded her. They screamed. So many screamed, but nothing gave her light, as if she'd gone blind or been swallowed by some monster. She knew their voices, their cries made her blood race. Kikyo. Elliott. Scorpios. Maltack. Elite...

Kiuno jolted, sweat caking her hair to her forehead. The thick furs were too warm. She threw them to the side and swung her legs over, trying to settle her breath. She cupped her face, wiping the tears. It'd been a while since her last nightmare.

The birds told her morning neared, so she walked from her room to tend the fire. It'd gone low, telling her Vincent was already gone. Throwing in a few logs she sat on the floor, letting her mind wander, but it only went back to the darkness. She couldn't stand it. Vincent couldn't spar that morning, and she didn't want to sit around thinking about the haunting voices.

Kiuno slid on her shoes, lacing them up the side and stepped outside. Vincent had given her a new pair as her old were worn and cracked.

The cold stung her damp skin, but she walked toward the gate, finding Liam already stretching and running in place. They'd started a routine of running every morning, at least when the snow allowed. He must have remembered Vincent's busy schedule.

They set off in silence, and she wondered if something in her expression gave away the long night or if he hadn't slept well either. Whatever the reason, she welcomed it.

Melting snow dotted the landscape. The temperature had risen though the wind still had a bite to it. None of them knew what to expect with winter, but it'd been three long months of cold, freezing rain and what felt like an eternity of ice.

Large snow drifts shut everyone indoors for days, forcing them to survive on what little they'd stored for emergencies. They would get a week of light snow, then the rain would set in, temperatures would dip, and snow would blow through again. It was an endless cycle of frigid nights.

Though Vincent was opposed to it, she helped the hunting parties whenever she could. He wanted her to rest and regather her thoughts, but she needed to move. Everything she did was based off a drive to keep going, and if she stopped, the darkness would catch up. She'd become another voice lost to its endless torment.

Their run started around the perimeter and then headed straight down a familiar path, the one her friends should have walked down. She always stopped by the burnt cabin, but said nothing. Maybe it was because Liam was with her, or maybe she just didn't know what to say. An apology wouldn't bring them back.

It wasn't until they had the walls in view that they slowed.

"Are you all right?" Liam asked.

"Just didn't sleep well." He didn't comment. He knew what that meant. Every day he was on her heels, even more so than he'd been with Vincent. It worried her. She didn't want any ties here.

Liam followed her back to the cabin, and she threw him a staff. She usually sparred with Vincent, but trained the child on occasion. He needed to learn.

The magic still frustrated her, and she'd all but given up on it. Maybe there was a limit and it'd finally run its course. Kiuno felt empty without it, especially knowing she wouldn't be able to defend herself against someone who used such.

Kiuno clutched her wrist, wrapping her fingers around the fabric that still hid her stone. She trusted them and maybe even allowed herself to love them a bit, but she'd never been able to convince herself to reveal the stone. She'd always trust Kikyo more, and he'd instructed her to keep it hidden.

After their session, the two went inside. She fed the fire and warmed up lunch. Food was mostly in the form of stew. It warmed the body.

The end of winter brought glorious relief. Flowers were beginning to break through the cold ground, and the trees were forming buds at the end of seemingly dead branches.

The thought of moving on was something she both looked forward to and dreaded. She needed to find Elite, among others, but that meant leaving Kikyo and Elliott behind. Once she escaped, that was it. There was no coming back. They'd never have a resting place in the real world.

Kiuno twirled the bracelets around her wrist. She'd never taken them off. It was a reminder of their sacrifice. She liked to think that maybe Elliott died for her. That perhaps he'd seen the shots coming and placed himself in harm's way. Then again, maybe not. Maybe that line of thinking was just a comfort to ease her own mind.

Six months…it was hard to grasp just how fast time flew. The last three were spent with Vincent as he helped her process the grief. He asked the villagers about her husband, but once again there wasn't any news. She couldn't imagine how far ahead they might be by now.

Vincent returned late that afternoon and wasted no time. He grabbed a staff and gestured her outside. Liam gave her a shrug, and both followed. She thought he might like to rest after a long day.

Standing before him, she twirled the staff in hand and stretched her shoulders. Her reflexes had improved and after all their practice Kiuno was sure she'd be able to outpace almost anyone.

Liam sat on a stump in the corner and folded his legs to watch. She gave him a quick smile and turned to Vincent to do the same.

He didn't return the greeting.

"We're going to do things differently today." He shifted back into a stance, and she mirrored him. "You're going to use your magic."

"You know I can't, I haven't been able to in months." Why was he suddenly so interested?

"You'll be able to, you just need to get past what's holding you back."

"That's the problem, I don't know what that is."

"The emotions you draw on are what dictate the response. You need to figure out what the correct trigger is."

"Don't you think I've been trying?"

"Not hard enough."

Her mouth fell open, speechless. Tears of frustration threatened as she asked herself for the hundredth time what the secret might be. If she knew, they wouldn't have died, and if she figured it out then it might not satisfy the reason she couldn't save Kikyo.

She tried to think of what might help. Anger wasn't the answer, and the adrenaline while they sparred didn't seem to help either. Did Vincent know something she didn't?

He was already in mid swing when she looked up, just blocking his unannounced attack. The sound of wooden staffs cracking against one another filled the area and she moved to keep up with him. This wasn't Vincent. He never came at her like this. His goal all winter had been to center her and allow her time to find herself.

Why was he doing this?

Brute strength beat her back until she twisted to the side and shoved him forward. "What the hell?" she exclaimed.

He turned without speaking, rushing her again. Liam sat forward, confusion written across his face.

"Focus Kiuno!" Vincent caught her ribs. Hard. She rolled to the ground wincing and barely pulled the staff up to block a downward strike. The impact stung her hands and she ground her teeth.

"Are you trying to kill me?"

"If that were the case, you'd already be dead. You are your worst enemy. You're the one preventing the magic."

"What are you talking about?" She shoved him, and his staff came up, just missing her chin. She took a few steps back, trying to catch her breath.

"I've waited, hoping you'd figure it out on your own. Spring is here, and I can't allow you to leave until I know you can defend yourself to your fullest potential. What happens if you need that magic and it doesn't work a second time? What if you can't protect someone else?"

Her heart dropped, the sinking fear settling in her gut like rotten garbage. She didn't need her nightmares voiced. "Stop it."

What was he doing? After all the time he'd spent building her up, why try to tear her down? Why remind her of that pain, like pouring salt on a wound?

"Why do you fight?"

She looked up as he ran to her again and struggled to block the movements. His speed increased as her mind slowed. It was a question that should have been easy to answer, yet—

His staff collided hard with the other side of her ribs, and she jumped back, dodging a second swing before their weapons collided again. "You can do better than that, why do you fight?"

Fear. Doubt. It all lingered, buzzing in her mind like an angry swarm. She fell on her back and threw him over when he sought to pin her. He didn't hesitate, charging her again and again. Her vision blurred as she was shoved back, hit, shoved back and hit again. Was she not strong enough? Had he been toying with her all along?

"Why do you fight Kiuno?"

"I don't know!" she screamed. How was she supposed to figure out the reason when he was pounding her into the ground? How could she think when so much threatened to break in her mind?

Vincent paused, the pair breathless as they stared at one another. "Then Elliott and Kikyo died for nothing."

Her breath hitched, and she finally felt the wall she'd been building crumble to tiny pieces. "How dare you."

Who was he to insinuate anything? She thought he understood, that he cared. Her doubt shifted to rage, the fear to a burning hatred. They were everything to her. Why would he defile the only thing she had left?

Kiuno rushed forward, anger flaring. Her staff hit his side, and she swept his legs out from under him. She watched him struggle to defend against her onslaught and relished in the pain she inflicted.

"Vincent!" Liam jumped to his feet and ran toward them.

"Stay there," Vincent commanded. Liam stopped, fear covering his face, but she wouldn't let up, not until she was satisfied Vincent understood the depth of her loss. She locked eyes with him again, and his strained smirk made her hatred boil.

"You find this funny?" she spat in disgust.

"No, but it worked."

She was about to retort when a flicker caught her eye. Flames danced around her as they once had, a familiar heat circling her body where she'd previously been cold. Kiuno took a few staggering steps back and let her eyes fall as she watched the shadows. "Is this what you wanted?" Her voice shook. That he'd go that far.

"I didn't want to hurt you. You've always wondered why the flames never responded and grew to believe that anger and fear are what make you strong, but that isn't true. It's the desire to protect that drives the magic in you. You carry regret for not being able to save them, but you'll protect their memories."

"Then why couldn't I save *him*?" she yelled, feeling the guilt crash down.

"You were injured, and magic is complicated. He could use the wind, and perhaps some part of your subconscious believed he could protect himself. When that didn't happen—"

The staff clattered to the ground, and she sank to her knees, letting the flames die. Was that the secret? After all this time, it was something so simple?

She thought back to the arrow pointed at Kikyo and the man that threatened Elliott. She thought the flames were an instinct to breaking away from Tyler, but her real concern had been for her friends.

When the feline attacked Kikyo, it wasn't the fear of him being mauled, but her desire to protect him that caused the flames to spark and spiral down her arm. With the slaves, she'd wanted to protect them and feared people she knew might have been captured as well.

Then there was the cabin—despite all the blood, she'd hoped it wasn't too late, that the cut hadn't been deep enough, and she still had time...

Vincent knelt in front of her with Liam close behind. "I'm sorry. It wasn't my intention to dishonor them, but it was the only thing you still have a desire to defend. I hope you can forgive me." She tried to hide her face. "They died protecting someone they loved, there's no greater sacrifice."

Gathering her courage, Kiuno looked into his eyes. Sympathy. He was the same man she'd spent all those nights crying beside, but still—

Kiuno punched him square in the face.

He fell back, grabbing his nose, the blood already dripping down his chin. "I deserved that."

She smirked through the tears, knowing he'd be able to heal himself. Looking at her palm, she pulled on the flames, the energy rushing through her body as though a veil had lifted. The fire ignited and spiraled around her hand.

He was right, no one she cared for would die again.

HORDE

REALM: 4
DAY: 197

Kiuno sighed in frustration. Despite a week of constant practice, she was no closer to controlling the magic. Conjuring it forth was no longer an issue, sending it in a general direction was even easier, but dictating where the flames went thereafter was uncertain at best.

After hours, she collapsed with sweat rolling down her neck. "It's just not meant to be." Kiuno looked up at Vincent who was supervising her progress.

He rubbed his chin. "You'll get it with time."

No, she knew the real reason, Eldridge told her before. It was uncontrollable and now she understood. Once it left her fingertips, she had no tie to it.

"So, what do I do?" she asked.

"Maintain distance. We both know you're more than capable of defending yourself by other means."

Vincent helped her up, and they made their way to his cottage. Due to the nature of fire itself, she trained away from the village, but it didn't stop a crowd from forming.

Liam jumped from the wall, to a roof and down to join them. "Any luck?"

She shook her head. "Same as always." The boy pouted.

They gathered by the warm fire that night to share in a final dinner. This would be the last time, at least for a while. Vincent's group decided to wait before moving forward. It would ensure they wouldn't get caught in a late snow and that someone would be available to guide anyone left behind.

"I want you to take Liam."

She stopped eating but wasn't surprised. The only thing Liam talked about was leaving, getting closer to the front. She suspected he was talking to Vincent behind her back. She looked at the boy and his hopeful expression, the fire glinting in his eyes, and something wrenched in her gut.

"What if I can't protect him?"

"I can protect myself," he said. "You've been training with me, you know I can. I don't have magic or anything, but I can still fight, and I promise not to get in the way."

Kiuno smiled gently. He thought he could defend himself, but it wasn't people she feared…or maybe it was. There were those that had gone insane and wouldn't care if a child were their victim.

"Considering your nightmares, it might be wise to take someone who understands," Vincent added.

She turned to the fire. She still woke screaming on occasion. He'd be able to wake her before the worst of it hit. It wouldn't do any good to alert an enemy in the middle of the night.

Kiuno sighed and turned back to Liam. "Only if you promise to do exactly as I tell you."

"I will!" He beamed.

"All right, now that things are settled, go home, pack and get some rest, we'll see you in the morning," Vincent said. The boy practically danced out the door, but her smile faded as it shut. There were things she had yet to encounter, monsters she had yet to see.

"Will I be able to take care of him?" He was so young. Maybe she should sneak out before morning. It might hurt him, but at least he would be safe.

"He'd follow you."

"Reading my mind?"

"I've come to know a thing or two. You'll be fine, in fact I was going to ask if you'd like to travel with a small group."

She leaned forward. "I didn't think anyone was leaving."

"There's a few ready to move on, they have family and friends just like you that are still missing. They'll stay in the next town a few days and then move toward the fifth realm. I'm sure they'd be happy to have you along."

"How far is the next town?"

"Only a day or so depending on how fast you move."

"I'd be happy to go." It'd be safer for Liam.

"I'll let them know in the morning."

"You're determined to stay then?" She'd been hoping she could convince him to come along.

"I have an obligation to the people here. We'll meet again, of that I'm certain."

"How do you know?"

"Because you won't be able to stay out of trouble."

She laughed, and a comfortable silence settled around them.

MORNING CAME too fast, and Kiuno woke before dawn. There was something she needed to do before leaving this realm behind.

It was too early for Liam to join, but that's how she planned it. This was a trip she had to make alone.

Kiuno stood before the cabin's burnt remains as the sun peaked over the horizon. The snow had melted, revealing the charred remnants of their memorial.

This was goodbye.

She wouldn't be able to run past and greet them every morning as she'd been doing all these months. If she were going to tell them anything, now was the time.

So many memories surfaced. So many things left undone. Guilt bubbled in her gut, like something sour that didn't quite settle. Vincent told her she needed to come to terms if she were to move forward. She needed to accept it, forgiveness would come with time. She just needed something...

"I'll live," she finally said. "I'll do the things you weren't able."

She knelt and placed a gentle hand on the wood, silent tears falling as she bid them farewell. She'd imagine the place full of flowers, alive and sweet, like the memories she'd always cherish. She'd imagine them together and tell the world about two men who helped mold her into who she'd become.

I'll live for you...

LIAM PACED by the gate and looked surprised when she ran down the trail.

"I thought you left." He crossed his arms and pouted.

"Just had something to take care of."

His expression softened. "You all right?"

"Yeah, does Vincent have breakfast going?" He nodded and led the way, but not before casting her a backward glance.

They ate the leftovers from last night's dinner, then collected their things. Kiuno was given a bow and a side pack that contained dried food and various medicinal herbs.

Spring was all around them. The air fresh. Vegetation littered the ground in green clusters, and animals were beginning to emerge from their winter dens.

It was a new beginning.

"Kiuno," Vincent called. "I have a gift for you." He disappeared in the cabin for a moment, and she exchanged a glance with Liam. He came back holding a staff like she'd never seen.

"I had someone make it." She took the weighted weapon, running her hand down the smooth surface.

"How?" She didn't remember a forger being around, or anyone possessing the skill.

"We have someone who's capable." The staff was made of steel. It was cold and heavier than she was accustomed, but nothing she couldn't acclimate to.

"It's amazing." She walked forward and hugged him.

"First embrace I get is the one where I have to tell you goodbye?"

"It's not too late to come with us."

He shook his head. "An old man like me would just slow you down. I'll travel with the slower lot."

"Don't wait too long, we'll need you."

He nodded, and they walked to the gate and said their final good-byes. There were about thirty people packed and ready to go with three carts of supplies. She didn't know what they were carrying, but with all the hunting through winter, animal hides were in abundance.

Horses pawed the ground in anticipation, excited to stretch their legs in the field. They set off. Liam tried to keep Vincent in his sight for as long as possible. Without a father, she wondered if he viewed Vincent as a surrogate.

"You're welcome to go back," she offered.

"No way." He shook his head and she tried to give him a warm smile, but his vision was drawn to the fading town. "He'll be all right, won't he?" Liam asked.

"He's free of your constant pestering, might even be able to get some work done now." Liam made a face and she laughed. They'd both miss him, but he had promises to keep. This wasn't the last time they'd see Vincent.

Kiuno used the staff as a walking stick, and they found themselves in the middle of the fields, following a thinning tree line. Before them, the sky met the ground in endless blue. It was nice to see something beyond dreary gray. A gentle breeze swept through the barren area, and she imagined it grazing the grassy tops that were sure to come in summer.

The journey was calm, and the wagons moved faster than she'd predicted. The horses played, shaking their manes and kept their heads high as they enjoyed the warmer weather.

The bumpy road made items shift and she helped with adjustments. Small groups chatted about the fifth realm and what surprises it might hold. Some of their predictions were a little too hopeful, but she could appreciate their optimism.

As the sun started to fall, she jumped into the back of a cart, leaning her head against a soft bundle. The jarring made it difficult to relax, but basking in the sun lulled her into a light sleep, at least until Liam shook her.

"Look," he whispered, and she followed his finger to the tree line. Concentrating on the barren trunks, she was about to question him when movement caught her eye. Kiuno leaned forward, grabbing her staff before jumping to the ground.

Whatever they were, they were quick and scurried along the ground in clusters. It wasn't until they were almost upon them that she heard the clicking and it sent her hair on end.

These were the monsters.

One man shouted a warning, and the entire group scrambled to grab their weapons and protect the cargo.

Kiuno thought she'd prepared herself, that nothing could surprise her after all the stories she'd heard, but she was wrong.

These creatures moved along the ground like insects, crawling on all fours. Their bodies resembled that of a human, but they were covered in pale gray fur and the skull split in half to reveal a mouth of jagged teeth. Pale, dead looking eyes sat on either side of the head unnaturally, feral, and with a hunger that wouldn't be sated.

Kiuno separated herself, moving on them and a strange hissing filled the air, like that of cicadas in the warm summer. The high-pitched whine made her skin crawl as they circled her, calling to one another.

When the first jumped, she cracked the staff over its head, and it landed with a snarling hiss, relocating the injury. It reminded her of a snake's jaw after it'd consumed a meal. Another lunged forward, receiving a similar injury. Both looked unfazed. She was reminded why Elliott had given them swords. The blades weren't for the human monsters.

Screaming made her turn to find the wagons surrounded and the horses bucking. A few already carried bite marks. Too much longer and the horde would jump them in unison. There were too many monsters to fight with weapons alone.

The river coursed through her body, and she erupted in flames as three more were almost upon her. They screeched in agony, writhing on the ground, and she let the fire spread effortlessly. It was so simple. She should have realized it from day one.

Kiuno threw flames to the nearest group, watching it burst, and the creatures scattered like insects. She hoped it would be enough to deter them, that their instincts would kick in and make them flee.

The flames surged to another cluster further away and they howled in anguish, those unmarred backing away. Their heads twisted back and forth like a bird's, each eye taking her in as they regarded her with caution.

"Kiuno!" Panic shot through her as she spun to find them closing in on Liam. He was alone, a young one separated from the pack. She wouldn't reach him in time and despite the risk Kiuno spun the fire down her arm and right at them. She made a promise. No one else would die.

The flames leeched from her grasp and those in the way crumbled in its wake, distracting the ones that remained from their former target. Liam ducked under the cart and suddenly all eyes, both human and not, were on her.

The creatures clicked to one another and their dead companions seemed to draw their attention before a low gargled howl echoed across the field. They scattered, crawling to the safety of the trees like a nest called by their queen.

She didn't waste time running to Liam. He sat under the cart, looking after them, clutching his arm.

"How bad is it?" She should have known better, maybe he could have fought them off while she ran to his side, but the image of him being eaten alive wouldn't let her pause.

"I'm fine." He tried to wave her off, but she grabbed his wrist, pulling it forward to reveal marred skin that snaked from the wrist to his bicep. She shouldn't have used her magic.

"That is not fine," she said. Kiuno dug in her satchel for the salve Vincent made. "I'm sorry, I thought I'd have better control." There was never a time where she had an inkling of control. The flames moved where they desired.

"I'm fine, it'll heal."

She sighed, the guilt gnawing at her. "It's going to scar."

He tried to smile as she smeared the sticky medicine over the wound. "Girls will like it." She returned a scowl.

The group started moving as soon as everyone was patched, and they didn't stop until they came upon the next town. Several men greeted one another like old friends, and she quickly felt out of place. She forced Liam to a doctor, where he was properly bandaged.

While the doctor worked on Liam, Kiuno went back to question about their departure. Vincent said they might stay a few days, and she didn't want to miss them.

"When will we be leaving?"

A few of the men looked up, but continued untying boxes while another stepped forward, a little hesitant. "We won't be, not until Vincent and the others join us."

"But I thought—"

"Look, I know you want to get to the fifth realm, so do we, but with those creatures still lurking so close we can't risk being attacked. We were lucky. If we wait it out, they might move on."

"And they might not." He only shrugged, and she turned back to the inn, full of disappointment. Liam got them a room next door. That night she fed the fire, thinking. If she'd known this would happen, she would have stayed with Vincent.

"We can still go," Liam offered.

"You're hurt." She reminded him.

"I'm fine, really, it won't keep me from moving if I have to."

It wouldn't be any different than when she traveled with Elliott, but being alone had led to their deaths. Vincent said they wouldn't be moving on for a few months so where did that leave her? Stuck here while those in other realms moved on?

She'd waited long enough.

"We'll leave in the morning then."

Liam woke her in the middle of the night several times, interrupting the nightmares that clawed at her subconscious. They shouldn't be this bad, but perhaps the thought of leaving on their own had her worried. She didn't want to go, but a nagging feeling kept telling her they had to. She was running out of time.

They left with dawn.

A man stationed at the gate pointed them toward a wood line, and they entered the trees with the sun at its peak. She watched the horizon, wondering if those creatures would come over it, but after entering the forest, her eyes wandered to the treetops. Maybe with it just being the two of them, they would go unnoticed. It could have been the horses they were after.

When the shadows lengthened, she felt a tug at unpleasant memories. Every sound drew her attention, every movement played on her
fears. This was another mistake, after all the times she had questioned
herself, why put them in the same situation again. Why—

"Kiuno." She took a breath before looking at him. "You okay?"

"Yeah." She didn't need him to worry.

Kiuno refused to light a fire that night, and Liam nestled against
her for warmth. It was cold, but nothing unbearable. He didn't complain. After seeing the creatures, he understood.

She checked his injury, adding more salve to ease the burn before
he fell asleep. Blisters stretched across the skin, and he grimaced when
she touched the area. Being desperate to control the flames didn't help
her do so.

A bright moon shone down, giving light to the surrounding shadow. She'd know firsthand if anything was out of place. They sat against
a tree with the barren branches of bushes as their cover. She welcomed
summer, at least there would be more places to hide.

Kiuno relaxed, letting her head lean against the tree when a familiar scent made her jerk.

Smoke.

She couldn't see it, but the smell was strong enough to make her
uncomfortable. Too strong for a campfire. Had the wind shifted? How
close were those responsible?

She woke Liam. "We have to move." At first, he was confused, but
quickly realized what had her heart racing. Kiuno had a hard choice to
make. She could try moving away or follow the scent.

Following it would tell her where a potential threat might lie. She
could eliminate them or try outrunning them and risk getting caught.
The latter wasn't an option.

Kiuno glanced at Liam's arm. He wouldn't be able to fight, that
much was certain. He tried to act tough, but the pain prevented him

from moving it much. He needed to hide. Maybe she could just scare them off.

"Keep distance between us," she whispered. "I'm going have a look around. If I run into trouble, stay hidden."

"I can fight," he protested.

"I can't if you're in the way." He crossed his arms and she turned a stern gaze on him. "You promised to do as I asked."

"Fine."

Kiuno gave him her pack and bow, pulled her hood up and walked through the woods with the staff in front. With the barren trees and full moon, anyone could see her, but she didn't want to appear as a woman. People were less likely to attack a male. He'd put up more of a fight.

She didn't walk far before finding the source. Burnt remains that were crumbling to ash. The embers still smoldered, but the area was devoid of bodies. Hopefully they'd escaped and not been taken as prisoners.

It reminded her how cruel some people could be.

She turned and scanned the trees for Liam. A lone soul, watching her from what shadows he could find.

Her skin prickled. Hair stood on end. Liam was close, waiting on her signal, but something was wrong. Someone else was lurking.

A branch cracked.

In one quick movement, she twisted the staff and the ring of clashing metal filled the air.

COMPANIONS

REALM: 4
DAY: 200

Kiuno ducked, swinging her staff to collide with his weapon, twisting in hopes of wrenching the strange things from his grasp. He turned with the movement, maintaining a firm grip and stepped back, the moonlight glinting from the blades.

She'd never seen the weapon before, a pair of sickle blades attached to short wooden handles. He twirled one in his hand, his stance low. She'd have to be careful. The way he moved would give him better mobility with the weapons. Maybe she should have gotten a sword after all.

"How dare you come back." He thought she was someone else and the hood didn't help. He wasn't much older than herself, but no doubt had suffered at the hands of the demented people who thrived here. Was the burnt village his home?

He charged before she could respond, his blades twirling in various directions. She dodged again and swung at his legs, but he moved beyond reach. The way he handled them made her wonder how many lives he'd taken…but that wasn't something she had a right to dwell on.

His strike made her spin, and a searing pain tore through her shoulder. She cried out, cracking the staff against his leg. The momentum shoved him forward, but the blade cut further down as it was extracted, her shirt already damp.

She took a step back, tears stinging her eyes. Fighting him directly was no longer an option, another strike like that would end this and if she lost too much blood…

Kiuno didn't want to kill him. He thought he was just defending whoever had been attacked, but she had Liam. If she passed out, Liam would rush in, and they'd both die. She couldn't let that happen.

When he rushed again, she let their weapons collide before the flames poured from her center. His eyes widened, and he jumped back to reexamine his opponent. She put them out, not wanting to draw more attention.

When his eyes darted to the trees, hers followed, worried that Liam had been spotted. She didn't consider if he weren't alone. Was Liam in danger? Kiuno peered through the woods, finding him a few yards out, pressed into a tree.

Her enemy took the distraction as an opportunity, and she narrowly escaped the swing. She wrapped one hand behind his neck, kneed him in the gut and twisted his arm behind, shoving him to the ground. Her body pinned his in place.

She drew the knife from her belt, hoping the feel of a blade would settle his movements long enough for her to question hi—

A sharp pain exploded in her side. She dropped the knife and rolled across the ground, barely grabbing her staff in the process. Kiuno brought the weapon high to protect her head and felt a hard hit that made her palms sting. He wasn't alone after all.

She clambered to her feet with her side screaming and blocked another strike from the left, only to be hit in the same tender area on her right. The speed was incredible.

With space between her and the newcomer, he paused, leaning down to check on his friend. The male before her was older and of Asian descent. It took a fraction of a second and he was on her again. The way he danced with his staff would have made Kikyo look like a novice.

She took another hard shot to the side, and it knocked the wind from her lungs.

"Scorp, fire!" She let the flames surround her, hoping for some reprieve, without it he was going to—

The staff cracked against her shoulder, and she cried out. Surprise made her movements slow. His skin didn't scorch as it should have, and his movements didn't falter. Was he able to use magic as well?

The first bit of real fear crept into her gut. Without magic, winning this fight would be impossible. His sharp eyes calculated every movement and reacted before she even knew how to counter.

Her foot caught a branch and only instinct had Kiuno rolling to her feet. Both men stood with weapons directed her way. She took another step back. The flames scared the first one, but it was the second that mattered.

"Watch the right Blue." She glanced, and Liam burst from the trees, colliding with the younger of the two. Names mixed with memories as the two fumbled across the ground. Liam was injured, he could be killed. She turned back to the one standing. This man would end their fight in seconds. However, if both were the people she thought they might be—

He slammed her against a tree, using the staff for leverage, the flames crackled around them, but still his skin didn't burn. This was her only chance.

"Scorpios?" His brow rose, questions glinting in dark eyes as the world froze. She tugged on the flames, pulling them into submission, but neither moved. The two on the ground paused, both watching their dominant counterpart.

He pulled the staff from her chest, allowing her to breathe. "Who are you?"

She pulled the hood back. "Kiuno."

"Kiuno?" The male wrestling with Liam threw the boy aside. "I can't believe it's really you!" He wrapped her in a tight hug making her wince. "Sorry, sorry." He stepped back. "Where have you been? Are you well? Where the hell did you learn to fight like that? You're hurt, do you remember me?"

She struggled with which question to address first, throbbing pain making itself known in both shoulders. "Of course, I remember you Blue, how could I forget? As far as being hurt I think you tore me open, and I'm fairly certain Scorpios might have cracked something." She could already feel the pain creeping along her sides as the adrenaline receded.

Both males returned an apologetic look. "Forgive me, after hearing Blue I thought he might be in danger. You were over him with a knife. I assumed the worst."

"I only wanted him to be still, I wouldn't have killed him."

He nodded. "How bad is the shoulder?"

She could feel the damp material rubbing against her skin, but in the dark, it was difficult to tell. "I'm not sure."

"We have a small camp nearby where we can stitch it up." She turned to Liam. He stood with his mouth gaping. A moment ago, the two beside her had been trying to kill them and now they were talking like old friends.

"This is Scorpios and Blue," she said. "I've known them for many years, long before we were dragged here. You can trust them." He nodded though still seemed reluctant.

"Are you going to introduce him to us?" Blue teased.

"This is Liam. I stayed with him through the winter."

"Nice to meet you."

Liam looked at her again and then back into the forest. "I left our packs back there," he said, still uncertain.

"Shall I help you get them?" Scorpios offered.

Liam looked to her for guidance. She had to remind herself that he was still a child and looked up to her. It might take him a while to warm up to the others. After seeing her wounded, she imagined his fear and the confusion he was feeling now.

Scorpios carried her pack and bow. She hadn't even thought about Liam using it, but was glad he hadn't.

"So Kiuno," Blue started again, his demeanor bright and cheery, "you didn't answer my question."

"Which one?"

"All of them, where did you learn all that?"

"Six months of practice."

He laughed. "That'll do it."

Still giggling at his banter of questions Kiuno explained where she'd been and what she'd accomplished along the way. She kept the details short, and a wave of nostalgia swept through her. It felt as though a heavy weight had been lifted from her chest. They were alive. That's all that mattered. If they'd survived, then surely Elite had as well.

In their gaming world, she relied on everyone, each watching her back and guiding her no matter how trivial the situation. These two were among the top players and shaped their foundation. She was confident they'd do the same here.

Back then, Scorpios functioned as her second in command, though he'd been reluctant to accept the title. He was always good at reading people and controlling tricky situations. He'd never failed to keep tabs on those that were a threat and his suggestions were things she took to heart. He was smart, kind and possessed every quality a leader needed. It made her wonder if he were their true lead and her nothing more than a pretty face.

Blue was the glue that held their little family together. His jokes and sense of humor brought out the best in everyone. She couldn't remember him ever being in a foul mood. His ability to work with others spoke for itself. He was excitable and energetic; someone she was glad to call a friend.

Silence fell for a moment as they walked. Her eyes drifted to the weapons now hanging from Blue's belt. "What *are* those?"

He glanced down. "They're called Kamas, I had someone make them."

"Dangerous is what they are."

His eyes fell, trying to examine her shoulder in the darkness. "That's the point, I just hope you aren't hurt too much."

"I'm sure it's nothing that isn't patchable."

A fleeting shadow caught the corner of her eye. She stopped to examine the humanoid figure and tensed at the thought of another fight. It wouldn't bode well for her. Kiuno glanced at the others, expecting to find suspicion and concern as they grabbed for their weapons. Both saw the figure, but neither moved. Confused, she turned back as he stepped into the light. A young face with dark skin.

"Maltack?"

"Is that you Kiuno?" It was her turn to run, to wrap her arms around someone she'd been praying would survive. After everything she'd suffered, after all the sleepless nights, she miraculously found herself in the presence of three people she loved dearly.

Maltack had been a young man of sixteen when they met, but he seemed to possess the maturity of someone older than herself. He was smart, level headed and navigated people much like Scorpios did. Always watching, learning. That was two years ago.

"Where have you been?" he asked.

"Out searching for all of you."

Scorpios interrupted as she wiped away tears. "She's injured, perhaps you can take a look?"

"Of course." Maltack gestured her forward and they came upon a dying fire.

"Mal has learned a lot concerning things of a medical nature. He should be able to help your shoulder," Scorpios said.

She followed him to the fire where Blue fed it to give them light. Scorpios sat against a nearby tree, observing. Kiuno cringed as he pulled back the bloody cloth and she fed her arm through the sleeve. Liam hovered, his worry palpable, watching Maltack's every move.

"Anyone else would need a lot of stitches," Maltack said.

"Anyone else?" Instead of replying, a faint light emitted from his fingertips, and an itching sensation crawled beneath her skin. In the firelight, she could see the area patch itself together.

"I won't be able to heal it completely, but it'll be enough to stop the bleeding. It should just feel bruised come morning." He rubbed a salve over it and helped her slip her arm back in the sleeve.

"That's a relief," Blue said.

"What about her ribs?" Scorpios asked.

Maltack moved his hands over her sides, prodding the tender areas. She winced, but tried to stay still. "They're all right, bruised I'm sure, but nothing is broken."

"I'm surprised," Kiuno said. "You shouldn't hit people so hard, Scorp."

"Perhaps you shouldn't lurk through the woods at night."

Blue interrupted, "So tell us where you've been, how did you end up here?"

Kiuno hesitated, anything up to that point included Elliott and Kikyo. "For now, let's just say it's been a long journey."

They were silent, exchanging glances before Scorpios spoke. "In any case, we're glad to see you alive and well. I ran across Blue in the second realm, then we found Maltack in the third. As of now, we haven't come across anyone else. Have you been able to locate Elite or Silver?"

She shook her head. "There were people that talked about some-one looking for me, but I don't know who they were. That was back at the beginning."

Blue said, "You think they stayed back or—"

"I think they're moving toward the front. We met some recruiters about a month in, but they hadn't heard of them. We were one of the last they visited from the first realm."

"Have you been told anything about the front?"

"Very little."

"They've amassed a few groups with their own leads. Smaller armies line the borders that operate on their own terms. They worked together to break through to the fifth realm. From what I understand they'll be there for a while," Scorpios said.

"They pushed forward through winter?"

He nodded. "I've talked to a few recruiters and they're pressing ev-eryone along. The first realm has been cleared, at least as far as they can tell. The second is almost empty, though my information could be dat-ed. Many are afraid to move to the more dangerous realms, especially with the amassing violence and murders."

"It's gotten worse?"

He sighed. "Unfortunately. It's my hope that supplies and food are the main motivators, but that doesn't always seem the case. We be-lieve that's what happened to the little village over there."

"Are you sure they aren't still around?"

"We didn't find anyone. The fire is pretty dim, and coals will burn for a while."

"I can't believe this is what we've come to."

"It's the world we live in now." Silence followed, the crickets sing-ing their nightly song. Blue moved back from the fire, folded his arms behind his head, and closed his eyes.

"I'll take first watch." Scorpios stood and sat beneath a tree, plac-ing his staff over his knees.

Kiuno walked closer to the flames and sat beside Liam, pulling her blanket from their pack. She imagined he felt uneasy being around strangers. She laid back and winced when she tried to lay on her side. Everything hurt, but exhaustion brought sleep, and she drifted off into the realm of nightmares.

OPAL

REALM: 4

DAY: 200

*K*iuno ran through the unrelenting darkness, a veil covering her vision. She searched for those missing, mind swirling in uncertainty. She had to find them, to prevent this threatening abyss from swallowing them forever.

She turned—

They stood at a distance, laughing amongst themselves. Blue playfully pushed Scorpios at some joke he made. Why couldn't they see the danger that surrounded them, the demons crawling from the shadows? Kiuno cried in desperation, but her voice remained mute as the flames lashed out and seared their bodies.

Blood dripped from an arrow.

A blade pierced tender flesh.

She bolted upright screaming, her heart racing as beads of sweat rolled down her face. Kiuno's eyes scanned the tree line, and everyone was on their feet, weapons drawn.

Silence. Nobody moved until they gradually calmed, turning to her in question. She shook her head apologetically. They looked at her concerned, but laid down and attempted to rest once again.

Scorpios sat against a tree in silence, the only one who hadn't jumped to his feet. She shuffled over to him and sat down. "I can take over."

"You didn't sleep long."

"I won't be able to now."

Questions hung in the air and she shifted, uncertain. Perhaps she shouldn't be so at ease with them. She'd known these people in a game. A world where none had interacted much beyond those imaginary borders. Who was to say it hadn't all been a façade? They shared the occasional story about their lives, but did she know them on a personal level? Her eyes drifted between them. Each seemed comfortable around the other, but what if—

"You've been through a lot," he said. She remained silent. "What were you dreaming about?"

"Someone I lost." He didn't comment, so she continued. "I met them in the first realm. I think Elliott reminded me of you in a way. He always kept an eye out."

"You said them?" She smiled to herself. Same old Scorpios. She'd never been able to get anything by him.

"Kikyo was much younger. Around my age."

"You bonded with them."

"I did. They taught me everything I know."

Scorpios looked off into the night, to a place beyond the trees. She was afraid he might ask for more details, things she wasn't quite ready to recount.

"This world is dangerous." His eyes fell to his staff, and he wrapped one hand around it. "This idea of a weapon is a joke, even for people like us who know how to use them. A blade could easily slice through it. I'm glad you thought to alter your own, especially with us headed to the front."

"It was a gift." Always observant. Considerate. She thanked his switch in conversation. "You plan on coming with me?"

"I can't let you wander away now that we've found you. We've been trying to track down our former team. If you think Elite is headed toward the bigger alliances, then that's where we'll go. There's too many untrustworthy people out there for friends to separate."

"I know."

"Have you been taught to use a sword?"

"Just the basics." Kiuno didn't want to elaborate. The thought of murdering anyone again left a bitter taste in her mouth. Regardless of their intension, killing someone wasn't the best option. Back home, it never would have happened.

"Then I'll teach you."

"You can do that too?" The way he used the staff was beyond anything she'd seen so far. Was he as good with a sword?

"I'm a bit rusty, but I spent several years training. I'm sure it'll come back to me."

"How about Blue?"

"If you remember, he practiced in the martial arts as well. Kama's are more his thing, and he's good with them. No reason for him to change. He can use a bow, but I think most have picked up that skill as a necessity."

"Was such a strange weapon just lying around?"

"No. He had a blacksmith make them. It was before we realized metal was scarce in the first realms."

"Is it more abundant now?"

"You could say that. I think the creators have a hand in the way things were distributed. I imagine they wanted to see who could survive without metal first."

"That's barbaric."

"Indeed."

"What about Maltack? Are you teaching him?" Kiuno tried to recall if he'd had a weapon.

Scorpios laughed. "Yes, but I don't really need to."

"Why?"

"He defends himself with magic."

Kiuno breathed a sigh of relief. "What kind?"

"Everything."

Her brows raised. "What do you mean?"

"He can manipulate all the elements and heal as well, though that particular skill is somewhat limited."

"Is that why you weren't burned?"

"Exactly, he protects us from the rear and usually settles most fights before they begin. You caught us off guard. Blue had simply gone out to relieve himself."

"In my defense, he attacked first."

"That doesn't surprise me."

She'd been worried over Maltack for nothing. If he could use all the elements that made him one of the most valuable people in the game. He could create barriers, attack, heal—

"What color is his stone?"

"It resembles an opal. Have him show you in the morning."

Not blue then.

"You know. Mal hasn't stopped worrying about you since we figured out you'd be here."

She felt the same. Kiuno looked at Maltack and Liam curled next to the fire. Both were gentle at heart and would hopefully form a strong friendship. They needed strong bonds if they were going to survive this place with their sanity.

THEY LEFT with first light, putting some distance between themselves and the burnt village. Each step made her feel more at ease. Scorpios said they'd reach the void by evening and her heart sped with the news. They were almost there. Almost to Elite.

Scorpios yawned as they walked, and she wished he would have let her take over, but their conversation had been a welcome distraction. Unlike herself, he remembered exactly what he'd been doing seconds before appearing in a forest. He'd been getting his young son ready for school when the world spun out of control.

At first, he hadn't been sure what to make of it. He thought he might have been hallucinating or perhaps was killed and brought to the afterlife. Without an explanation and nothing else to do, Scorpios wandered and found a settlement that, just as her own, couldn't provide answers.

"How did you say you ran into Mal?" she asked.

"It wasn't until the third realm. When I saw what looked to be a firework display, I got curious."

"Fireworks?"

"It was the first time we'd encountered magic. Fire was shooting in all directions and it seemed items were being thrown from thin air." He couldn't suppress a smile.

"What did you do?"

"Helped the poor kid of course. He seemed to be holding his own, but these—" he paused, "things, were chasing him. He'd been traveling on his own, mostly observing and had about as much information as I did. He's quite amazing." The pair looked at their young friend who held an odd expression.

"You give me too much credit," Maltack said.

Scorpios laughed. "Rather, not nearly enough. I can't count the times you've had our backs."

"That's gone both ways," Maltack reminded him.

Kiuno couldn't help but smile. Their playfulness and ease around one another reminded her of happier times. It was only meant to be a game, something she'd dabble with occasionally. Her cousin had been the one to introduce her to it and convinced her to create an alliance. Before anyone knew what happened, they'd turned into a family.

Good times, bad times, they shared it all. Maybe they were the same, maybe she had nothing to worry about. Maybe for once, she could breathe.

"Scorp told me about your stone," she said.

Maltack shifted his pack and pulled back his sleeve. It was a beautiful, almost transparent opal, with fire shooting through the core. Various shades of blue and green lined the red in a powerful display.

"Beautiful," she said.

"We've come across a few that were similar, but none of them could use all the elements. Even Mal has trouble with earth and he can't use water unless there's a source," Scorpios said.

"Is water created from the body's energy like fire?" she asked.

Maltack shook his head. "Those that use it generally pull the molecules from the air, but I find it too slow. I imagine if they were in a desert, they couldn't use it at all."

"That makes sense. How does earth work?"

"By pulling from the ground, but it's—" he paused, searching for the right word, "heavy."

She laughed.

"I noticed your fire was a little strange, do you know why?" Maltack asked.

"What do you mean?"

He seemed to think. "Everyone I've come across uses it directly, but yours doesn't follow a pattern I could grasp."

She glanced at Liam, remembering Vincent's mention of something similar. If Maltack could manipulate magic, then he should be able to explain a few things but—she gripped her wrist. Kikyo wanted her to keep it hidden.

These people were her friends, but could she trust that they hadn't changed? What if they reacted like Tyler? Scorpios would be strong enough to subdue her and with Maltack at his side, the magic wouldn't help. Then there was Liam's safety to consider.

"Kiuno?" Scorpios caught her attention and his eyes shifted to her wrist.

Shit.

She tried to force a smile. "Sorry, lost in my thoughts, I'm not sure, I've never had much control."

"What color is your stone? he asked.

Her heart jumped as she tried to divert her eyes from Scorpios. He already knew something was up. How could she deter them without causing suspicion? Should she just tell the truth?

Kiuno took a calming breath. "It's nothing special, just a cloudy red." For a moment she thought he wouldn't buy it.

"I haven't run across anyone unable to control it. I'm sure there will be others once we reach the front that can explain it better."

She turned back to Scorpios, but his intense gaze hadn't shifted. He knew. He knew she was lying. She hadn't been able to lie to him in a game, what made her think she'd be able to in person?

"You don't have any control?" It wasn't the question she expected. Her gaze drifted to Liam. When were his bandages last changed? All eyes fixated on her until Liam caught her stare.

"I'm fine Kiuno."

She sighed. "Not much, I burned Liam a few days ago when we were attacked."

"How bad?" Maltack asked, turning to the boy.

"Bad enough to scar," she said, feeling sick with herself.

Liam waved both hands, trying to deter Maltack. "I'm fine, really, there's no need to get worked up—"

Maltack grabbed his wrist, making him wince. "Burns can get infected, let me look at it."

She watched in wonderment as Maltack unwrapped the bandage, cleaned the wound and set to work on knitting the skin.

"How bad is the control?" Scorpios asked.

"I can send it in a general direction, but after that I lose connection."

"Are the wild flames harmful to you?"

She shook her head. "Just things around me."

They watched Maltack re-wrap Liam's arm. "Can you predict how far they travel?"

"Not really."

Scorpios approached the boys. They'd moved to sit on a fallen log. "Mal, we'll need you to shield us if Kiuno has to use her magic."

He looked back at Liam's arm. "I can try, but it might be better if she doesn't use it at all. It burns hotter than others I've encountered and blocking all four of us will be hard."

Scorpios rubbed his chin. "Then we'll distance ourselves. I hope to avoid confrontation, but if it comes down to it..."

She nodded. "I'll be careful." They shouldn't be having this conversation. Her friends should be able to rely on her.

"Don't think on it too much," Scorpios said. "Remember, Maltack can shield us long enough for you to get space if the time comes."

"Now that that's out of the way," Blue interrupted. "How are you feeling?"

Everyone turned to her as they remembered what happened last night. She'd been trying to hide her discomfort.

"I think I know what it feels like to be hit by a truck." The group laughed.

"If you need to rest, let us know." Blue said a little more seriously.

"I'll be all right, it won't stop me from walking."

"Until Scorpios tries to take out your knee," Blue snickered.

"I've apologized a hundred times."

Upon her confused look, Blue explained. "We were sparring and Scorp took a cheap shot, sweeping me with his staff. Let's just say wood colliding with your leg is *not* a pleasant feeling."

"I assumed you'd be able to block, don't blame me for your lack of focus."

"I blame your speed. Wait till you spar him Kiuno, you'll know what I mean."

"I think I already do. Wood colliding with your ribs isn't exactly pleasant either."

She'd never seen anyone move like Scorpios had. It'd taken all her strength to block the few attacks she managed. There'd been no hesitation. Not when he thought his friend's life was on the line. Not when the flames raged around him. He had confidence in Maltack's ability and trusted Blue to have his back. Would she be able to trust them as they did one another?

Trees shifted to meadow as the sun faded. Pines littered the area in small clusters, but the grass still hadn't grown, leaving it mostly barren.

They were close to the halfway point. Close to the fifth realm. She wondered if it would take another six months to get home. Maybe with the growing realms it would take a lot longer than any of them hoped. How would it feel to finally step back into the real world?

Sharp hissing sent her hair on end. Kiuno gripped her weapon, turning, hoping the sound was just the annoying insects of summer.

Blue turned with her. "Something wrong?" The sound grew closer and they all stopped to watch the horizon. The forest was a few miles back. Surely, they hadn't followed—

Crawling shadows rose over the hill, pale skin visible against the fading light. There were only five, but she knew there'd be more.

They sprinted on all fours and the first leapt, jaws wide and teeth gleaming, but fire shot from behind, catching it before it came into range. It writhed on the ground, screaming. She turned to Maltack, the fire fading from his fingertips as fast as it'd come.

The second lunged, and he made quick work of that one as well. Scorpios broke two of the creatures' necks while Blue sank his blades deep into the fifth.

"What the hell are those things?" Blue exclaimed. Even with the last dead, the chirping didn't cease. It grew louder, and they took a few uncertain steps back, each casting glances at one another.

Her heart jumped when they came over the hill in vast numbers, like an angry swarm whose nest had been disturbed. They crawled with deadly speed, snapping their jaws, ready to relish in the taste of their prey.

"Run!" None questioned Scorpio's command. It would be impossible to outrun them, but if they made it through the portal, they might stand a chance. Jumping through would let them fight a few at a time.

The whistle from Scorp's staff flew past her ear, catching a creature that jumped after her. He spun the weapon while running, colliding with a few others, and she let the fire catch the grass in her wake. As long as her friends were in front, they'd be fine. All she needed was for the flames to act as a deterrent.

"Up ahead!" Blue yelled and she pushed her pace.

"Kiuno!" She turned, spinning her staff to take out another one as the wind swept past to knock three more back.

Everything froze.

Instead of creatures she saw men, their swords poised and ready. Turning around, Kikyo stood with his arrow drawn, screaming for her to pay attention. This wasn't real, she knew it wasn't. Her vision clouded as she turned back—

"Kiuno." Liam hit the man coming for her and reality slammed back as he twisted to all fours. Fire laced through Maltack's fingertips, the wind spinning to create a fiery vortex around him. She twisted her staff and bashed another in the head before shoving Liam toward the portal.

"Go through," she commanded. All but Scorpios obeyed. He stood in the mist as she pushed the fire to surround them, creating a barrier around the portal to buy some time.

Sharp fangs yanked her arm and a pair of crazed eyes seemed to smile in its triumph. Scorpios brought his staff down hard, yanking her wrist and plunged them both into the icy air. When her feet hit the ground, she rolled and turned back, ready. They all stared at the swirling vortex. Her mind spinning with it.

Seconds ticked by, and she hoped the flames were killing as many as possible, it gave them time to collect themselves. Seconds turned to minutes and with exaggerated relief they all relaxed. It appeared the beasts wouldn't be able to pass through after all.

Kiuno let herself fall back on the cool ground, her breath coming in gasps. Her arm burned as much as her lungs and the queasiness sat heavy in the pit of her stomach.

"Are you all right?" Scorpios knelt beside her. She signaled that she needed a moment and they waited in silence.

"The portals make me sick," she finally answered.

He seemed to understand. "How's your arm?" He pulled the fabric up before she could move, and her heart sank as he lingered on the two bracelets. Without comment, he wiped the blood and examined the skin. "Just a few puncture marks."

"That was crazy," Blue said, still trying to catch his breath.

"We were lucky to be close to the portal." Scorpios stood and examined the surrounding area.

Once again, trees surrounded them, but one thing was vastly different. A path cut clean through the center, with fallen logs laid out on either side.

They were so close now. The fifth realm. It's what they'd been striving for. Elite was here. Everyone had to be here. Right?

"What's that smell?" Blue asked.

"Sulfur," Scorpios said. "Follow me."

Though reluctant, Kiuno followed him into the trees. Maybe he wanted to settle away from the main path for the night.

The landscape took on a rockier feel and a few minutes later the group came upon a handful of boulders that jutted from the ground. Mist rose from their center in small wisps that disappeared in the darkening sky.

Scorpios pointed. "That's what you smell." Clear water flowed between three pools.

"A hot spring?"

Blue already had his shirt off before she could turn around. "I'm still here," she reminded him.

"Oh," he fumbled. "Sorry, guess I'm just used to us guys."

Scorpios laughed and set his pack on the ground. "We shouldn't all go in at once."

"Since Blue is already halfway there you boys can go first."

"I'll go with Blue, and the younger two can stay with you," Scorpios said. "You can go last and stay in as long as you like."

"Why does she get special treatment?" Blue whined.

"Because she's our queen."

Kiuno burst out laughing. In the game, Scorpios had referred to her as such. Hearing it from him now reminded her how close they'd been and how much fun they had with one another.

Blue sighed. "Guess I can't argue with that."

Kiuno lit a small fire and watched the landscape darken as the sun faded below the trees. The stars dotted the sky in a beautiful splendor of sparkling lights.

She eventually convinced Maltack and Liam to join the others as her magic would be rendered ineffective with them around. Plus, it wasn't as if they wouldn't hear her should she need them. She went about collecting wood and sat against the flat rock listening to them laugh. They joined her after about an hour, hair dripping, but spirits lifted.

"It's all yours Kiuno and you're going to love it," Blue said. Only Scorpios and Liam followed.

"Where's Mal?"

"He's going to sit by one of the smaller pools, just in case. The rest of us will be here."

As she expected they would be protective, and Kiuno realized she'd never be alone again. Loneliness had been a plague back home, something that tried to drown her whenever it got the chance. It wasn't that her husband was inadequate, in fact, when he was around she didn't feel the ache at all. But when she was alone, that's when it attacked. Maybe she'd been depressed. It was hard to know.

Kiuno made her way to the larger pool, passing Maltack who dangled his feet in the water. He sat with his back pressed against the rock that separated one pool from the other. He gave a little wave before closing his eyes again, content to sit in silence.

She removed her shoes and dipped one foot into the steaming liquid. After going so long without a proper bath, she would be able to relax. Heating water took too long and over the winter, they'd only heated small bowls.

Kiuno glanced at the fire that flickered a short distance away. It wasn't likely any would peek, but that didn't stop her from undressing as fast as possible and jumping in. Her self-conscious nature didn't care for being naked in the open. She hissed as her body slowly acclimated to the heat.

The bottom was rough, with random stones that promised a stubbed toe, so she settled in a corner. Blue was right. She did enjoy this. Kiuno pulled the braid from her hair and allowed the water to wash away the dirt. Her wounds burned, and she realized how the rest of her body must look.

Even though Maltack had healed it, the skin on her left shoulder was swollen, a nasty scar forming. She had another small scar on her right side where she'd been stabbed the night Kikyo died. Random cuts lined her arms from training and the few battles she'd been part of.

In only six months she looked as though she'd been through a war. Maybe she had been. It felt as though this world was becoming part of who she was.

Kiuno lifted her gaze to the moon and let her mind wander to Elite. Perhaps he was looking at the same sky, wondering if she was safe. She willed him to be, to know that everything would be all right. They would find one another and escape this nightmare together.

She had to believe, if she could survive this far, then he could too. He was stronger, but then...so was Elliott...

Kiuno dipped her head beneath the surface, letting the warm water rush across her face. She resurfaced and fixed her gaze on the bracelet. Could she tell them? Maybe it didn't matter. Maybe others had been found that carried the same stone and she was making a bigger deal about it than she should. Eldridge could have been wrong.

"Kiuno?"

She startled, he'd been so quiet, she almost forgot Maltack was there. "Yes?"

"We'll find the others."

He knew. Maybe they all did. Scorpios said finding everyone was their goal. They were just as worried. Of the fifty people in their original alliance, only five had come together. There were so many beyond that group as well. It seemed doubtful they'd find even half.

"Thanks Mal."

TRUST

REALM: 5
DAY: 202

Watching the sun rise on another day Kiuno took the chance to breathe in this moment of stillness. They were finally here. The fifth realm. There was no doubt in her mind now. She'd see Elite soon.

Kiuno tilted her head letting her eyes fall on Maltack. Yesterday was eventful. She never thought magic would trigger her fears, but when that gust of wind shifted, she'd seen Kikyo again… Liam brought her out of it, but what would happen if such a thing became a regular occurrence? She'd known it to be an illusion, but still.

Kiuno turned back to the sun, reminded of Kikyo's magic and how it manipulated the flame in her palm. There was so much they could have accomplished together.

Taking a breath, she stretched and sat up, sore muscles protesting. Her body was covered in bruises. Maybe they let her sleep because they'd caused most of said injuries. Though she appreciated it, she couldn't let their favoritism turn routine. She wasn't helpless.

"We still have a good way to go before we reach the main settlements. There's a village or two along the road. We can stop for information," said Scorpios.

"You mean you don't know where we're going?" she asked.

"My information ended the moment we passed through that portal."

"That's surprising," Blue said. "He's usually three steps ahead."

Kiuno smiled. "We can't all be perfect."

Blue laughed. "I think she just insulted you."

"That's fine. She can go hunting with you."

Kiuno accompanied Blue into the woods with less confidence than when she'd first fired an arrow. She hadn't used her bow in a month. When she missed their fourth potential meal, she knew he'd never let her live it down. Blue claimed they'd all starve if it were up to her. As they made their way back, he seemed inclined to share his discovery.

"Kiuno is a horrible shot," Blue said.

"Shut up."

The three looked up, and Scorpios cracked a teasing smile. "How bad?"

"Bad enough that if your life depended on it, you'd better pray she doesn't try saving you."

"I didn't know you could use a bow," Liam said. She stared at him. What did he think she used while hunting?

"I don't claim to be great and I should have stayed up on my practice but—"

"Practice? You completely missed four targets. I think the kid could shoot better than you."

"Hush or I'll kick your ass again."

"You think you beat me?"

She placed her hands on her hips. "I wasn't the one on the ground and if not for Scorp trying to break my ribs, you would have stayed there."

Scorpios laughed. "It seems you two will need to settle this matter."

"Yes, though I'd prefer to do it without sharp objects." Her eyes fell to the blades dangling at Blue's waist.

Maltack interjected. "Neither of you are solving anything until Kiuno is healed."

"Fine," Blue stated. "But you don't get to use your magic either. I'm not down for being scorched." There was a moment of silence before they burst out laughing.

They ate, stored the leftovers and set off following the straight path laid out for them. Two days passed without much excitement. She was banned from hunting, but could help with skinning rabbits. While cutting and tearing at the flesh, she wondered why it had bothered her before.

Wooden walls promised refuge as they climbed a hill. Large gardens lined the outskirts and several animals were tethered to posts that surrounded the gate. Were they preparing to spend the whole summer here? Surely, they wouldn't be trapped in this world long enough for a harvest.

"Put your hood up," Scorpios said before they reached the gate.

"Why?"

"Best if people don't think a woman is traveling with us." Instead of arguing, she did as he asked. Maybe he knew something she didn't, or he just wanted to be cautious. She knew what people were capable of. If something as simple as this helped safeguard them then she'd gladly oblige.

Scorpios greeted the four men at the front with a smile and commented on the weather. They nodded in turn, but their gaze lingered on her, the only one hidden from view.

The atmosphere took Kiuno by surprise. She'd grown accustomed to the feel of a small town, but this was more like a war camp. Everyone held a weapon of some sort and though the men laughed amongst themselves, it was strained, the mirth not quite reaching their eyes.

Blue asked about an inn, and she followed him to a building on the far side. Once inside, the atmosphere shifted again. Singing, dancing, and the loud strum of instruments filled the air. A band, if one could call it such, played in the corner by a stone fireplace, and the stench of beer and sweat lingered through the air.

"I'll be back." Scorpios made his way through the throng, and Blue guided them to a table at the end.

"Where's he going?" She had to lean close for him to hear.

"See if they have any rooms open."

"And if not?"

He shrugged. "We'll make do." Scorpios came back informing them of their poor luck, and they tried two other places with the same outcome. They weren't the only ones headed toward the main front. People were anxious after sitting through the winter months, they wanted to be done.

She tapped her foot, waiting, hoping they wouldn't have to sleep outside. She'd rather be a hundred miles from people if they didn't have a roof over their heads. The groups outside didn't exactly give off a peaceful air.

"She only has one." Scorpios looked at her apologetically.

"Good, I'd rather us stay together anyway, it's safer than sleeping out there." She gestured.

"I was hoping we wouldn't have to invade your privacy."

She scoffed. "That flew out the window the day we arrived."

Scorpios left once again to drop their belongings off while Blue forced them to take a seat near the fireplace. Though it was still crowded, they could at least hear one another over the banter. Original music still played with whatever instruments could be found.

Once again Kiuno tapped her foot as they waited for Scorpios. Growing worried, she looked around and found him in a far corner with another group of people.

"What's he doing?" she asked.

Maltack followed her gaze. "Getting information."

"Does he know them?"

"I doubt it. Scorp just has a way with people. They always seem inclined to answer his questions."

"That's convenient."

Blue stood, stretching his arms. "In about an hour we'll have all the information we need, but for now I'm starved."

When Blue left, she turned to Maltack. "Do you think we'll be here long?"

"No, we usually move pretty fast. The faster we get there the faster we figure out what the real plan is."

"I bet Scorp is dying to know."

Maltack laughed. "He likes to see how people think."

"His intelligence and kind nature make people listen too. Sometimes I think he got us out of more trouble than I got us in," she admitted.

"Don't be hard on yourself, you were both great."

Kiuno jumped when Blue sat a plate of bread and meat on the table along with a few mugs he was attempting to balance.

"All this for us?" she asked, eyeing the beverages.

"Yep, they told us to enjoy." He slid a mug to her and sat on the stool.

"Is this a good idea?"

He downed half the drink before responding. "We're safe, there's no need to worry."

She was about to protest when Scorpios returned. "There's a few groups taking supplies to the front soon. We can travel with them. They like having an escort."

"Monsters?" she asked, feeling a shiver run down her spine.

"Not near the town, but a few caravans were attacked recently."

Her thoughts were interrupted as two mugs slid across the table. "We can worry about monsters tomorrow. Tonight, it's time to have fun."

Scorpios shrugged and drank to Blue's invite. Taking her own, she tried to smile, but cringed when the bitter burn ran down her throat.

"That is disgusting," she said, wiping her mouth.

"You don't drink for the taste," he laughed.

"I think I'd rather just watch you make a fool of yourself."

"Not gonna happen. I don't drink alone." Blue scooted the mug toward her again.

Scorpios bumped her and his sudden shift in position had her eyes darting between tables. She followed his nod to a group of young men whose gazes were fixated on them.

"Be ready, but avoid the magic," he whispered. Her skin crawled.

"Hey there," one called. "Why hide the lady? We all deserve to see that pretty face."

His slur indicated his drunken state. Kiuno's friends sat pensive, all scowling at those who leered. She needed to diffuse the situation before it got out of hand.

"Care for a little dance?" he asked, extending one hand.

Pulling the hood back and taking a breath, she returned the sweetest smile she could manage. "I appreciate the kind offer, but I'm a bit tired. I think I'll just rest here."

His smirk twisted her gut. "I could help you relax more."

Snickering, he elbowed his friends and they encouraged the behavior. Their drunken state made them too bold for their own good, or plain stupid. She guessed more of the latter.

"No thank you." She tried more forcefully. The male pouted. She turned away, ignoring his burning gaze until something of more interest caught his attention.

Kiuno took a sip of the poison Blue enjoyed and caught Liam with balled fists, still glaring as though he might spring any moment.

"Relax Liam, no harm came of it." It took a moment for his eyes to turn, and he took a breath to settle himself.

"Here kid." Blue planted a mug in front of him. "Take a drink, it'll help."

"He can't have that, he's a child." Kiuno grabbed the mug and pulled it toward herself.

"Says who? It's a free world, let him have a drink." Liam looked at her as if asking for permission, and for a moment she was torn. He was a child, but Blue was right. This wasn't home, so what did it matter?

She sighed and slid it back. "Just go easy." He looked at the mug, and she couldn't stifle her laugh when his nose crinkled from the taste. Blue patted him on the back and Liam spluttered. He'd been pensive around her friends until this point, though she wasn't sure Blue was the best of influences.

Blue got more drinks in Kiuno than she would have cared for and pulled her to the floor, twirling her in beat to the strange song. Scorpios was next in line followed by Maltack.

Each laughed as they danced, outside fears forgotten. By the time Liam joined them, Blue was showing him moves that had the whole place in an uproar. She clapped along, keeping time.

Kiuno eventually caught on to Scorpios and Maltack's trick of switching their mugs with Blue's. He never seemed to notice, but she'd already had too much before realizing it was an option. Clever tricksters.

As the night waned, Blue kept his pace on the floor, flirting with women who indulged his advances. Liam sat in a chair with his head down, the bitter liquid making his stomach turn while Maltack and Scorpios simply observed the crowd, content with the entertainment their friend provided.

Though she had had a few drinks too many, she was glad Blue brought them here. He wanted to defuse. If she wasn't nursing too bad of a headache, she might thank him come morning.

Her mind spun as she told Scorpios she'd be back in a moment. Kiuno had been watching where people exited for a restroom and headed through the dancers in search of it.

An arm wrapped around her waist. At first, she thought it might be Blue, even if the action was a bit bold, but she turned to a stranger's face.

"Finally decide on that dance?" His breath reeked of stale beer, and she struggled to control the contents of her stomach.

Scorpios stood, and she caught his eye, but she simply pushed the man away. "Actually, I just needed some fresh air." Hopefully he would get the hint.

"I'll escort you, wouldn't want a pretty face like that outside alone."

She forced a smile, working to pry his wandering hands from her body. "I'm sure I'll be fine."

"Come on, why not let—"

She gripped his arm, letting the intensity of her gaze be a warning. "Let me go."

He returned the hold. "Don't be like that sweetheart, we can head up to my room. I have a fire going."

"I said no." His grip tightened as he pressed his body against hers. The proximity made her heart race. Dark thoughts clawed to the surface. It was too familiar, too much like—

Her throat constricted, there were too many people, too much noise. She turned to Scorpios only to find a face that made her heart stop. Kikyo marched toward them, an angry scowl marring his face. She couldn't let anything happen. Not again.

Kiuno wrapped one hand behind her assailant's neck and slammed a knee into his groin followed by another to his face, then shoved him to the ground. Everyone around them took a few steps back.

"You stupid bitch!" he bellowed, trying to cover the blood streaming down his face. A few other men turned her way but Scorpios and Maltack stood at her side. Scorpios moved to place himself between them, but she pulled him back. One drunken idiot wouldn't get the best of her.

With blood still pouring from his nose, he stood, smearing the red liquid across his face. In anger, he rushed forward, but she sidestepped, grabbing his wrist and kicking his knee out. His face planted to the floor.

A burly man attempted to aid his friend, but Scorpios stepped between them. Despite his size the man recoiled with his hands high.

Four men stepped from behind the counter. Two of them grabbed the one she'd injured while the others escorted his friends out the door.

"Thank you." A round woman, close to Scorpios's age, beamed at her. "We should have thrown them out earlier. I'm sorry they caused you trouble."

"It's all right." Kiuno said and took a few steps back to their table.

"Be sure to have all you like," the woman called. Kiuno had never seen Blue so happy.

Another hour and a few too many toasts later, Kiuno found herself half asleep with her chair pressed against the wall. It was nice to forget, or at the very least, let the troubles of tomorrow slip to the back of her mind.

She stiffened when a hand wrapped around her shoulder. "It's just me," Scorpios assured. "Come on, let's get you to the room before you fall over." She'd already fallen over. The wall just saved her from the humiliation.

Without argument, she let him help her up. Even this late, people still danced and carried on as if their tolerance was limitless. She wondered how long Blue would hold out.

Scorpios kept a firm grip around her waist, and she let her weight lean against him. The world spun, and she tried to keep her eyes on the floor for some stability. She'd be cursing Blue come morning.

"Don't throw up on me." Scorpios lifted her into his arms and she wrapped her hands around his neck and buried her face in his shoulder. The world still spun, but at least she couldn't see it.

He climbed the stairs and closed the door to their room bringing about sweet silence. He set her on the bed and she unwound herself from him. Scorpios sat on the edge, probably wondering if she would be sick.

She drifted, but when Kiuno felt him shift, she grabbed his arm. "Don't go." He hesitated, but she moved over, and he laid beside her. Scorpios stiffened when she curled next to him.

"I don't think—"

Kiuno couldn't stifle her laugh. "Relax, Scorpios. I'm not that kind of drunk. I just…miss him." He paused, seeming to wrestle with something before wrapping one arm around her shoulder and folding the other behind his head. His breathing filled the space between them and she focused on it.

"We're going to find Elite."

Her throat constricted. "How do you know?" So much time had passed. So much could have happened.

"If he's half as stubborn as I know you to be, he won't rest until you're in his arms."

She smirked. "I'm not that bad." She knew he'd be smiling, but couldn't lift her head to look. "Will you stay until I fall asleep?"

"I can't very well leave you by yourself. We left Maltack with the worst of it. He has a professional drunk and a child who is going to be twice as miserable tomorrow."

She giggled. "Once we get home Mal will probably never visit a bar again. Are you going to carry them up too?"

"Not a chance, they can sleep on the floor if they can't climb the stairs."

"That's cold, you carried me."

"Because someone could take advantage of you."

"Someone could take advantage of them."

He let out a hearty laugh. "Somehow I doubt any of them would mind."

She giggled again. "I guess not."

The silence lengthened and her mind drifted.

"Kiuno?"

"Hmm?"

"There's a few questions I've been wanting to ask. Would you prefer to answer them now or in the morning?"

"Why didn't you ask earlier?"

"I wanted to be away from the others. I don't want you to feel cornered."

She propped her head up with one hand, trying to focus on his face. "What is it?"

"I know you lost your friends," he hesitated, his eyes tracing her face to gauge her reaction. "Do the particulars of that situation still affect you?"

Kiuno's mind felt sluggish as she tried to piece together his meaning. "I'm not sure I understand."

"When we fought the creatures, there was a moment where you seemed caught off guard. Liam brought you out of it and just tonight, downstairs, it happened again. I only waited because I thought you'd be able to handle the situation, however, when I saw your eyes…you weren't looking at me."

Kiuno wasn't sure how to respond. Observant Scorpios.

"No, I wasn't," she whispered. It was the truth, in that split second, she'd seen those blue eyes again.

"You have flashbacks?"

"A little."

"Does it happen often?"

"No, it's usually just the nightmares. Be thankful I didn't burn the place down."

At first, he smiled before realizing she was serious. "I'll keep that in mind. How bad are the nightmares?"

"What you saw the first night is pretty consistent."

"You've slept well since then."

It was only now that she realized he was right. She hadn't woken screaming in a few days. Maybe having familiar people around eased her mind. Maybe that's why she didn't want him to leave. If he did, the abyss would swallow her all over again.

"I have a second question, but I want you to know you're free to decline an answer."

What did he think could be worse than the previous? "I'm listening."

"What color is your stone?"

She froze, but it shouldn't have surprised her. Trying to hide anything from Scorpios was like a three-year-old trying to hide something from their mother. He saw everything, paid attention to the smallest of details. He must also know she had her reasons.

"In the morning?" she tried. She was too tired and though a bit of apprehension formed in her gut, she knew Scorpios wouldn't look at her wrist while he slept. He had too much respect.

"All right, I'll hold you to that. Now get some sleep." She laid her head on his chest, allowing his rhythmic breathing to lull her into a place of colored dreams.

STONE

REALM: 5
DAY: 205

Kiuno groaned when the light woke her, a splitting headache bringing the first of many regrets. She turned to find Maltack asleep at her side and Scorpios settled near the fireplace. The rest of them lay sprawled just inside the door.

The image of Scorpios or Maltack having compassion and dragging them up the stairs made her smile, though she hoped neither were kept up long. Kiuno sat up, holding her head to ease the pounding. If the others were going to wake to the same, she hoped they'd sleep longer.

Her mouth was dry, and a bad aftertaste prevented further sleep. She needed something to wash it away. Creeping to the door, Kiuno struggled to squeeze through without bumping Liam and tiptoed down the stairs.

The atmosphere from last night had shifted. It was quiet, the air not quite as thick. The building was empty, save for the few who slept on the floor. Someone had cleaned up and even covered those unable to make it to their beds.

"Are you hungry?" Startled, she turned to a heavy-set woman behind the bar, who ran a cloth through a mug, inspected it, then rubbed it down again.

"A little." Her stomach growled, but she wasn't sure how much she could hold down.

The woman disappeared and returned moments later with a plate of bread and mug of hot tea. "I trust those boys are taking care of you?" A stern gaze searched for signs of distress, and Kiuno briefly visualized this woman chasing Scorpios with a frying pan.

Kiuno giggled. "Yes, they're good friends of mine."

"Good. Thank you again for your help last night."

"No problem." Kiuno nibbled on the bread while the woman busied herself elsewhere. The tea helped ease her headache, but as the night came back to her, Kiuno's heart raced. Scorpios was asking questions, and it would be impossible to hide the truth. He had a keener eye than Elliott.

What did she fear? That Scorpios wouldn't turn out to be the same person? Did she fear him and the others changing? Maltack and Blue were both themselves. If they were playing off a ruse, then it was an elaborate one.

Kiuno shook her head. They'd keep her secret safe. Her friends wouldn't betray her. Kiuno's heart sank, and she dropped her head to the table. They wouldn't...right?

"You shouldn't leave without telling us." Scorpios sat on the stool next to her.

"I didn't go far. Did you have compassion on them after all?"

"No, Maltack did, I just helped them in the door."

"Explains things, I almost couldn't get out."

He chuckled. "It's good for them to unwind, especially Blue. Being serious too much takes a toll on his humor."

"I wouldn't think anything could effect that." She took a sip of tea. "I'm glad he enjoyed himself."

"He wasn't the only one."

She smiled. "At least until the middle of the evening."

Scorpios laughed. "I was impressed and glad to know you can handle yourself."

"I held up against you."

"You certainly did, but it was nice to see you do it without the magic. Sometimes we rely too heavily on one method of fighting." When she didn't respond, he glanced at her. "Something I said?"

She twisted her hands together. "I couldn't use it until recently." Her voice turned to a whisper. "I stayed with Liam and a man named Vincent through the winter. He helped me." She knew the answer was vague and could see him struggle, wanting to ask more questions.

"You remember what I asked last night?" he started.

"Yes."

"But you're still hesitant."

She eyed her wrist. "Last time someone saw it, people almost got hurt."

"Your friends?"

"Yes, but that's not why—" She shook her head. "The situation was handled."

Silence filled the space again.

"I know it's been tough for you, so I won't force you to do anything, but just know you can trust me. I'd never do anything to hurt any of you."

His words brought tears to her eyes. Trust. Yes, she could trust him. This was Scorpios. He was the last person who'd ever betray her. He'd always been by her side even with the offer of joining stronger alliances. If he could be that loyal in a game—

Kiuno slid her arm under the table and untied the knot. Her heart clenched. She'd forgotten it'd been Kikyo's. Scorpios's eyes traced over the lines that etched her name on the smooth surface. His lips parted, but he didn't speak. Instead he retied the knot and sighed, "I was afraid of this."

"What do you know about it?"

"Just hearsay. Many think the stone plays a key role in getting us home but I think their hope is misplaced."

"Why?"

He shrugged. "They want an easy answer, but from what I've seen, I don't think it'll be that simple. The rules are clearly stated, we still have to make it to the tenth realm."

"Rules?" She hadn't heard it put that way.

"The book everyone talks about. It states what has been explained to most. It talks about the ten realms, magic, the beasts and small details of that stone with a simple caption attached, 'Fire from the Sky'. It's mentioned to be uncontrollable, yet the strongest, but that's too vague a description to put my hope in."

"You think they're giving people false hope? That's cruel."

"Cruel, yes, but without it, many would have given up. Whoever put us here didn't want that. They left too many supplies and hints for us to stay put. They want us to find a way out."

"But why, what's the point?"

"Hard to say."

"If I find out we're part of some crazy military experiment, I'm going to be really upset."

He laughed. "You watch too many movies. There's people from all over the world. Look at *us*. We lived across the globe." That was true.

"What else then?"

"Could be a single person with an elaborate plan to entertain himself."

"Or herself," she added, "but entertainment just seems so…"

"Sadistic?" he offered.

She nodded. Thinking about some crazed person hiding in the shadows laughing at their trials felt too much like a horror movie.

"What if getting out is a lie, what if—"

"We have to hope it isn't." She fell silent. Could they make a life here if that was their only option?

Both turned to the sound of their friends trudging down the steps. Each plopped into empty stools without a word. Liam and Blue were both pale with dark circles under their eyes while Maltack simply appeared tired.

"How are you feeling?" she asked. It was hard to stifle a giggle when Blue shooed her away, and Liam's pitiful gaze made Scorpios burst out laughing, their serious conversation forgotten.

"I'm never drinking again." Liam dropped his head on the table.

"That's what we all say." Blue laughed, gladly taking the tea offered.

"Where you headed?" the woman asked, placing several bowls of warm broth before them. Kiuno turned to Scorpios, expecting his response, but he was staring at her, as were the others.

"To the front," she said, eyeing them. "There's still a few people we need to find."

"I suspected as much. There's a small caravan headed that way tomorrow. The ruffians we chased out last night were part of the escort. I wondered if you might be willing to fill in."

"We'd be glad to," she said.

"I wouldn't ask without offering something in return. We have plenty of weapons. I'll have someone show you later, and you can take what you need."

Kiuno was about to decline when Scorpios interrupted. "We appreciate that, what do you know about the front?"

"They're doing well, which is why there has been a large effort in moving everyone. They've come across large stone structures with thick walls. The protection they offer isn't something we can pass up and the land is fertile enough to promise an abundance of food."

"Stone walls? We haven't seen anything like that since the first realm." Scorpios wrinkled his brow.

"Which is why everyone is headed there. The leaders are doing great, working together to bring about some order to this chaos."

The news seemed to comfort the woman, so Kiuno didn't speak until she was well out of earshot. "You don't like the idea?"

"I don't like the sudden shift. The wooden walls have become less elaborate the further we've traveled, and some places didn't have them at all. Why make things easier? What do we need protection from?"

A chill ran down her spine as she thought about the feline and chirping creatures. She'd been lucky to only encounter those few. Is that why this place looked like a war camp? Were they preparing for something?

After breakfast, they returned to the room. Color was finally returning to Blue's face, but Liam fell onto the bed.

"Scorp, what do you know about the front?" she asked. "Specifically."

"I know five leaders are collaborating with one another, but each function separately and numerous smaller groups reside on the outskirts."

"Do you know any names?"

He shook his head. "People don't seem to be interested in names."

"How do the smaller groups help? Surely they aren't just hanging back."

"I'm told they trade food for weapons."

"If Elite isn't with the main five, finding him is going to be harder than I thought," she said.

Would she be able to meet with the leaders? Kiuno wasn't anyone of significance, not like she'd been in the game. They had a small band and nothing to offer, unless she was willing to reveal the stone. If it was the only way to find her husband, she might not have another choice.

"You're too young to worry so much. Elite will turn up." Scorpios added, "Would you like to catch the others up?" Everyone looked at her, their curiosity peaked. Once again, Kiuno untied the cloth and let it fall to her lap.

"Fire from the Sky," Maltack whispered.

"She was afraid to tell us and rightfully so. People are looking for that stone and the less they know, the better. We'll keep this between us, unless Kiuno suggests otherwise," Scorpios said.

Liam stumbled over to examine it with the rest of them.

"Well," Blue said. "Kiuno has the mystery stone. That figures, but it doesn't change our original mission."

"Agreed."

"Are we going to take advantage of the weapons?" she asked.

"Yes, sorry, I didn't mean to interrupt you, but I know you can be reluctant to accept a gift," Scorpios said. "Blades cut whether in the hands of an expert or novice. I prefer us to be the former."

They nodded in union.

NIKITA

REALM: 5
DAY: 205

That day, they helped everyone pack supplies and build new pulls for the horses. Each picked out a weapon under Scorpios's watchful eye. She found a thin sword, light enough to swing, with a dark gray scabbard. Two daggers hung on the other side of her belt with a third stuffed in her shoe. They were taking no chances.

Scorpios began working with her that night. He positioned her feet differently and had her doing more evasive movement than she was accustomed. He taught her how to read the body and pay attention to shoulder and hip rotation. They switched to using sticks after she almost tripped onto Blue's sword.

The carts were slow as they made their way across the hilly terrain. The weather had warmed, and she could finally move without a heavy cloak.

Liam warmed up to them, and she was delighted to watch him work with Scorpios on his balance. He handed Liam a short sword and

Liam seemed more comfortable with it than the staff. Maltack could swing with more force than she'd given him credit.

If she were to compare Scorpios's training to the horrid routines Elliott put her through, she'd have to say Scorpios's were easier, but more tactful. He wasn't as concerned with strength as he was with technique. Though the activity was serious, they kept a light heart, laughing together whenever someone fell or missed their target.

Nostalgia crept into her heart. If only they could see her now. If only Elliott could have long talks with Scorpios and eventually meet Elite. If only their lives hadn't ended so soon.

As they laid back for the night, the open sky drew her attention. She'd never get over the clarity. If there was one thing she'd miss about this place, it'd be this. Maybe in time, she'd have to move somewhere with a clearer view, somewhere away from the city.

Blue helped recover her lost archery skills, and she was reminded of the early days. Her arm burned from the pull, the muscles still healing as she worked them. Maltack still checked on her shoulder every night.

A wheel fell off a wagon and occasionally the horses would startle, but overall their journey remained uneventful. She was happy as long as they didn't run into any more of the cicada creatures.

As she was retying a rope that'd come loose, a white shift caught her attention. At first, she'd assumed it to be a bag or pant leg, but then she saw a tail flick to one side. Kiuno gestured for Scorpios to follow as she jumped from the wagon and crept forward, so as not to scare whatever lurked around the corner.

Deep, growling huffs made her pause.

In front of the cart, a man walked with a white tiger stalking behind, but something about it was off. Feathered wings rested on either side with tints of gray stripes running all the way to the tips. It only stood a few feet tall.

She'd always imagined the creatures here to be evil and foreboding, but this creature was neither. It was majestic. The feline paced between the wagons, low growls echoing from deep in its chest, but the man walking in front didn't seem bothered.

Scorpios took the initiative. "Hey there." The man turned, the tiger-like animal growling as it circled to place itself between the two. "Does it belong to you?" He nodded to the feline.

The male grinned, reaching down to pat the white fur. The skin rippled and it let out another panting growl. "You could say that, though she's not exactly a pet. She won't harm you."

Scorpios approached, but the cat kept her distance, its body low to the ground, ears flattened, and wings pulled close. "What's her story?"

"Pulled this little gal from a trap, been following me around ever since. Was nice to have her around for winter. She's a great hunter."

"You were outside all winter?" Kiuno joined her friend, surprised anyone would stay out in the awful snows that had passed.

"Yep, sure did."

"She's beautiful." Kiuno tried to inch closer, bending to her level, but was greeted with a firm snarl.

"Her name's Nikita, she doesn't take too kindly to strangers though. We've come across some rather unpleasant individuals."

"I understand." She'd met her fair share. Up close, emerald eyes darted between her and Scorpios, daring either of them to move in a way she didn't see fit. Why would someone bother to create something so beautiful in a world where, so many things were evil?

"What's your name?" Scorpios asked.

"Jim."

"I'm Scorpios and this is Kiuno," he said.

Jim halted, his companion letting out an audible huff. "You're joking." His eyes fixated on her.

"Wait, you're *that* Jim?" Scorpios asked.

A wide smile broke across his wild features and the two embraced with loud clasps to the back. "It's about time I ran into someone I know. You've no idea how many people call themselves Scorpios. However," he turned to her, "as far as I'm aware, there's only one Kiuno."

She returned his warm smile and gave him a light hug. "It's great to see you too."

Another one, within a week, she'd found another major player in their alliance. Scorpios, Jim, and Blue were always causing light heart-ed trouble. They never ceased to make her laugh.

"Have you any more of our troop with you?" he asked.

She nodded. "Blue and Maltack."

"My man Blue is here?" They walked around the wagon, Jim's ex-citement feeding her own.

"Blue," she called, "Jim has been here the whole time."

"Seriously? How are you man?" The two shook hands and he greeted Maltack much the same. Liam waved, looking between them a little wary.

"Holy shit, what is that?" Blue exclaimed, his eyes darting from Nikita back to them.

"Well, I'm not really sure what kind of creature she is, but I call her Nikita."

Blue knelt, trying to call for her, but another growl greeted them.

"Sorry, she's not fond of strangers. Seems to be too many crazies."

"I hear you, Kiuno knocked one out the other day." Heat rose to her cheeks and they laughed at her expression.

"I wouldn't expect any less from our fearless queen." Jim's eyes met hers. Kind and gentle, yet firm. Just like Scorpios. "So," he continued, "you're headed to the front then?"

She nodded. "We're still looking for Elite, these people needed an escort, so we decided to tag along."

Around the night fire, stories of days long past floated between them. About how a little alliance rose in ranks and strove to be the best.

The innocence of a gaming world.

"Blue, did you know Scorpios was suspicious of you when you first joined?"

Blue turned to him. "Seriously? Man, and here I thought you'd been my friend."

"You did come from an enemy alliance," Scorpios reminded him.

"Because they were trying to kill me! I had to change my name and everything." He pouted, but smirked thereafter. Each knew how strong their bonds had become.

"Oh, I got one," Blue started. "Do you remember when that Korean chick attacked Jim and I?"

Kiuno laughed. "Yeah. I asked K.J. if he wanted to have some fun."

"That was awesome! He chased her around the whole map!"

"That's about the time we realized how serious other people took the game," Scorpios said.

Kiuno nodded. "And how small we were in comparison."

"We didn't stay that way." Scorpios leaned back. "I think we started to shift when you took on an alliance ten times our size."

"Well, I hadn't intended the entire alliance to attack ours over one castle."

"What did you expect to happen after hitting the leader?"

"Some recognition."

Blue burst out laughing. "We got that all right. And five days of hell along with it. I couldn't even work with my phone buzzing constantly."

"I don't think anyone slept," Scorpios agreed.

"If only things were still that simple," she whispered. The nights they'd stayed awake watching out for one another paled in comparison to why they had to do it now. It wasn't a game anymore.

After a long silence, Jim recounted Nikita's story. He'd been walking through the trees when a whining drew his attention. She'd only been a foot long then and had her foot trapped in a snare.

She'd been tiny and though she'd likely chew an arm off now, she wasn't much of a threat then. He threw a shirt over her, released the trap and put her in a makeshift cage for a week to ensure the wound didn't get infected. Nikita snarled, resenting her savior the whole while.

Being so young, he expected the mother to return, but he never heard anything outside the deep cavern. He knew he couldn't keep it locked up all winter and released the creature to face the elements on her own.

She wandered back within a few hours and stalked him from the shadows. Food earned her favor and they formed an inseparable friendship. Throughout winter, they hunted together, and he learned her language. He witnessed her first kill and even saved her when she tried to take on something three times her size.

Nikita now lay at his side, curled in a ball. She'd grunt whenever Jim laid his hand on her side.

Conversation dwindled as each of them drifted to sleep. None were on watch tonight and with Nikita by their side she felt more secure than ever.

THE NEXT morning consisted of more training. Jim functioned as their newest addition and became Scorpios's teaching tool. The two shared similar fighting styles, though it was obvious Scorpios was more versed in the technicalities. Jim moved like a cat, evidence of too much time spent with one.

Kiuno passed the days watching Nikita fly, losing her unease as she soared at a safe distance above. The villagers had taken a liking to her as well after being assured she wouldn't cause any trouble. She was mystical, something that promised this world wasn't as dark and sinister as it seemed.

A harsh tremor shook the earth and Scorpios grabbed her arm to steady her. They exchanged worried glances as a murmur swept through the crowd. Everything fell silent.

When the second tremor hit the horses reared and Nikita took flight. Kiuno fell to one knee with Scorpios at her side and she exchanged quick glances with the others.

"Any idea what's going on?" Jim asked. All eyes followed Nikita as she frantically circled and made the worst sound Kiuno had ever heard.

"Not a clue," Scorpios said.

Kiuno scanned the ground, hoping it wouldn't split open. All they could do was wait and hope another wouldn't hit.

Those responsible for the horses tried to calm the animals, but they were having none of it. Their hooves beat the ground and they reared, trying to break free from the carts. Yelling ensued as one split the pull. All the while Nikita kept making an awful high-pitched whine.

Particles of dirt flew in every direction. Kiuno shielded her eyes, and Scorpios grabbed her arm and pulled her behind a cart. A second eruption sent two nearby wagons in the air. Several screamed until they collided with the earth.

A dark shadow rose, rocks falling from its enormous body. Spiraled teeth flexed and hundreds of legs too small for such a creature wriggled against itself.

She froze, body trembling as the massive creature tilted toward them. Everyone scattered.

Kiuno drew her sword, but their weapons would do no good here. She looked at Maltack and he nodded, fire already sparking at his fingertips.

The two ran, spacing themselves away from people, flames spiraling around their bodies. Scorpios called after them, but another explosion threw her to the side, and she skidded across the ground. Despite the burning pain, Kiuno rolled back to her feet, but it loomed above, its focus on her.

She stared, menacing teeth turning her blood to ice. The fear crippling. It dove at her, but her legs wouldn't move.

Kiuno pulled hard at the river that surged within her veins and burst the energy forth as a monstrous force collided against it, rock splaying up and hitting her on all sides. Her knees sunk to the ground and rock bit into her skin as a high-pitched screech filled the air. She covered her ears and pushed harder, the darkness pressing in. The force receded, taking the screeching with it, and daylight surrounded her once again.

Flames spread throughout the area as the creature writhed in pain and dove back into the depths of the earth, the thunderous movement throwing everyone off balance.

Kiuno sat back and trembled as she tried to pull in a shaky breath. That darkness. She'd been so sure that was the end. She watched as the other creatures tore through the caravan, their monstrous bodies diving at innocent people and crushing them.

Maltack rested a hand on her shoulder and startled her. His expression looked worried, but they didn't have time. Two more centipede creatures combed the area. The villagers fled in a vain attempt to escape. Scorpios, Blue, and Jim were charging the one on the right.

Kiuno swallowed her fear and let Maltack pull her up. He looked her over once before they charged the second beast. Both released fire, and Maltack shifted the wind to blow their flames forward in a wave that towered almost as high as the creatures. She might not be able to control the flames, but he could.

The demon let out a long screech as the flames enveloped its body, and it retreated with the last close behind. It was difficult to tell whether Scorpios had driven it back or if the other communicated the need to flee.

Breathless, their eyes fixated on the seemingly endless holes, the depths enough to make her skin crawl. Seconds ticked by as their adrenaline ebbed. They were so quick to leave. Did the beasts decide they weren't worth the trouble?

Her strength faltered and Kiuno sank to her knees. She was dangerously close to that time with Kikyo and the camp. Her head spun. She was certain only adrenaline kept her aware of the surrounding area.

She turned to assess the damage. A single cart remained, but the others had been shattered. Five horses stood in the distance, the rest crushed or their bodies scattered. The supplies they carried were meant to earn the favor of those up front, but now they'd be arriving empty handed and injured, nothing more than burdens for those still fighting.

Kiuno struggled to stand and a man pointed his finger at her. "You—" his voice shook, "you were supposed to protect us."

His gaze fell to a charred body beside one of the split wagons, wood still burning. It was impossible to tell whether the victim had been male or female. "She would have gotten away, it wasn't after her!" A blade grazed the front of her shirt, but Scorpios pulled her back and twisted the man's wrist, sinking him to the ground.

"If not for her magic, most of you would be dead. You should think before acting on impulse," Scorpios chastised.

"Did my wife have to be sacrificed for that?" Tears streamed down his face. None answered, and Scorpios released his grip.

She turned to the body, the repercussions sinking in. Was it possible? But when? Taking the lives of those trying to claim your own was one thing...but innocent blood? How did she get that out of control?

Kiuno balled her fists. How would she feel if someone killed Elite? How angry would she be, even if it were an accident? Tears spilled down her cheeks as she watched the man mourn his wife. The cruelty of this world...there was only so much hope to cling to and she—

"There's more," another said. At least two others lay blackened. Whether they'd been killed by the magic or the creature was difficult to tell, but it was clear who he cast the blame on. She was no better than the monsters in his eyes.

"I've run across several that could use magic," he started. "But none have accidentally killed anyone. I can't help but question your motives. Maybe we would've been better off with the lechers."

The sound of scraping metal filled the air. Kiuno stood, and a gentle hand on her back steadied her.

"We don't want trouble," Scorpios said.

"Neither did we." Scorpios gripped his staff. She didn't want them fighting for her.

"I'll leave," Kiuno said. "They're not the ones at fault."

WATER FLOWS

REALM: 5
DAY: 217

K iuno?"

She brushed by Maltack, not turning to his worried call. They were free to choose. If they wanted to follow, they could, if not, they could travel with the villagers.

You were supposed to protect us.

She'd failed them. Failed her friends. Maybe she wasn't meant to protect anyone.

His grief echoed through her mind, a reminder of what she feared most.

Kiuno took off running to the tree line, seeking refuge beneath the thick branches. It was the only shelter she could pursue, the only thing that promised some relief. She wanted to hide from the world. Becoming part of the chaos had never been her plan.

Kiuno tripped on a branch and caught herself by grasping a tree. She pressed her body into it and sobbed. Her side burnt, both knees hurt, and her heart ached for things of the future and past.

Running off…who was she kidding? Being alone was as bad as the guilt.

Kiuno didn't know how long she stood there, but the rustling of leaves drew her attention.

"You shouldn't keep your back to potential danger." She glimpsed Scorpios's scowl and watched as the others followed single file, each casting her small smiles and sideways glances. She turned, trying to hide the tears as rough bark bit into her skin.

"We'll stay here for the night." None spoke, but the movement told her they were settling in. Conflicted emotions surged. Did they stay out of loyalty?

"Come with me." It was commanding, but not unkind. She watched Scorpios walk past, moving between the shrubbery, but she hesitated. A horrible speech wouldn't do her much good, but it had to be better than the stares of pity.

Kiuno followed him down a hill until she heard running water. He knelt beside the creek, his fingers dipped below the water's surface. At first, he appeared to be washing his hands, but the liquid slowly traced up his arm, rushing over his skin as if he were the rocks it moved across every day.

She stood mesmerized, watching it shift between his palms, like something that breathed in rhythm to his movement. He knelt again, letting the liquid roll back, but his fingers didn't leave the water.

"How are you holding up?"

She pulled her gaze away, hugging one arm into herself. Different emotions played in her mind. The guilt of killing someone, angry that she could have prevented it and scared that one of them might be next. She'd already injured Liam.

"I don't know."

He was silent, letting the sounds of nature engulf them. "Maltack believes those capable of manipulating even one element have the potential to use them all."

She stayed quiet, so he continued. "It's not likely to have practical uses, but I've found another purpose." He gestured her forward. "Water, for instance, can help clear the mind because it requires absolute calm to manipulate. In my opinion, this makes it one of the more difficult elements to master."

He took her hand and pulled her down, dipping her fingers into the cool liquid. He sat there a moment, letting her feel the push of the small current. "Fire uses the fast energies within the body. For someone who is used to this, moving a calmer element would be difficult, however," energy pulsed up her arm in waves, like something melting against her skin, "it can be worth learning."

The sensation was that of pure tranquility. Instead of a sudden rush, the energy he fed through her arm moved slower, methodical. It pulled the strain that seemed to ebb into her soul away and let the deep-rooted coil unwind. He gently released her hand, letting the water trickle back to the creek, but the residual feel of his magic didn't vanish.

"There's no need to blame yourself," he said. "Many things have been left unexplained. Magic is largely one of them."

"I killed her, Scorp."

"You defended yourself and those around with what you saw as best."

"That doesn't stop his grief."

"If you'd hesitated, you'd be dead, as would several others. Maybe even all of us. You reacted out of self-preservation, and Maltack shielded us from the aftermath."

"Is he hurt?" she asked.

"No, just tired." She sighed in relief, but still averted her gaze. The magic wasn't practical. It was dangerous. Maybe if she stayed closer to Mal—no that wouldn't work. It reacted against her will. No matter what she did, she risked the people around her.

"Kiuno." He placed a hand on her arm. "You carry far too much guilt on those young shoulders."

"It's nothing I don't deserve."

"Deserve?" he protested. "Just because people make mistakes doesn't mean they deserve to drown in them."

She shifted away, almost whispering, "I've killed too many already Scorp, I've been in this place less than a year and killed more than I imagined I was ever capable."

"Killed too many?"

She wanted to curl into herself, hide from the unjustified guilt that always threatened to swallow her. Scorpios was silent, waiting for her to explain, to confess.

"I've been in situations that caused people to die. How do I know they weren't decent before being thrown into this chaos? I know we have to do what's necessary to survive, but where is the line drawn? And then there's—" her voice cracked, "Elliott and Kikyo…if I'd just been stronger. I could have prevented their deaths."

There… She finally said it.

"Now that *is* a shame." Scorpios shook his head.

"What is?"

"You blame yourself for those two?"

She gave him a confused look. "Why wouldn't I? I have all this power, yet I wasn't able to use it." The anger from that night bubbled to the surface. "I couldn't prevent those men from taking his life. We all know this isn't a game. Even if Elliott's death couldn't have been prevented, I could have saved Kikyo, he would still be here if I would have—"

"Kiuno." She met intense, dark eyes. "You dishonor their memory." Her world cracked a fraction. "They died protecting you, don't take that from them. They willingly gave their lives, so you could live."

"I took away their future."

"They died for something they believed in, *someone* they believed in. Your personality attracts others, making them want to protect you, guide you, push you. I may not know the whole story, but I can tell how much you cared for one another. Let them keep their dignity in death. They wouldn't want you suffering."

Her body trembled once again as she struggled with his words, then his arms wrapped around her and she cried. Just like that time she'd cried on Elliott. So much fear was pent up and he knew it. Scorpios could see right through her.

She took a steady breath, her body too exhausted.

He smiled. "Let's get back. I'm sure Maltack is worried, and we can't let him have a heart attack at his youthful age." She smirked through the tears.

When they came through the trees, a fire was going, and each looked up in turn. Kiuno knew they'd been talking about her, but Maltack's worried expression told her it was nothing but the concern of good friends. She had people who cared for her again, people she could rely.

"The knife only left a scratch, nothing to worry over."

"And your other injuries?"

She sighed and let Maltack work.

UNEXPECTED ALLIES

REALM: 5
DAY: 217

Despite Scorpios' kind words, when the stars emerged in the sky, the nightmares began to creep into her mind, ready to terrorize. It made Kiuno wonder if she'd ever be rid of them. A reminder to a time better forgotten.

Scorpios sat against a trunk, scanning the tree line as he normally did. She doubted he ever relaxed when his shift came around, it was his job to keep them safe. Maybe he was the one who carried too much on his shoulders. She laughed to herself, thinking about a time when she'd be able to chastise him. It wasn't in his nature to make mistakes. Kiuno moved over to join him.

"You should be sleeping. No one wants to be carrying you tomorrow."

"I know." She laid her head against his shoulder. His head turned, but he didn't object. She needed someone to protect her, only in a different way. His presence warded off the nightmares. She felt six years old again, a child in need of a security blanket. In his eyes, she probably looked like one.

The sickness from using the magic assaulted her once again, though it wasn't nearly as bad. Maybe she just had to grow accustomed to it.

Once again, they allowed her to sleep past dawn. The rest helped ease her headache, but her body still felt heavy. Blue poked at Jim and the older man grumbled about it being too early. Each of them packed up and started off.

"Where's Nikita?" Kiuno asked. She expected to see the animal on Jim's heels.

"Off hunting I'd imagine. She can track our scent, no need to worry." Jim stretched and looked over the horizon. "How close are we now?"

"This should be the last of the forest we have to pass through. After that it's field and rock."

Almost there.

Days passed, and they continued as if nothing happened. No one mentioned the incident, and she wondered if Scorpios forbad it. Kiuno had to let go and push the guilt to the back of her mind. The memories could haunt her when she returned home. A therapist would probably laugh at her once they escaped, thinking everything she told her had been some elaborate dream.

As dusk settled, they came upon a small valley where Scorpios indicated they would sleep. Maltack had a fire going moments later, then the jokes began.

Blue's impersonations had everyone in an uproar. She was sure half the realm could hear Jim's bellowing laughter. When Blue started another round, Scorpios jumped to his feet, and for a moment she thought he might join them.

"Scorp?"

"Shhh." They all froze, every eye following his beyond the trees. He grabbed a weapon, the others following suit, and her heart pounded. They backed into one another, peering into the darkness.

There was a growl, a yelp, then silence.

Nikita came through the trees, her white jaw stained red. The hair on the back of her neck stood on end, and her wings were tucked close. Firelight danced across emerald eyes.

Small orbs appeared through the brush. Hundreds, all crouched low. As they crept closer, the growls sent a chill down her spine.

Something resembling a dog with gray matted fur came into the firelight. Double fangs curled beyond the jaw, lips pulled back in a snarl. She took a step back. If there'd only been a few, she might have been able to separate herself but with the numbers—

They jumped from all angles and the violence exploded with Nikita ripping the throat from the nearest one. Jim cut another in half and she twisted her staff to knock one in the face. Maltack ignited the area while Liam stayed behind her. He was frozen, wide eyes telling of his fear. She knew what that felt like.

As Maltack's flames shot through the forest, it revealed more beasts than she cared to count. She couldn't help. Not with Maltack so distracted and Liam frozen. Leaving him wasn't an option in his state.

Fangs sunk into her leg and she cried out, striking the creature with her staff.

A cry rang through the night as men jumped from the shadows. Blades struck several of the canines, and Scorpios pulled her behind him as they tightened their circle.

The masked figures beat the animals back until they retreated. Nikita continued to growl and pace before Jim, daring any of the men to come forward. Maltack's flames shed light for them to see the few dozen men.

"Be still boy." Kiuno turned to the voice, and her blood ran cold. A blade glinted in the night and pushed at the base of Maltack's throat. She tried to push toward him, but Scorpios gripped her wrist and the others pushed against her. Arrows raised, and they stilled. Liam clutched her arm.

Kiuno glanced at Maltack. It was taking everything in her to contain the magic. With them so close, it would be impossible to use it. If she could get closer, Maltack could shield the others. She just had to—

A few of them lowered their bows as two men made their way through. "Who's your leader?"

"I am." Scorpios said.

The man pulled off his mask, revealing scruffy hair. Each carried several weapons at their sides and wore animal hides over their clothing.

"Where are you headed?"

"To the front."

"I said be *still* boy." Each of them turned to the one holding Maltack as the blade bit into his skin. A trickle of blood ran down his neck.

"Your friend should—"

"Let him go."

Scorpios looked back at her with a warning, but she pushed him aside.

"I don't think you're in any position to be demanding, princess."

Kiuno glared at him as fire sparked at her fingertips. Scorpios took a step back. She wouldn't let another die. Not by a group of stupid barbarians.

"I don't think you realize who you're dealing with." If bluffing was her only option—

"Kiuno, I'm fine," Maltack said. "Don't do anything." Was it a warning that he couldn't help the others, or did he think she would reveal her stone?

"Kiuno?" The man before her looked confused. His gaze shifted to the man holding her young companion.

"Is that you Ki?"

There was only one group of people who'd ever called her Ki.

"Reece?" A broad grin spread across his face as he told his men to lower their weapons. The one holding Maltack released him and sheathed the knife.

"Are we going to do away with the flames?"

Kiuno looked down at her hands and took a few breaths to calm her racing heart.

"Sorry kid." Maltack and the man who'd held him hostage walked toward them.

"How you been Ki?"

She looked at Reece and he pointed. "Nsane." Ah, his right-hand man.

"I've been better," she admitted, glad to have Maltack before her. She lifted his chin despite his protest, but the cut was small.

"Sorry Kiuno, I didn't mean to cut him."

She glared at Nsane. "Do you always put a blade to a stranger's neck?"

"In this world? Yes."

Reece interrupted them. "What are you doing out here?"

"Passing through. Headed to the front just as Scorpios said."

He clicked his tongue. "It's too dangerous for that in this realm. Those things are nothing compared to others."

"We know." Kiuno still felt she could hear the screeching of the centipede creatures.

"Why don't you come stay with us?" Reece offered.

All eyes fell on her. She turned to look at Scorpios whose eyes barely met hers. He scanned them, searching for anything out of place. Nikita still paced at Jim's side, but he nodded his approval. Maltack and Blue agreed and Liam still appeared shocked.

"Sure."

Reece nodded and headed toward the front of the group.

"Are you okay?" Scorpios asked. She nodded, but didn't elaborate. The image of Maltack stung. Whether Nsane intended to kill him or not would remain a mystery, but she'd be hard pressed to forgive him.

Scorpios and Maltack knew these people, but perhaps not as well as she did. Or had. It'd been quite some time since she'd last spoken with Reece. Scorpios's caution would be appreciated here.

As they passed through the trees, it became apparent that Reece was their leader. She'd been afraid Nsane led them. Maybe Reece had found those loyal to him from the game.

The trees parted to a camp with a dozen fires and people surrounding them. Reece fell back to join them. "I'm guessing you understand the gist of what's going on?"

"You mean with this world?" she clarified. He nodded.

"If someone hasn't then they're an idiot," she said. Kiuno watched Nsane wrap his arms around a woman, kiss her, then rejoin them.

"Meet Kiuno," he said. The woman's eyes flew open and strong arms pulled her into a hug.

"I'm so glad to see you alive, we've been looking for you. Reece never shuts up about it."

"Marci," Reece groaned.

"My wife." Nsane answered her unspoken question. Kiuno felt her anger fading at the site of him with his loved one. He wasn't a monster, just someone trying to get back to their family.

"It's nice to meet you." Kiuno smiled and then turned to Reece. "Anyone else I might know?"

"Just the ones you see." His gaze fell on the group behind her. "Are you going to introduce me?"

She turned. "I'm sure you remember Scorpios and Maltack."

"I do." Reece smiled at them and shook their hands.

"The others back there are Blue, Jim and Liam. The older two are people we knew in game, but I met Liam over the winter."

Reece squinted. "What the hell is that standing by them?"

"Her name's Nikita, she's Jim's companion."

"I wondered. Glad no one shot her."

"That would have complicated things a bit." She couldn't imagine Jim's reaction if someone hurt Nikita.

"Are you part of the front line?" Scorpios asked.

"Sort of. We deliver food for one group."

"Why haven't you joined them?" she asked.

"Found a bad leader a while ago and had some problems. Staying out here suits us better. Why are you eager to head there?"

Her expression turned solemn. "I haven't found Elite yet."

"Your husband?"

She nodded. "I'm hoping he might be there."

"Have you had any problems with the leader you're sending supplies to?" Scorpios asked.

"No. In fact, he threatened the other leader to steer clear of us. He must be held in high regard since they listened."

"Do you think I'd be able to talk to him?" she asked.

"Don't see why not. We've never entered the gate, at his request, but people come and go all the time."

"Do you trust them?" Scorpios's gaze fixated on him.

Reece shrugged. "Couldn't say, I just know they keep things pretty tight. They won't let too large of a group in all at once."

"I can go. I won't be seen as a threat and might have a better chance to talk to the leader if I act as though we have something to give."

Scorpios gave her a skeptical look. "You don't have anything to give."

"They don't know that."

Reece chuckled, but Scorpios's eyes fell to her wrist. "That's risky Kiuno, even for you."

Though still smiling Reece seemed to agree. "He's right, what if they decide not to let you go?"

"I'd have no problem escaping, and being alone would just make that easier."

"How?" Doubt and intrigue mixed in his eyes. "Because they don't know who they're dealing with?" He smirked, mocking her.

"I have my ways." She smiled when he looked to Scorpios for an answer. He'd never give up her secrets.

"Well, if you're determined to try, we might be able to come up with something agreeable during the trade. Then you can see if Elite is there, but you know Ki, you're always welcome to stay with us."

"I know. I just have to find him first."

"I understand, make yourselves comfortable. We'll head out in the morning. It shouldn't take us more than a few days to get there. If you need anything, just let myself or Nsane know."

"We will, thanks again," she said.

"Anything for you." The way he said it made her face heat and she turned away, thankful for the cover of darkness.

Everyone sat around a crackling fire as silence settled over the camp. Nikita paced, growling at anyone who tried to get too close.

"What do you guys think?" she asked.

Jim replied first. "We'll follow you anywhere Kiuno. If you feel they're trustworthy, that's good enough for me." Flattered, she turned to find them all in agreement.

"I remember Reece," Maltack started. "He was a cool guy, I don't think we have anything to worry about." His statement seemed to comfort Scorpios a bit, but he still glanced around more often than she thought necessary.

Lighthearted conversation returned, and they laughed at one another as if nothing had changed, but changes were coming fast. Soon, they'd arrive at their destination then they'd have to figure out what to do next.

Kiuno moved to sit beside Scorpios, hoping to ease his mind. "You don't trust them, do you?"

He sighed. "That among other things. I have trouble trusting anyone, but the numbers and their experience is worth consideration." The fire crackled between them and Blue roared with laughter at something they weren't privy to. "Going there alone is incredibly stupid."

"I'll be able to handle myself, even more so if no one is with me. I won't have to worry about holding back."

"What happens if you get hurt? How will we know? It's not that I doubt your fighting abilities, I've seen the magic first hand, but an entire army isn't something to be taken lightly. They made it to the top for good reason."

"I won't be fighting, I'll be running."

"And if they catch you?"

"I still have the stone. I won't be killed."

He sighed in frustration. "I do hope you reconsider, killing people isn't in your nature, and if you go you might be forced to do just that." His tone shifted to something softer. "Your soul isn't dark, you're too kind for your own good, really. For someone like you, killing will eat away at your soul. I don't wish such ill feelings on anyone, especially you, my dear queen."

She smirked and shoved his shoulder playfully, but the words struck deep. "Just promise you'll watch the others until I get back."

"How will I know if you're in trouble?"

"I'll burn everything in sight."

"And your flashbacks?"

Her mind shifted to the knife. It hadn't sent her back to that time, but the anger had resurfaced. "Better."

"Good. Your nightmares have also lessened."

"I haven't had them much since I've been with you guys. Is that odd?"

"It's not odd to yearn for protection. It allows the mind to rest. You worry too much for those around you."

"I can't help it."

"You aren't responsible for everyone, remember that. Don't burden yourself, the world is a heavy thing to carry."

They added another log to the fire and laid back. He was right, but how could she not concern herself with the people she loved?

DEPTHS

REALM: 5
DAY: 222

With the sunrise, everything in Kiuno tightened at how close they'd been to a ravine. Reece should have mentioned something like that. What if one of them had fallen to their death?

The forest stood to their right and stretched thin the farther it came into the meadow. Hills of grass stood before them with rock outcroppings scattered along the path.

Those in the camp put out fires and packed their things. Reece mentioned they'd be leaving come morning.

Kiuno watched in fascination. Without a place to call home, they thrived and almost seemed to enjoy it. Everyone carried a handful of weapons and the clothing didn't appear quite so odd in the light. Kiuno giggled.

"What's funny?" Maltack asked. He appeared refreshed and the thin line on his neck had vanished. Perhaps he'd healed himself.

"I thought of these people as barbaric last night."

"You just haven't been with us long enough." Reece stood with one hand lightly resting on his sword. "You ready?"

"Always."

Groups of twenty went into the thinning forest as they moved. Reece said it would take another day before the trees disappeared, and they would hunt until that time.

Several wagons carried furs and crates full of other items. Weapons were probably the only thing they needed from the main group, that and information. To her, it looked as though they fared well on their own.

Her heart sped faster when she neared the ravine, a thick layer of mist blotting out the bottom. A fear of heights had been ingrained in her from birth.

"A river runs at the bottom that has some great fishing." Nsane walked next to her. Perhaps he was trying to ease her ill feelings from yesterday. Kiuno doubted she hid it well.

"How do you get down?"

"When we're almost to the first settlement you'll be able to see down, but the water is too shallow, so we have to venture back to about this point. Pools are great, just inconvenient to get to."

"How far is the drop from here?"

"Couldn't tell you. Far."

Screams echoed from the forest as a panicked group of men broke through the branches. Reece's people surrounded the wagons and drew their weapons. Reece and Nsane shouted commands and jumped into the fray with several more following. She locked eyes with Scorpios before drawing her sword.

Scorpios grabbed her wrist. "Don't rush in." Though reluctant, she nodded, trying to keep her mind rational. Several of the attackers broke off from the main group and headed toward the supplies.

Scorpios told her to stay before rushing the enemy with Blue, Maltack and Jim at his side. Kiuno looked around for Liam only to find him in the wagon with a group of other children. One of Reece's members must have grabbed him.

Why was she the only one left behind? She could fight without her magic. She glanced around, waiting for an opportunity until Kiuno saw a lone man struggling. She ran forward, sinking her sword into his opponent's back. The man nodded his thanks, but their victory was short lived as three more took his place.

None laughed in mockery as so many others had. They looked angry, desperate, as if everything had been stripped away from them. Had Reece done something to deserve such brutality?

One kept her occupied while the other two cornered and killed the man at her side. The adrenaline thrummed through her body as all three launched themselves at her. It didn't matter if she was a girl. They simply wanted to eradicate everyone here.

Kiuno glanced around for Scorpios. He was too far to call, and most fought within the larger crowd. She was on her own. The one to her right swung and she ducked, pushing the flames out to create space. She had to maintain control.

Each of them studied her now and rushed in together. A sharp pain lanced through her upper arm, and her hand reflexively grabbed the shaft of an arrow. She took a step back to avoid another blade when her foot slipped.

Kiuno's stomach dropped as the ground slid from under her. In a split second, she saw Scorpios turn, then he was replaced with a blue sky that fell away faster than she thought possible.

She'd forgotten the ravine.

SCORPIOS

REALM: 5
DAY: 222

Leaving her alone was one of the stupidest decisions Scorpios had ever made. He turned a moment too late, watching the young woman he should have been protecting, disappear off the edge. He watched Reece dive after her, though for what purpose he couldn't comprehend.

Scorpios knocked his opponent down, desperate to run where she'd fallen, Maltack on his heels. The three men peering over the edge felt the wrath of the weapon he bore. Their actions unforgivable.

Thick mist obscured his vision, rolling as clouds undisturbed. Maltack fell to his knees in defeat, tears already falling from the young man's face.

Was that it? A life put out so quickly? His mind churned with possibilities. There was water at the bottom, they'd mentioned a river, and Reece jumped. Despite Kiuno's trust, Reece wasn't the type to throw his life away.

What didn't he know?

Scorpios looked back at the battle, their victory all but won. Nsane made his way over, wiping the blood from his sword. The calmness in his eyes filled Scorpios with some hope.

"Is it safe to assume Reece has a plan?" His voice sounded too desperate.

Nsane cocked his head, a smirk playing on his lips. "Reece has his ways."

Maltack stopped sobbing and looked at Nsane. Scorpios wasn't one to lose his temper, but the prospect of losing his dear friend had him on the edge. "This is hardly the time for vague details."

Maltack's despairing gaze seemed to disturb Nsane. "I'm not certain I'm at liberty to tell."

"Then give me what you're able."

"They're alive. Reece is proficient, you don't have to worry."

He *was* worried. Though Kiuno trusted the man, he didn't. He had minimal interactions with these people at best. He hadn't been given proper time to study them, learn their habits and how they lied.

Scorpios fought with himself, looking back into the mist. They'd revealed themselves after learning Kiuno's name. That meant something.

He glanced at Nsane. They were a wild group, not quite governed by the same laws most followed. He questioned their nomadic existence. What made the leader of people like these so keen on following Kiuno? How much would they listen to her now?

"Don't look so worried." Nsane tried to comfort his young friend. "Ki means a lot to us, Reece will ensure she is safe." Though tears still fell, Scorpios could see the boy calming down.

"How long before we can reach them?" Scorpios asked.

"A few days. Once the land levels out, the mist will clear, and we'll be able to see down."

"And if they aren't there?"

"Then we'll hunt them down. This isn't the first time Reece has jumped into something on his own and it certainly won't be the last.

He knows what he's doing, that's why we follow him. He wouldn't have jumped if he thought they would die." Nsane rejoined his companions who were celebrating their victory.

"You think they're okay?" Maltack asked.

They'd all grown to care for her over the years and even he felt the sharp pain of grief at the possibility of losing her. Scorpios looked to where Blue and Jim were piling up bodies. He doubted they even realized what had happened yet.

"I know one thing. Reece wouldn't throw his life away."

"You don't have to worry about Reece. If they're safe, he'll take care of her." Scorpios looked from his young friend back into the mist. Maltack watched people as much as he did. He was smart. Clever. If he trusted Reece that much, then maybe...

Stay alive Kiuno.

EARTH BINDS

REALM: 5
DAY: 222

Reece jumping over the edge was the last thing she expected, but she clasped his outstretched arm and allowed him to pull her close.

Fear gripped her soul. Death was never part of the plan. Burying her face in his chest, she tried to separate her mind and force it into a happy memory. Somewhere safe.

A tightness gripped her entire body but Kiuno kept her eyes shut and prayed. Waiting felt like an aching eternity.

The rush in her gut slowly ebbed, and she realized they were slowing. It took a moment for her to risk a glance over his arm. Green vines surrounded their bodies, lowering those in its clutches to a riverside. Confused, she looked to Reece for answers, but the strain in his face told her everything.

He had no plans for either of them dying.

His hold slipped when they were mere feet from the ground and they dropped and fell back as he placed his body over hers to protect her from the falling vines.

"That was way too close," he said, breathing heavy.

"What just happened?" He moved off her and untangled himself from the greenery.

"You aren't the only one with magic." Reece's head dropped to his hands as his body shook.

"Are you all right?" His face turned pale, and she wondered if he would pass out. She understood the repercussions magic could have.

"Yeah, I just need a minute." They sat in silence and the adrenaline ebbed. A sharp pain in her shoulder reminded her of the arrow.

He looked up when she winced. "You're hurt." Reece moved to sit behind her, placing one hand on her arm and wrapped the other around the broken shaft. "Ready?" She looked away and her breath hitched when he yanked.

"Sorry, I must have broken the front when I grabbed you."

She scoffed. "Trust me, I'd rather that than the alternative."

Reece tore the bottom of his tunic and pulled a string from his belt pouch. He wrapped it around the wound and tied the fabric. "I'm sure that's going to hurt later, you probably need some stitching, but I don't have the means to do it. You're lucky it missed the artery."

"I think I'm lucky for a lot of things, Maltack can take care of it when we get back."

"He can stitch it?"

"He can heal it."

Reece looked surprised. "Kid is full of talent."

She laughed. "You have no idea." Kiuno looked at the vines, the foliage fresh with leaves sticking out from the base. "So, you grow things?"

"Earth." He waved his wrist, but let his arm flop back to his side. "I enhance the growth of things, they don't just spontaneously appear."

"Odd."

"I thought so too, figured earth would involve tossing boulders around. Was a little pissed at first. What the hell can I do by growing a flower? But, I can't complain about it now."

Kiuno looked up, trying to see the ledge they'd toppled over through the thick mist, along with those she was sure would be mourning. "I don't suppose you can lift us back up."

"With how I feel, not a chance."

"You said it levels out upstream?"

He nodded. "I'm sure Nsane knows we're all right. He'll lead the others in that general direction."

She sighed. "Scorpios is probably freaking out."

"He doesn't trust easy, does he?"

"He's just cautious."

"And rightfully so."

She looked up again and then to the small path that followed the river. "How long will it take?"

"About a day and a half before I can get us to the top. We'll have plenty in the way of food and water."

"How did you get to me so fast? Last I looked you were with Nsane."

"The fire caught my attention. At first, I thought it was the kid, but he was on the other side. When I saw you alone, I thought you might need some help."

She looked at her hands. "Thank you, Reece, really."

He smirked. "Don't get all mushy on me now, you'd have done the same if our roles were switched. Honestly, I'm surprised your group is so small."

"I've just been trying to get to the front as fast as possible. I haven't really stuck around to make friends."

He seemed to understand. "I'm curious. Now that I've seen your magic, I can't help but wonder why you didn't use it when the pack attacked you guys. I saw the kid using his."

She started to respond before pausing. "How long were you watching us?"

He rubbed the back of his head. "We saw you set up camp and kept our distance. I figured you all to be magic users since you were traveling so small, but when they attacked, it was only the kid who displayed any ability. At that point, I figured we'd help." He met her gaze. "We have to take care of our own too."

"I understand, I wouldn't do anything to endanger Scorpios or the others."

"Somehow I doubt that. I'm willing to bet you'd run to someone's aid, damn the consequences." She was about to protest before remembering the slaves and how Elliott had scolded her. "I'm right, aren't I?"

She laughed. "Yeah, yeah."

"So, tell me." He pressed. "Why didn't you use it?"

"They were too close."

"Ah, yes, I noticed Scorpios playing protector. I'm guessing they don't throw you up front to fight then."

At that she laughed. "You think Scorpios would do that?"

"No, I suppose not."

"They try to protect me even though we've only been together a few weeks. We were lucky you came along. If you hadn't, I would have been forced to try and Maltack would have attempted to shield the others."

"Are you kidding? He can do that too?"

She nodded. "He can do just about anything. I fought Scorpios, Blue and him all at once, though I didn't know Mal was there. He prevented my fire from burning them."

Reece waved his hands through the air. "Hold up, you fought Scorpios? How did that happen?"

"They mistook me for someone else. It was dark."

"Who won?" He asked, a playful glint in his eye.

"Three on one, who do you think? Scorpios kicked my ass." Both laughed, stood and started walking. Her arm throbbed, and Reece still looked worn, but color had returned to his face.

Kiuno watched the crystal surface, only broken by the occasional insect. Plant life grew in abundance despite the rocky soil, and small animals scurried between the rocks as they neared. A hidden oasis.

"We don't have to worry about anything coming out of that water, do we?" After seeing the worms and canines, she wondered if danger could lurk around every corner.

"We've never had any trouble."

"Good," she sighed with some relief. "How long have you been traveling with a group that big?"

"Most are still originals from the first realm, never could quite shake them."

"And Nsane?"

"We didn't meet until the fourth. Naturally, he was looking for his wife, just as you are for Elite." He laughed to himself. "Woman almost killed him when we found her."

She was horrified. "Why?"

Reece turned away a little. "Well, we don't always play by the rules so to speak." He glanced at her before continuing. "When we came across them they had the option to join us or give up their belongings."

"Reece!" she exclaimed.

He held up his hands. "We aren't exactly living in the greatest of circumstances. Sometimes things have to be done, however, the leader of that group wasn't happy about the idea."

"It was her."

He nodded. "We tried to stay concealed and she was ready to slit his throat when he recognized her voice. You should have seen her face."

"I can only imagine." Her mind wandered to Elite. How would they finally meet? Hopefully something a little less violent. She couldn't imagine almost slitting her husband's throat, but she never imagined having to fight Scorpios either.

"Elite will turn up if he's at the front. If he's not with this first group, I'll send some riders to the other three. I can't imagine he'd stay with the crazy one."

They filled the day with small talk about their home lives. Reece worked with computers and ran his own business, but without much knowledge on how such things worked, he did a lot more explaining than should have been necessary. She laughed when he vowed to never lay his hands on another game. That wouldn't last long.

When dusk settled, Reece used his abilities to form a net and sunk it in the water to catch their dinner. She would have loved to watch him do more, but the toll it took for that simple task made him break out in a cold sweat. It was only sheer will that had him walking. Though he was exhausted, he bloomed a few flowers for her entertainment.

The nervousness about meeting them seemed incredibly childish now. Just like the others, he appeared to be the same person she remembered. Maybe she'd picked good friends after all.

They pulled a few dead branches, set a fire and cooked dinner. Afterwards, the two sat in silence listening to the water slosh against the bank. The cool night air brushed against her skin, lulling her to sleep as she gazed at the stars.

"Go ahead and get some rest Ki."

"You're the one who should be sleeping."

"I will, I'll wake you in a few hours."

Kiuno took him up on the offer.

Again, and again. It was always the darkness, a deep cavern that never seemed to end. They never saw it and she didn't understand how they couldn't feel the crawl beneath their skin. The warning. It was coming, no matter how hard she fought, it always came.

There were more, figures around the others she didn't recognize, Scorpios and Maltack among them. One image had their arms bound. Another, they were laughing. Glimpses of them played in the shadows, some dancing, some cold, some mocking.

That knife was always there, the cold unforgiving blade she could never warn them about, but this time she didn't wake when the metal slid across his throat. She was forced to watch as the others fought harder, trying to escape the web they'd been trapped in. Scorpios was thrown in the crimson puddle, the next to be—

Scorpios's name reverberated off the walls as sweat rolled down her neck. Reece's pale face was the only thing to remind her that this was reality.

"Kiuno?" He stood a few feet away, his body positioned defensively as flames surrounded the area. She pulled them back, taking several breaths to calm her racing heart.

"Are you hurt?" she asked, still trying to catch her breath.

"No, but are you okay?"

She nodded.

"Does that happen a lot?"

"Sometimes, but I've never experienced the fire along with them."

He sat back down and was silent for a time. "I guess we've all been through some pretty rough shit."

"You could say that."

"You're worried," he stated.

"I know Nsane will keep them safe, but..."

"It's hard, I get it."

She nodded. "Get some sleep."

"Wake me if you get tired, you didn't rest long." He curled next to the fire and her eyes were drawn to the flames as she thought about her dreams.

Reece woke well before sunrise and urged them forward. He had more energy today and wanted to cover as much ground as possible.

Dusk settled, her feet ached and stomach growled, but just as she thought they'd be spending another night below the rocky cliffs, her friends came into view.

"Kiuno!" Maltack's voice rang through the air and he waved his arms frantically.

"Someone's excited to see you." Reece smiled, pulling her close. She stiffened. "Just relax." The vines burst from the ground and wound their way up her legs and both their bodies pressed into one another. Feeling her feet leave the ground had her clutching Reece tight, making him smirk.

Maltack had his arms around her as soon as the vines let her go. He blubbered about how scared he'd been, and she returned his embrace, trying to calm the child. He started on her arm as soon as he saw the makeshift bandage.

When he was finished, she turned to Scorpios who also wrapped her in a tight embrace. He lingered for a moment, and she wondered if he thought she'd really died. Maybe he felt responsible for leaving her behind.

"I'm glad to see you're all right, mostly." His gaze dropped to the wound, which was now another scar that marred her skin.

"I'm glad Reece is quick on his feet," she said.

Scorpios looked her over once more before turning to Reece. "I apologize for doubting you."

A smile broke across Reece's face. "You aren't the only one who used to call her queen."

They all burst out laughing.

Over the next few days, Maltack fussed over her plans with the leader and Scorpios voiced his opinion on her going alone. After telling them both she'd be fine, Maltack stopped pestering her and Scorpios fell eerily silent.

When the towering stone walls came into view, she ran ahead with Maltack and Liam on her heels. A massive castle stood at its center, with walls that looked as though they could withstand the might of a thousand armies. It was something only a grand king would have occupied if they still lived in those times.

Scorpios' concern returned to the forefront of her mind. Why did they need something so elaborate? What danger hadn't they faced?

"Impressive, isn't it?" Reece stared at the building, far less moved by its presence. "All five leaders have taken refuge in similar structures. It's like five were planned to come all along."

"There's others as big as this one?"

"Yep, but all are separated by a few days ride on horseback."

"How close are you allowed to get?"

"Not much closer than this, we keep a respectful distance. They'll come out to meet us once the flag is seen. We're expected." He nodded to the full wagons.

"You've really never been in?"

"Not that one, but I imagine most operate the same. They have gardens and animals on the outskirts which is part of the reason we stay back."

Reece turned, but she lingered, trying to imagine the person it took to run something so enormous. The extensive planning, ensuring everyone had a place and that they were all fed. It had to be an amazing team.

Kiuno followed Reece and helped set the fires while they prepared dinner. They ate, sharing their food despite her not doing anything to earn it. She'd have to remember to repay their kindness.

"That was quick." Nsane stood and they followed suit. It'd only been an hour since he tied the banner between two trees. It didn't say anything, but she imagined they'd be able to see it clearly.

Four men rode toward them on horses. The rear two pulling a small cart. Were they really trading all they had for something so small? Reece greeted one of the men as if they were old friends. They shook hands and began discussing the terms of items and weapons.

Reece pulled a few blades from the back, running his hand along the edge and nodded in satisfaction. Likewise, the other man inspected the crates and furs. Kiuno sat on the sidelines while the two did their business. They talked for a while, but once things seemed like they were settled, she made her move.

"Excuse me." He turned to her with one brow raised. "Would you mind if I accompany you back?"

The man glanced at Reece. "What for?"

"I have a few questions for your leader and might be interested in joining him within the walls. We all know how dangerous it is out here."

"Aren't you with this group?"

She looked back at Reece, trying to seem indifferent. "They helped us a few days ago, but I'm a leader of my own." Like she said before, it was of no concern to them how big her group might be.

An Asian man in his thirties stepped forward. "I'll take you."

"Kiuno." Scorpios rested one hand on her shoulder, a plea in his eyes.

"I'll be all right." She smiled at him, but he didn't return it.

"She'll be in good care."

Scorpios met his gaze, dark eyes burrowing into the man's soul. Whatever he found there, must have been enough to convince him. "If she's not back by nightfall, I'm coming for you." The intensity he put off sent a shiver down her spine. He told her she couldn't take down an army, but could he?

SHADY

REALM: 5
DAY: 225

Riding with strangers was unnerving, but Kiuno was also excited to see the castle. Eldridge hadn't been exaggerating about there being plenty of food and shelter.

On the outskirts, peopled tended gardens and animals. Horses were everywhere, most grazing freely on the wild grass. In the distance, magic sparked as soldiers practiced perfecting their skill.

As they rode through the large gate, she realized just how thick the walls were. An arch loomed over the gate with iron bars crossing the inside of the massive wooden door.

The clanking of metal strummed through her ears, breads and the smell of cooked meat wafted through the air and people scrambled from place to place. It was impressive, organized and well-guarded. Everything she had hoped for. Whoever led this place knew exactly what they were doing.

They rode up to another set of steps, passing several buildings that lined the walls and streets. The man helped her dismount from her horse and she smiled at him, trying to seem passive. He returned it, but his expression wasn't naïve. He knew there was more to her. Perhaps that's why he agreed to bring her along.

"Iggy, who is this?" They both turned to a rough voice. Finally, she had a name.

"She wants to speak with our leader."

"We're taking requests now?"

"I was told to bring anyone who might add to our ranks."

The short, stout man gave her a scrutinizing gaze. "Where did you find her? Weren't you assigned to meet with the outsiders?"

"I did, she was with them."

"And you brought her here? She could be one of them." His face darkened. Reece never mentioned animosity toward their group. Was he unaware?

"I'm not—"

"I don't recall speaking to you," he said. Kiuno bit her tongue, trying not to lash out. His worry was justified, not everyone could be trusted.

Iggy cleared his throat. "She's here now, we—"

"Bind her." Kiuno's heart jumped.

"I don't think—"

"I don't care, we don't know who she is, bind her." Iggy shifted beside her, hesitating before taking a rope from his saddle bag.

"I hope you can forgive this." She considered refusing, but his hesitation led her to cooperate. It wasn't like a rope could hold her back anyway.

Iggy...where did she know that name?

With bound wrists, they started toward the stairs, but the man wasn't satisfied. He decided his escort was needed to ensure she remained a prisoner. Kiuno sighed, but again, tried to reason with herself. Everyone was wary, they had a right to be.

Kiuno tried to focus on what their leader might be like. Iggy was kind, compassionate, capable of fair negotiations. The other one was hard, stern, even a little rude. With such opposite demeanors, he could be either. Hopefully more of the former, she didn't feel like dealing with an arrogant ass.

The inside opened into a massive hall, tables set in long rows with benches neatly tucked underneath. They led her down a side hall and up a twisted staircase. Should the need to run arise, she'd have to remember this particular route. Nothing covered the walls. Just plain gray brick. It was a clever way to keep the enemy running in circles.

They passed a few people, and she paused to look at them, but the gruff man shoved her forward. Kiuno took a breath, trying to fight her rising temper. Was that really necessary?

Two more turns and another set of steps later he shoved her again, causing her shin to collide with the hard stone. She cursed and turned on him. "Do not touch me again."

It was the only warning he'd get.

"Or you'll do what?"

I'll burn a hole through your chest, you arrogant prick.

Heat moved through her, making its way to her fingertips. Kiuno tried to remember the feeling of Scorpios's energy, how it radiated in soothing waves.

She'd love to knock that smirk off his face.

Iggy placed himself between the two thereafter, casting his companion a degrading look before giving Kiuno an apologetic smile. Something about him made her relax.

Displeased with the interruption, the short one shoved past, pushing the doors open to a smaller hall.

This room differed from the rest. To their right sat a pair of closed wooden doors, plain and new. Cushioned seats lined the walls to the left with a flower vase set on a small round table. Colored tapestries hung around the walls and for a moment Kiuno thought she had everything wrong. Didn't Reece mention the leader was male? This place definitely had a woman's touch.

Iggy asked her to stay put and walked up the stairs, cracking the door to whisper of her arrival.

"Thank you, Iggy, I'll see to it soon." Definitely male.

A dark-skinned man standing a full head taller than the rest followed Iggy through the door. He stared at Kiuno a moment before positioning himself in a corner where he set to examining the lines in the floor as if he'd never seen them. Everything about him radiated dominance, daring anyone to question his motives. It made her even more curious.

Iggy's bright eyes drew her attention. "He's in a meeting."

"How long?" The rude one asked. She'd almost forgotten he was there, though her shin certainly hadn't.

"I'm not sure."

The male sighed, frustrated. "We have jobs to do, lock her up, he can send for her later." Her stomach dropped. Lock her up? In a cell? No way. She needed a way to escape, she promised Scorpios she would return.

"He wouldn't approve," Iggy said.

"That man is too damn sentimental to women, she'll be fine for an hour, it won't kill her."

Kiuno scanned the three men in the room, weighing her odds. Iggy could be reasoned with, the one in the corner was questionable, and the other just needed his teeth knocked out. She wished their bracelets weren't covered, though she didn't expect any less after seeing the organization. A major detail like that wouldn't be overlooked.

"He's going to be upset," Iggy said.

"So?" They turned to her.

"If you think I'm going to let you stick me in a cage, you're sadly mistaken." Kiuno took a few steps back and clenched her fists.

Iggy tried to reason. "It's only for a short while, I'll escort you myself and keep you informed. You must understand, it's for our safety."

"Against one woman?" He fell silent.

"You'll do as you're told and wait as long as we see fit. If you resist, I'll drag you myself."

Kiuno smirked. "I'd like to see you try."

He reached for her and that was the last thing she could handle. Fire melted her bonds, and she punched him in the mouth, feeling the satisfaction in her fist as he stumbled. She jumped back when they drew the weapons.

Iggy held a staff, perhaps if she could wrestle it from him, she'd be able to fight them off. His stance told her such a thing wouldn't be easy.

The one in the corner worried her more. He stood straighter, but hadn't drawn his weapons. Two swords, one on either side and well-defined arms spoke of rigorous training. Did he feel Iggy could subdue her? Even with the magic? That meant he had his own. She needed to be cautious.

The unnamed male charged forward, but she sidestepped his body and shoved him into the nearby table. A vase fell, shattering on the floor, at least that could give her a makeshift weapon.

Iggy tried to placate her. "Kiuno, let's talk about this, we'll wait here if you—"

"Like hell we will." His lip bled, but it was hardly enough to silence his loud mouth. She'd hit him harder next time.

"Hunt, stand down," the man standing in the corner commanded. Hunt ignored him and ran at her again. She pulled at the current beneath her skin.

Water slammed her back and a staff planted itself in her side. Kiuno ducked under the second swing and took a few steps back. Iggy followed her movements flawlessly and hit her a second time, knocking the wind from her body. Scorpios would never let her live this down.

She tried to move around him again, but she was shoved against the cold stone, a blade pressed to her throat. Kiuno stilled. Dark eyes held her in place, their intensity daunting. Her flames didn't touch him.

Double doors slammed open and a thundering voice echoed against the walls. "What is going on out here?" His voice brought everyone to a halt. Determined eyes swept the scene. Kiuno wasn't sure whether to be frightened or relieved. This was their leader.

The one pinning her pushed back and sheathed his knife. "Hunt provoked her."

"Typical." Piercing eyes shifted to her and suddenly the names fell into place. Hunt. Iggy.

"Blade." The dark-skinned male furrowed his brow at her, then they both turned to his leader. There was no question.

"K.J."

His face softened as he studied her. "Kiuno?" All eyes sparked recognition. The flames faded, and everyone relaxed as she tried to restrain herself from bounding up the steps.

"Do we shake hands or am I allowed to hug you without being mauled?"

He smirked, giving her a brief embrace. He was alive, along with those that always stood by his side. In the game he'd led an alliance stronger than her own and managed to pull those same people together, creating a group just as powerful in this world.

Like many of her other gaming friends, they'd known one another for years, though her relationship with K.J. ran deeper than most. They had a friendship that went beyond the game, sharing both dreams and fears of their future. Countless sleepless nights passed between them and he'd grown to be more like family. Her only regret was not being able to meet him in the real world.

She'd been suspicious of most of the people she came across, wondering if they were the same in this world as they'd been in the gaming world, but if there was one she would never have to question, it was him. He was cunning, commanding, able to talk his way into any-thing. Some claimed him manipulative, but those loyal enough knew he could be relied on.

"What kind of trouble are you causing out here?" he asked, look-ing at the overturned table, the broken vase and a tapestry that had a small charred corner. The other three followed his eyes, and Kiuno wasn't sure how to respond.

"Hunt tried to put her in a cell." Blade crossed his arms.

"Explains things." K.J. gave Hunt a meaningful glare and nodded to his lip. "I'm sure you earned that."

Tension shot between them and for a moment she wondered if he might try coming after K.J. next. It seemed like her friend was hoping for it. Instead Hunt wiped the blood from his mouth and stormed off, cursing under his breath.

K.J. turned back to the others. "Thank you, Iggy, I've got it from here."

He nodded, gave her a smile and followed Hunt. Blade joined them in what looked like a study.

K.J. gestured to a chair. "Have a seat, do you need anything?" She shook her head, but he eyed her with doubt. It dawned on her how bad she must look. How long had it been since she saw her own reflection?

"I'm fine really, just been traveling for a while."

"I trust you weren't alone."

"The others are waiting with Reece."

"Yes, I know him."

"He claims you've never met."

"According to him."

She smirked. "Shady as ever I see."

He burst out laughing. "Eyes and ears everywhere Kiuno, some-times even my own. He seemed like a good man."

"He is."

"You know him well?"

She shrugged. "We played Chronopoint together so as well as I know anyone."

"And they let you come alone?"

"I didn't give them much choice, though Scorpios is plotting how to take the place down if I don't return."

"I'd like to meet the one crazy enough to attempt such. I'll send someone for them now. Blade, would you mind?" The man nodded and left the room.

She stared after him, a sense of fondness growing at how Blade watched his friend. "It seems like you found everyone."

"Most found me."

"Not surprising, you've always had a way of attracting people."

"We're similar in that regard, how many are with you?" he asked.

"Just a handful."

"You don't have your own army yet?"

"I've been looking for my husband, so I haven't stayed in one place too long. Those with me are the ones I was closest to in the game. I think you remember me mentioning Scorpios and Maltack."

"Sounds familiar, how did you convince Iggy to bring you?"

"I might have failed to mention my group was on the small side."

"And you claim I'm shady." Both smiled and turned when the doors opened again.

A beautiful woman with a puzzled expression waltzed in. "Should I ask what happened in the lobby?" She was gorgeous. Blonde hair tied back in a tight braid, long legs and startling bright eyes.

K.J. smirked. "Hunt tried to put Kiuno in a cell." Kiuno turned to him, waiting on an introduction, but a strange expression crossed his face. His eyes sparked as he looked between the two of them.

"She's a fighter, I like her already." The woman winked, putting her hands on her hips. "You may not remember me though."

Kiuno shook her head, once again turning to K.J. for some direction. "I'm sorry."

She waved her hand. "Perhaps he didn't mention me as much as he claims. I'm Palindrome, it's a pleasure to meet you."

Kiuno's heart flipped and she turned to K.J.'s broad grin. Palindrome, one cause of the many sleepless nights.

He loved her, spoke highly of her until one day she just vanished with a promise to return. She never did. He wanted to find her, convince her to just talk with him, to let him help with her suffering. As time passed, their hope of finding her dwindled and everything led to a dead end. Now, here she stood, just as glorious as all claimed her to be.

Kiuno stood and took her hand. "It's good to finally meet you." Questions raced through her mind, most out of curiosity, but she held back. There was plenty of time, she doubted she'd be leaving anytime soon.

Palindrome informed K.J. on the supplies from Reece and brought him up to speed on a few details she didn't quite understand.

Kiuno couldn't stop staring, wonderment filling her at the site of two of them together. Palindrome's eyes were her most startling of features. Bright. Adventurous. Challenging.

"I'll let you two catch up, I look forward to talking with you later Kiuno. K.J.'s told me a lot about you."

The room fell silent when the doors shut.

"You found her." Kiuno finally managed.

"Again, she found me, Hunt is only here because he was with her. I'm not fond of him, but if he's willing to put himself on the line for Palin's sake, I'll tolerate his presence."

"When did you meet up?"

"Third realm," he said, laughing. "Her army was twice the size of mine."

"Did that surprise you?"

"Not really." He seemed to drift before coming back to reality. "Where have you been hiding these past months?"

"I could ask you the same," she said. "Do you realize no one even knows your name?"

"It's intentional."

"Why?"

"Prevents those I don't want from finding me. Most within the walls know who I am, but beyond that it's only the other leaders."

"Don't want your crazy fangirls breaking down the walls?"

"Hell no."

"I'm sure Palindrome would chase them off."

His expression darkened. "No, she wouldn't, I've come across one crazy and that woman told me to handle my own crap."

"You're alive and uncaged, seems like you managed."

"Barely."

She laughed again. "I ran across Scorpios and the others in the fourth realm. Took me longer to find them than I expected."

"Did you travel on your own before that?"

She paused. "No."

He continued as if not noticing. "What about your husband, any luck?"

"That's why I'm here. I planned to meet with each leader, see if they had any news."

"What's his name? I'll have the record keepers take a look."

"He'll be going by Elite."

K.J. paused, looking up from a note he started. "You're sure?"

"Have you heard from him?" Her heart quickened.

"Do you know anyone named Silver?"

"My cousin! Are they all right?" Kiuno was out of her chair, heart beating wildly as she leaned on the desk.

"I only met Silver, but he mentioned his co-command as Elite. Your cousin appeared to be in good health and he didn't mention anyone needing medical attention, though that might change. He is incredibly reckless."

"Why, what happened?"

"They sought my help in clearing a piece of land." He stood, shuffling a few papers.

"You declined?"

"I mentioned getting a team together, but he didn't want to wait. When they set off, I thought they were only fighting a small group of monsters, but there's more headed that way."

She didn't think her heart could beat any faster. "How bad?" The doubt that flashed across his face made her gut wrench.

"Optimistically, they could walk out with at least half still standing."

"When were they here?"

He shuffled a few more papers. "Yesterday morning."

So close.

"I'm going to pull Blade in here, and organize a group to leave immediately."

"You'll do that?"

He paused and looked up. "Of course, they're important to you. Sit tight, we'll be back in a day or two."

"I can help."

"I don't doubt it, but you look dead on your feet already. Just wait here." K.J. started calling for people as soon as he exited the room.

Helpless. She hated that feeling. Kiuno knew he wanted to keep her safe. To prevent her from acting rashly with her husband so close. She clenched her fists. After all this time, after all the battles she'd fought.

He was risking his life, what difference did it make if she risked her own?

'FIRE FROM THE SKY'

REALM: 5
DAY: 225

Awoman arrived a short while later and led Kiuno to a small room where she was told to make herself comfortable. A small bowl of water and towels sat in one corner, with a bed and fresh cloths in the other. It would be nice to settle down, let herself relax, but only after she had Elite.

The running back and forth continued for another hour, then the halls fell silent. Kiuno peeked around the door. No one in sight. The hardest part would be finding her way out.

She trotted down the hall and peered around the staircase before bounding down the steps. A few men walked through the next hallway, and she followed them. Hopefully they would lead her out.

Ten more minutes passed before the doorway came into view. Once outside, she paused. When K.J. said he'd organize a march, she didn't envision him having an entire army. Most were outside the main gate already.

Looking to be sure no one saw, Kiuno ducked into the crowd and made her way around the guards. Most seemed preoccupied with the soldiers leaving. She found a corner that let her see them and crouched behind the wall to wait. When they were far enough out she'd go. Kiuno wasn't sure what she'd be able to do, but she couldn't just sit idly by.

A hard grip spun her around.

"Going somewhere?" She blinked at Scorpios, Maltack and the others coming up behind him. He appeared out of breath. Kiuno looked at the retreating army and bit her lip. There wasn't time to explain.

"I have to go."

"Why didn't you to begin with?"

She pulled away. "There isn't time." Her panic must have thrown him off and he followed her gaze.

"You weren't going to wait for us?"

"I didn't ex—" She shook her head. "I'm sorry, do you have everything you need?"

"Never had time to unpack."

Kiuno took off running, the others on her heels. Scorpios, Maltack, Blue, Jim, and Liam all chasing an entire army. She imagined the guards laughing behind them.

"THE GUY that came for us didn't do much explaining," Blue said. "Care to fill us in?"

"K.J.'s the leader."

"Why are we chasing them?" Scorpios asked.

"Because he knows where Elite is, and if we don't get there in time they're going to be in a lot of trouble."

"He's just willing to grab an army and go?" Scorpios asked.

She smiled. "He is." Scorpios seemed surprised, but her ties with K.J. ran deep. She'd do the same if it were Palindrome.

K.J.'s quick pace forced them to jog to keep up, but she was thankful. She didn't want Elite and Silver fighting the odds alone.

It wouldn't be long now.

That night her group avoided a fire and camped behind one of the larger stones. Kiuno wasn't sure how K.J. might react should he see her, and she wasn't about to be sent home like a child.

Fear gripped her heart. What if they arrived too late? What would she do if she found him out on the field motionless?

She looked at each of her companions. Did they know what they were following her into? Her gaze lingered on Liam, the nervousness in his expression. What if she lost them because she hadn't listened to K.J.? What if she lost Elite because she had?

"You're nervous." Scorpios sat beside her.

"What if this is a mistake?"

"Decisions like this are never easy. Your mind wanders to what might happen, what terrors the future could hold, but we're here because you feel we should be. Something tells you you're needed, and we'll help you with whatever that is. Instinct has gotten you this far."

"Scorp," she started. "I'm not anyone special. Just a normal girl thrown here like anyone else. You guys followed me in a game, something innocent and fun, but this isn't a game anymore."

"Whether you realize it or not, you're a natural leader. That's what drove us to follow you in the first place. There were hundreds of alliances, and you drew in the best. Do you think that was coincidence? You listen, people are drawn in by your character. Inside the game or out, we trust you, and if your decisions are ever questionable, you've always listened to reason...mostly."

She tried to smile. There was no one she trusted more than Scorpios. He had something to go home to. A son. A reason. She doubted anything would prevent him from doing just that. If he trusted her decisions, then she ought to trust in herself.

"You're right, thank you."

K.J. moved with the dawn.

They followed, closer now, and before long, spotted smoke rising over the horizon. Her heart thundered. Were they already too late?

When K.J.'s scouts left a hill side, she bounded up the slope, veering from his army's path. From the top she'd be able to see—

Kiuno froze.

Curling smoke rose from the remains of a village, the surrounding trees still on fire. Despite the horror of those likely killed, her attention was drawn to the hundreds of men around it. Hundreds of men that surrounded another group. Elite.

The numbers didn't add up. K.J. said there were more headed that way, but he didn't mention how many. They wouldn't survive against those odds.

Bellowing war cries echoed across the valley, and the enemy closed in around them. K.J.'s army barreled down with weapons drawn, but it only pulled the attention of half.

It wouldn't be enough to put the odds in Elite's favor.

Those in the center were scattering. The enemy forcing their way through the ranks.

They fell, one after another. By the time K.J. reached them, half would already be dead.

Clouds billowed overhead, the rain preparing to wash away the aftermath of gore from the earth.

Her breathing hitched. The panic pulsing through her body. What could she do with only five people? Rushing in would just ensure their deaths. Was she helpless to just watch this horror unfold?

Thunder pulsed through her chest as lightning cracked across the sky and cold rain drops hit the ground one by one. Every second sent an overwhelming urgency coursing through her.

So close, yet she might never see her husband alive again, never feel the warmth of his touch, his gentle kiss, the surprised look on his face she'd envisioned so many times.

Another fell.

Then another.

Searing rage tore through Kiuno's body, lighting her veins on fire. The magic pulsated like she'd never felt before and instantly she knew.

This is what it meant to be uncontrollable. This was the fire they all feared.

It strummed through her body again, like a dangerous creature that roared against a cage, her body acting as the cell. Fierce, powerful, and feral, it craved release. There was nothing she could do to contain it.

She'd kill them all.

Kiuno shot down the hill, letting the momentum carry her into the fray. She gripped the metal staff that had defended her so many times.

There would be no defense today.

A cry fell from her lips that drowned the pleas for her to stop and a searing sensation shot from her fingertips as everything exploded in a field of electricity.

The bolt swept over the area in a wave of death, knocking whatever it touched to the ground. Her skin radiated with the blue static, her body exhilarated. There was so much to pull from, like an endless sea of power.

Elite's army stood on the other side. For once there was a safe distance. There was no one to worry about. Another wave pulsated through the crowd, driven by the momentum of her staff. Bodies melted, skin seared, and the sickening smell of burning flesh wafted through the air.

Lightning cracked behind her again, and she brought the storm upon them.

WITH RAIN pouring over them, Maltack grabbed Scorpios when he made to run after her. The lightning sparked as soon as she took her first step, and Maltack knew it was too late to stop her. The prospect of such magic had crossed his mind, but on this level?

They watched her sprint down the hill, bolts of lightning crackling around her body like fierce snakes before exploding in a wave that brought everyone to their knees. He feared the consequences of that magic. How long could her body hold out?

"Mal?" Scorpios fell silent again as they watched her in awe. "How long can she keep that up?"

Maltack studied her. "I'm not sure, I've never seen anything like this."

"Can we get close?" Maltack shook his head.

"Can you block it?"

"You're kidding, right?

Clicking his tongue, Scorpios turned to the army breaking through the enemy's ranks. "I'm going to K.J., keep an eye on her, try to drag her out if she falls." Scorpios turned to Liam. "You, stay put." The frightened boy didn't look as if he needed convincing. "Signal me if she collapses, I'll get a team here as soon as I can."

Scorpios took one last look before heading off and Maltack hoped the anger that burned through her would be enough to keep her going. That the drive to save Elite would end up saving her as well.

HE RAN along the hill top and skidded down the slope when he came upon those positioned to guard the rear. They hadn't engaged in battle yet, but raised their weapons when he approached.

"I need to speak with K.J., it's urgent." They looked between one another.

"Who are you?"

He held his hands up, trying to steady himself. "A friend, I have information he needs." Scorpios pointed to the lightning, the currents visible even from here.

"Please." He wished he could just push past, but he wouldn't be able to fight his way through.

"Follow us." They led him down a path, half running, half walking and instructed two others to take their place.

Bodies were already piling up. People carried the injured to the back, while healers rushed between them, some using magic, others bandaging lesser wounds. Pale faces left a haunting image and blood-soaked rags created a stench in the air. At least half of the wounded wouldn't see dawn.

"Wait here." One man molded into the crowd. Scorpios prayed K.J. hadn't rushed in with the front soldiers. The guard returned minutes later with a tall man, of average build and dark hair, trailing behind.

"You have information?" Calculated, determined, it was no wonder Kiuno had been drawn to him.

"My name is Scorpios, I'm wi—"

"She came anyway." Scorpios nodded. Apparently, he wasn't the only one who knew her to be stubborn and reckless. "Dammit, where?" His eyes drifted as another bolt cracked across the ground.

Scorpios pointed. "There."

"What do you mean?"

"Those waves, they're coming from Kiuno."

K.J.'s expression shifted from confusion to shock and then relief. "She can use that sort of magic?"

"As of ten minutes ago. Maltack isn't sure how long she can keep it up. There are four others watching, but I'm doubtful they'll be much help if she falls."

K.J. only thought for a second before pushing his way to a nearby group of men. "I'm moving east, you go west, and we'll converge at the center." He turned back to Scorpios. "That should diminish the numbers around her."

"Her magic isn't something she can control, so keep your distance."

"What's her current state?"

"Rage."

"That'll keep her alive." K.J. looked back over the field as another pulse shot across the area. "I think she's taking out more than her cousin's entire army. Is there another magic user with her?"

"Just one, he's been instructed to signal if something happens, but he's not fighting with her."

"Has she been in a fight like this before?"

Scorpios shook his head. "Not that we know of, Maltack is afraid she'll push too far."

"I know. How long before she passes out?"

"I don't know."

K.J. drew his swords. "Best we give her a hand then."

K.J.

REALM: 5
DAY: 226

K.J. cursed. This was taking too long. He'd hoped to reach her in only a few minutes, but the hollows continued to race toward them, their eyes fearless in the face of death. It had unnerved him the first time he encountered one. They looked like people, but outside of battle they were soulless.

His sword cut through an arm, but the hollow smiled and reached for him with the other. His blade sliced the head from its shoulders.

These beings didn't respond to pain, nor did they fear death. None screamed when tortured and wouldn't speak if interrogated. They simply held an eerie smile that mocked their enemies' efforts. He'd rather fight people, at least when captured, they produced information.

Following Scorpios, they met up with his small group of four. Two were little more than children, but one possessed magic. If they were loyal to Kiuno, they'd be with his group shortly. She wouldn't leave after this.

By the time they reached her, his men had pulled back. None dared to come within reach of the deadly electric field that shimmered at random intervals. The battle was won, the last of them killed, at least those fortunate enough to be far from his friend.

Kiuno was a raging storm, the epicenter of crackling lightning that struck her enemies with enough force to blow them back...or to pieces. He hoped she knew what they were, otherwise her guilt would be the next storm he'd face.

"She should have collapsed by now." Maltack looked at her with worry and he shared the concern. He'd seen them push too far, be in a coma for days, their bodies drained to the brink.

How far was she willing to push herself?

He stepped forward, but a hand pulled him back. "She'll hurt you."

There was no end to the frustration. "Can you shield it?"

"I can't promise anything."

He sighed. "Cover me."

KIUNO BROUGHT her staff down on the head of another, the skull splitting with a cracking sound that reverberated through her teeth. Bodies littered the ground, blood stained her clothes, and the smell of burnt flesh filled her nostrils. Her body cried, begging to stop. Her very skin felt as if it were on fire as the magic coursed through her veins like molten liquid.

Her hands tingled, numb, barely able to hold the staff. Kiuno's body looked marred, or maybe it was just her vision. Or was it blood?

She spun when a hand grabbed her shoulder, the pool in her body depleting further as it screamed in agony. Just one more. There's always just one more.

"Kiuno." She met his gaze and reality slammed down on her as the tormenting flames faded.

If he was here, then—her legs buckled, but he kept her from colliding with the ground.

Broken bodies lay beneath her feet. Bodies she'd put there.

None of them had faltered. None had screamed. They just kept coming like animals.

Her body shook and K.J. supported her weight as they walked across the field. He seemed to know exactly where she wanted to go. She stumbled, fighting for control. Everything burned, her body yearning to collapse.

Not yet.

Hollow eyes followed every step. So many had been willing to throw their lives away and she'd gladly taken them.

So many...

K.J. tapped her side and she looked up.

Elite ran toward them. He looked different, stronger, aged. Maybe she looked different too. He skidded to a halt and pulled her in his arms, holding her tighter than he'd ever done.

Fear melted and the cord that had been strangling her heart unwound. He was here. He was safe. Elite pulled back, his hands tracing her face before the welcoming shadow of darkness took over.

ELITE

REALM: 5
DAY: 226

Elite held her close, his arms wrapping around the woman he'd been seeking for nearly a year. She looked thinner, sick, and right now he feared for her life. Kiuno's entire body burned beneath his fingertips, almost as if she'd sat beside a furnace too long, but it wasn't this mere fact that had his heart racing.

Stretching from both wrists and crawling beneath her clothes were burns like he'd never seen before, the skin completely raw. It almost looked like frost on a glass window pane.

Elite barely paid attention to the man who'd carried her, but followed him on command. Had she been the one to bring this army to their rescue?

He knew it'd been a stupid decision to move this way, but they hadn't been expecting the hollows. They were fierce and unyielding creatures. At least the normal monsters felt pain.

"Lay her here." Elite glared at the man, reluctant to release his wife, but he did as instructed when another woman ran to their side.

"What happened?" she asked, running her hands along Kiuno's burnt skin.

Elite was about to reply when the other man spoke. "Exhaustion from the magic, but the reason for the burns isn't clear."

"This is bad," the woman whispered.

"Will it heal?" Both turned to Elite as if they'd forgotten he was there.

The woman's eyes went back to Kiuno. His wife flinched, and he wished she'd just open her eyes. "I don't know..."

"Is she all right?" A young man with dark skin stopped short, his breath coming in rapid gasps. Six more followed, two who were clearly guards.

"They claimed to be with Kiuno," one guard said, his voice uncertain. The man who'd been carrying Kiuno held up one hand and two of the men dismissed themselves.

The young boy knelt beside Kiuno then looked up at him. "Are you Elite?"

He nodded once, and the boy held out his hand. "Maltack." Elite took it and looked at the others. So, she hadn't been alone after all. All this time he'd been worrying. Afraid for the worst. She didn't do well alone, she never had.

Another stepped forward and extended his hand. "Scorpios."

At that, Elite finally smiled. Scorpios always had Kiuno's back. "I'm glad you were with her."

They turned back when the woman stood. "That's all I can do for now. Take her somewhere to settle for the night, and I'll be by to bandage her wounds later." Her eyes scanned the area, cries of pain filling the air.

"Come with me, I'll get something set up."

"You are?" Elite asked.

The man turned to him with a sly smile and cocked his head. "K.J."

KIUNO COULD hear their whispers.

What happened?

Will it heal?

I don't know...

Pain shot through her limbs in the dark room, but a comforting hand rested on her abdomen. A familiar scent clouded her senses, and heat radiated from his skin. Or perhaps that was her own. She tried to sit up, but he gently pressed down.

"Elite?"

"I'm here." Kiuno tried to wrap her arms around him, but she cringed from the slightest movement.

"Where are we?"

"Still at the valley."

She struggled to wrap her mind around the darkness. "Everything's over?"

He nodded.

"Where's Maltack and the others?"

"They're safe. Everyone is sleeping."

"I need to see him." Kiuno pushed against his arm, but the pain took her breath away.

Elite sat up. "I promise, they're fine."

"Please." She had to know. What if they were trying to placate her so she would rest? What if her stupid decision had led to—

"Wait here." Elite kissed her temple and carefully removed himself from the blanket.

She listened to the quiet, straining to hear anything that might tell her if someone were coming. Despite the lack of flames around her, it still felt as if the magic pulsed beneath her skin, trying to burn her from the inside out.

"Kiuno?" Maltack's voice enabled her to take a breath. He knelt beside her. "You should be resting."

"I just needed…" she trailed off.

"Everyone's okay, you don't have to worry. Palindrome is taking care of us."

She nodded, but didn't release his hand as he moved to leave. He stayed put, kneeling as she traced the bandages with her fingers. He'd gotten hurt.

"Kiuno." She tried to look in his eyes, but the darkness wouldn't allow it. "It's okay." She took a breath and released him. He was alive, she'd let that soothe her mind for now. Elite whispered his thanks as Maltack left.

"I'm sorry," she said.

"There's nothing to apologize for." He pulled the blanket back and laid next to her, his hand wrapping around her own.

"What happened after I passed out?"

"You didn't miss anything."

"Are we headed back?"

"In the morning."

An eternity had passed since she'd last felt his skin, heard his voice, and yet it felt as though nothing stood between them. "I've been looking for you," she whispered.

"I'm here. Sleep, you're safe." His lips grazed her temple, and for the first time in almost a year she honestly believed those words.

ACKNOWLEDGMENTS

Kyle—You've always listened. Even during those horrid first drafts, you listened to my story as it developed and took form. Your encouragement kept me going through the three long years of this journey, and I can't ever thank you enough.

Paige—Somehow you came into my life at exactly the right time and you were one of the first to dive into my world. Watching your laughter, tears and excitement makes this whole journey worthwhile. I hope to see others react as you have and touch some small corner of their hearts.

Brent—Your friendship means more to me than you know, and your interest in my book is heartwarming even if your ability to pick me apart through its pages is a bit uncanny. I look forward to our future discussions on Kiuno and the world I've thrown her into.

Allex, John, Mal, Reece and the many, many friends who I've had the pleasure of meeting through our gaming world— You guys are the best, and without your influence this world wouldn't have been possible.

Catherine with Quill Pen Editorial—The developmental editing you did with this story is beyond words.

Fanfiction fans—Your kind words encouraged me to create an original work.

To all the people who created the Final Fantasy world— Thank you for making my childhood magical.

ABOUT THE AUTHOR

J.E. Reed lives in Cincinnati, Ohio with her husband and two cats. She's always had an interest in writing, but didn't explore that talent fully until 2015. During the day, Reed works as a Licensed Massage Therapist in the quiet town of Anderson. She graduated massage school in 2009 and has spent the last three years building her small business as well as developing her writing craft. She enjoys swimming, yoga and the occasional mud run with friends. *Running With the Wolves* is her first novel.

CPSIA information can be obtained
at www.ICGtesting.com
Printed in the USA
FFOW02n0619250618
47223725-50022FF